STRANDED

The *Ray of Hope* darted around the asteroid belt, trying to elude the Solar Patrol. Suddenly the ship's five passengers felt a huge blast.

Lona, the computer expert, spoke: "Their sensors locked their battle computer on us, and let loose a ball of pure energy. They didn't just shear away our engines—they blew away our reactor too." She told the group that the ship had a few weeks' rations.

"Will our power last that long?" Samantha asked in a hollow voice.

Lona was silent . . .

The "prequel" to Stasheff's popular *Warlock* series, *Escape Velocity* tells how and why the original colonists of Gramarye left Earth. An exciting story in its own right, it introduces one of SF's most stunning and original worlds.

ESCAPE VELOCITY
Christopher
Stasheff

ACE SCIENCE FICTION BOOKS
NEW YORK

ESCAPE VELOCITY

An Ace Science Fiction Book / published by arrangement with
the author

PRINTING HISTORY
Ace original / October 1983
Third printing / June 1984
Fourth printing / October 1984
Fifth printing / September 1986
Sixth printing / December 1986

ISBN: 0-441-21603-X

Ace Science Fiction Books are published by The Berkley Publishing Group,
200 Madison Avenue, New York, New York 10016.
PRINTED IN THE UNITED STATES OF AMERICA

To
Gail Crellin

who wanted to know
why Horatio Loguire's ghost
didn't recognize the time machine
as being, at least, a machine

1

She was a girl. Dar knew it the moment he saw her.

That wasn't as easy as it sounds. Really. Considering that she was shaved bald and was wearing a baggy gray flannel coverall, Dar was doing pretty well to identify her as human, let alone female. It would've been a much better bet that she was a department-store mannequin in one of those bags that are put on them between outfits, to protect them in case somebody with a plastic fetish comes along.

But she moved. That's how Dar knew she was human.

And he was just in from a six-week trading tour and was just about to go out on another one (Cholly, the boss, was shorthanded this month; one of his traders had been caught shaving percentage points with Occam's Razor). Which meant, since the Wolmar natives didn't allow their womenfolk to meet strangers, that for the last six weeks Dar had seen things that were human, and things that were female, but never both at the same time; so he was in a prime state to recognize a girl if one happened along.

This one didn't "happen"—she strode. She nearly swaggered, and she stepped down so hard that Dar suspected she was fighting to keep her hips from rolling. It sort of went with the gray jumpsuit, bald head, and lack of makeup.

She sat down on a bar stool, and waited. And waited. And waited.

The reason she waited so long was that Cholly was alone behind the bar today and was discussing the nature of reality with a corporal; he wasn't about to give up a chance at a soldier.

Not that the girl seemed to mind. She was ostentatiously not looking at the two privates at the other end of the bar, but her ears fairly twitched in their direction.

"He niver had a chance," the gray-haired one burbled around his cigar. "He but scarcely looked up, and whap! I had him!"

"Took him out good and proper, hey?" The blond grinned.

"Out! I should say! So far out he an't niver coming back! Mark my words, he'll buy the farm! Buy it for me yet, he will!"

The girl's lips pinched tight, and her throat swelled the way someone's does when they can't hold it in anymore and it's just got to bust loose; and Dar figured he'd better catch it, 'cause the soldiers wouldn't understand.

But Dar would. After six weeks without women, he was ready to understand anything, provided it came from a female.

So he sidled up to lean on the bar, neatly intersecting her line of sight, smiled with all the sincerity he could dredge up, and chirped, "Service is really slow around here, isn't it?"

She got that blank look of total surprise for a minute; then her lip curled, and she spat, "Yes, unless you're looking for death! You seem to dish it up awfully fast around here, just because you're wearing a uniform!"

"'Uniform'?" Dar looked down at his heavy green coveralls and mackinaw, then glanced over at the two soldiers, who were looking surprised and thinking about feeling offended. He turned back to the girl, and said quickly. "'Fraid I don't follow you, miz. Hasn't been a killing around here all year."

"Sure," she retorted, "it's January seventh. And what were those two bums over there talking about, if it wasn't murder?"

She had to point. She just had to. Making sure Dar couldn't pretend she'd been talking about two CPOs walking by in the street, no doubt. To make it worse, judging by their accents, the two privates were from New Perth, where "bum" had a very specific meaning that had absolutely nothing to do with unemployment.

The older private opened his mouth for a bellow, but Dar cut in quicker. "Points, miz. You can believe me or not, but they were talking about points."

She looked doubtful for a fraction of a second, but only a fraction. Then her face firmed up again with the look of someone who's absolutely sure that she's right, especially if she's wrong. She demanded, "Why should I believe you? What are you, if you aren't a soldier?"

Dar screwed up his hopes and tried to look casual. "Well, I *used* to be a pilot . . ."

"Am I supposed to be impressed?" she said sourly.

"They told me girls would be, when I enlisted." Dar sighed. "It's got to work *some*time."

"I thought this planet was an Army prison."

"It is. The Army has ships too."

"Why?" She frowned. "Doesn't it trust the Navy to do its shipping?"

"Something like that."

"You say that with authority. What kind of ship did you pilot—a barge?"

"A space tug," Dar admitted.

She nodded. "What are you now?"

Dar shrugged, and tried to look meek. "A trader."

"A *trader*?" She spoke with such gleeful indignation that even Cholly looked up—for a second, anyway. "So *you're* one of the vampires who're victimizing the poor, helpless natives!"

"Helpless!" the old private snorted—well, roared, really; and Dar scratched his head and said, "Um, 'fraid you've got your cables crossed, miz. I wouldn't exactly say who's doing the victimizing."

"Well, I would!" she stormed. "Stampeding out here, victimizing these poor people, trying to take over their land and destroy their culture—it's always the same! It's all part of a pattern, a pattern as old as Cortez, and it just goes on and on and on! 'Don't give a damn what the people want; give 'em technology! Don't give a damn whether or not their religion's perfectly adequate for 'em—give 'em the Bible! Don't ask whether or not they own the place—herd 'em onto reserva-

tions! Or make slaves of 'em!' Oh, I've heard about it, I've
read about it! It's just starting here, but you wait and see! It's
genocide, that's what it is! It's the worst kind of imperialism!
And all being practiced by the wonderful, loyal soldiers of our
miraculously democratic Interstellar Dominion Electorates!
Imperialists!'' And she spat.

The two soldiers swelled up like weather balloons, and the
weather was going to be bad, so Cholly yanked himself out of
his talk and hurried down to the end of the bar to put in a
soothing word or two. As he passed Dar, he muttered, "Now,
then, lad, whut've I told ye? Reason, don'cha know, now, Dar,
reason! Try it, there's a good fellow, just try it! An' you'll see.
Sweet reason, now, Dar!'' And he hurried on down to the end
of the bar.

Dar thought he'd been trying reason already, and so far it
hadn't been turning out sweetly; but he took a deep breath, and
set himself to try it again. "Now, then, miz. Uh, first off, I'd
say we didn't exactly stampede out here. More like a roundup,
actually."

She frowned. "What're you talking about? . . . Oh. You
mean because this is a military *prison* planet."

"Well, something of that sort, yes."

She shrugged. "Makes no difference. Whether you wanted
to come here or not, you're here—and they're shipping you in
by the thousands."

"Well, more like the hundreds, really." Dar scratched
behind his ear. "We get in maybe two hundred, three hundred,
ah . . ."

"Colonists," she said sternly.

". . . prisoners," Dar finished. "Per year. Personally, I'd
rather think of myself as a 'recruit.'"

"Doesn't make any difference," she snapped. "It's what
you do after you get here that counts. You go out there, making
war on those poor, innocent natives . . . and you traders go
cheating them blind. Oh, I've heard what you're up to."

"Oh, you have?" Dar perked up. "Hey, we're gettin'
famous! Where'd you hear about us, huh?"

She shrugged impatiently. "What does it matter?"

"A lot, to me. To most of us, for that matter. When you're
stuck way out here on the fringe of the Terran Sphere, you start

caring a lot about whether or not people've ever heard about your planet. 'Be nice to feel even *that* important."

"Mm." Her face softened a moment, in a thoughtful frown. "Well . . . I'm afraid this won't help much. I used to be a clerk back on Terra, in the records section of the Bureau of Otherworldly Activities—and a report about Wolmar came through occasionally."

"Oh." Dar could almost feel himself sag. "Just official reports?"

She nodded, with a vestige of sympathy. "That's right. Nobody ever saw them except bureaucrats. And the computer, of course."

"Of course." Dar heaved a sigh and straightened his shoulders. "Well! That's better than nothing . . . I suppose. What'd they say about us?"

"Enough." She smiled vindictively. "Enough so that I know this is a prison planet for criminal soldiers, governed by a sadomasochistic general; that scarcely a day passes when you don't have a war going on. . . ."

"Holidays," Dar murmured, "and Sundays."

"'Scarcely,' I said! And that you've got an extremely profitable trade going with the natives for some sort of vegetable drug, in return for which you give them bits of cut glass and surplus spare parts that you order through the quartermaster."

"That's all?" Dar asked, crestfallen.

"All!" She stared, scandalized. "Isn't that enough? What did you want—a list of war crimes?"

"Oh . . ." Dar gestured vaguely. "Maybe some of the nice things—like this tavern, and plenty of leave, and . . ."

"Military corruptness. Slackness of discipline." She snorted. "Sure. Maybe if I'd stayed with the Bureau, a piece of whitewash would've crossed my desk."

"*If* you'd stayed with them?" Dar looked up. "You're not with BOA anymore?"

She frowned. "If I were working for the Bureau, would I be here?"

Dar just looked at her for a long moment.

Then he shook himself and said, "Miz, the only reason I can

think of why you *would* be here is because BOA sent you. Who could *want* to come here?"

"Me," she said, with a sardonic smile. "Use your head. Could I dress like this if I worked for the government?"

Dar's face went blank. Then he shrugged. "I dunno. *Could* you?"

"Of course not," she snapped. "I'd have to have a coiffured hairdo, and plaster myself with skintight see-throughs and spider heels. I had to, for five years."

"Oh. You didn't like it?"

"Would *you* like to have to display yourself everyday so a crowd of the opposite sex could gawk at you?"

Dar started a slow grin.

"Well, I didn't!" she snapped, reddening.

"And that's why you quit?"

"More than that," she said grimly. "I got fed up with the whole conformist ragout, so I aced out instead."

"'Aced out'?" Dar was totally lost.

"Aced out! Quit! Got out of all of it!" she shouted. "I turned into a *Hume*!"

"What's a 'Hume'?"

She stared, scandalized. "You really *are* away from it all out here, aren't you?"

"I've kinda been trying to hint about something along those lines, yes. We get the news whenever a freighter lands, about three times a year. So until they invent faster-than-light radio, we're not going to know what's happening on Terra until a couple of years after it's happened."

She shook her head in exasperation. "Talk about primitive! All right . . . a Hume is me—a nonconformist. We wear loose gray coveralls like this to hide our bodies from all those lascivious, leering eyes. We shave our heads, so we don't have to do up a pompadour everyday. And we don't submit to those prisons society calls 'jobs'; we'd rather be poor. We've put in our time, we've got some savings, and between that, our GNP share, and whatever we can pick up at odd jobs, we manage to keep going. We do what *we* want, not what the I.D.E. wants. That's what's a Hume."

Dar nodded, lips pursed and eyes slightly glazed. "Uh. But you don't conform. Right."

"I didn't say that, gnappie! I said we're nonconformists."

"Uh—right." Dar nodded. "I see the difference—or I'll try to."

She turned on him, but Cholly got there first. "Do thet, lad! Do thet, and you'll make me proud of you! But you see, you have to know the history of it, don't you? Of course you do; can't understand nothing wot's happening in human society if you don't know the history of it. The first who was called 'Nonconformists,' see, they started showing up toward the end of the 1500s, now. Shakespeare wrote one of 'em into *Twelfth Night,* called him 'Malvolio.' Puritans, they was, and Calvinists, and Baptists, too, and Anabaptists, all manner of Protestant sects what wasn't Church of England. And the Anglicans, they lumped 'em all together and called 'em 'Nonconformists' (the name got put on 'em from the outside, you see, the way it always does) 'cause they didn't conform to the Established Church (what was C. of E., of course). Yet if you sees the pictures of 'em, like Cromwell's Roundheads, why! they're like to one another as bottles in a case! Within their opposition-culture, you sees, they conformed much more tightly than your C. of E.s—and so it has been, ever since. When you call 'em 'nonconformists,' it doesn't mean they don't conform to the standards of their group, but that their group don't conform to the majority culture—and that's why any opposition-culture's called 'nonconformist.' Now then, Sergeant . . ." And he was off again, back to the reality case.

The Hume stared after him, then nodded thickly. "He's right, come to think of it . . ." She gave herself a shake, and scowled at Dar. "What was that—a bartender, or a professor?"

"Cholly," Dar said, by way of explanation. "My boss."

The Hume frowned. "You mean you work here? WHOA!"

Dar saw the indignation rise up in her, and grinned. "That's right. He's the owner, president, and manager of operations for the Wolmar Pharmaceutical Trading Company, Inc."

"The boss drug-runner?" she cried, scandalized. "The robber baron? The capitalist slave-master?"

"Not really. More like the bookkeeper for a cooperative."

She reared up in righteous wrath, opening her mouth for a crushing witticism—but couldn't think of any, and had to content herself with a look of withering scorn.

Dar obligingly did his best to wither.

She turned away to slug back a swallow from her glass—then stared, suddenly realizing that she *had* a glass.

Dar glanced at Cholly, who looked up, winked, nodded, and turned back to discussing the weightier aspects of kicking a cobble.

The Hume seemed to deflate a little. She sighed, shrugged, and took another drink. "Hospitable, anyway . . ." She turned and looked up at Dar. "Besides, can you deny it?"

Dar ducked his head—down, around, and back up in hopes of a sequitur. "Deny what?"

"All of it! Everything I've said about this place! It's all true, isn't it? Starting with your General Governor!"

"Oh. Well, I can deny that General Shacklar's a sadist."

"But he *is* a masochist?"

Dar nodded. "But he's very well-adjusted. As to the rest of it . . . well, no, I can't deny it, really; but I would say you've gotten the wrong emphasis."

"I'm open to reason," the Hume said, fairly bristling. "Explain it to me."

Dar shook his head. "Can't explain it, really. You've got to experience it, see it with your own eyes."

"Yes. Of course." She rolled her eyes up. "And how, may I ask, am I supposed to manage that?"

"Uhhhh . . ." Dar's mind raced, frantically calculating probable risks versus probable benefits. It totaled up to 50–50, so he smiled and said, "Well, as it happens, I'm going out on another trading mission. You're welcome to come along. I can't *guarantee* your safety, of course—but it's really pretty tame."

The Hume stared, and Dar could almost see her suddenly pulling back, withdrawing into a thickened shell. But something clicked, and her eyes turned defiant again. "All right." She gulped the rest of her drink and slammed the glass back down on the bar. "Sure." She stood up, hooking her thumbs in her pockets. "Ready to go. Where's your pack mule?"

Dar grinned. "It's a little more civilized than that—but it's just out back. Shall we?" And he bowed her toward the door.

She spared him a last withering glance, and marched past him. Dar smiled, and followed.

As they passed Cholly and the sergeant, the bartender was saying earnestly, "So Descartes felt he had to prove it all, don't you see—everything, from the ground up. No assumptions, none."

"Ayuh. Ah kin see thet." The sergeant nodded, frowning. "If'n he assumed anything, and thet one thing turned out to be wrong, everything else he'd figgered out'd be wrong, too."

"Right, right!" Cholly nodded emphatically. "So he stopped right there, don't you see, took out a hotel room, and swore he'd not stir till he'd found some one thing he could prove, some one way to be sure he existed. And he thought and he thought, and it finally hit him."

"Whut dud?"

"He was thinking! And if'n he wuz thinking, there had to be someone there to do the thinking! And that someone was him, of course—so the simple fact that he was thinking proved he existed!"

"Ay-y-y-y-uh!" The sergeant's face lit with the glow of enlightenment, and the Hume stopped in the doorway, turning back to watch, hushed, almost reverent.

Cholly nodded, glowing, victorious. "So he laid it out, right then and there, and set it down on paper, where he could read it. *Cogito, ergo sum,* he wrote—for he wrote in Latin, don't you see, all them philosphers did, back then—*Cogito, ergo sum*; and it means 'I think; therefore: I exist.'"

"Ay-y-y-y-uh. Ayuh, I see." The sergeant scratched his head, then looked up at Cholly again. "Well, then—that's whut makes us human, ain't it? Thinking, I mean."

The Hume drew in a long, shuddering breath, then looked up at Dar. "What is this—a tavern, or a college?"

"Yes." Dar pushed the door open. "Shall we?"

They came out into the light of early afternoon. Dar led the Hume to a long, narrow grav-sled, lumpy with trade goods under a tarpaulin. "No room for us, I'm afraid—every ounce of lift has to go to the payload. We walk."

"Not till I get an answer." The Hume planted her feet, and set her fists on his hips.

"Answer?" Dar looked up, surprised. "To what?"

"To my question. This boss of yours—what is he? A

capitalist? An immoral, unethical, swindling trader? A bartender? Or a professor?"

"Oh." Dar sat down on his heels, checking the fastenings of the tarp. "Well, I wouldn't really call him a capitalist, 'cause he never really does more than break even; and he's as moral as a preacher, and as ethical as a statue. And he's never swindled anybody. Aside from that, though, you've pretty well pegged him."

"Then he *is* a professor!"

Dar nodded. "Used to teach at the University of Luna."

The Hume frowned. "So what happened? What's he doing tending bar?"

Dar shrugged. "I think he got the idea from his last name: Barman."

"'Barman'?" She frowned. "Cholly Barman? Whoa! Not Charles T. Barman!"

Dar nodded.

"But he's famous! I mean, he's got to be the *most* famous teacher alive!"

"Well, notorious, anyway." Dar gave the fastenings a last tug and stood up. "He came up with some very wild theories of education. I gather they weren't too popular."

"So I heard. But I can't figure why; all he was saying was that *everybody* ought to have a college education."

"And thereby threatened the ones who already had it." Dar smiled sweetly. "But it was more than that. He thinks all teaching ought to be done on a one-to-one basis, which made him unpopular with the administrators—imagine having to pay that many teachers!—and thought the teaching ought to be done in an informal environment, without the student realizing he was being taught. That meant each professor would have to have a cover role, such as bartending, which made him unpopular with the educators."

The Hume frowned. "I didn't hear about that part of it."

Dar shrugged. "He published it; it was there to read, if you managed to get hold of a copy before the LORDS party convinced the central book-feed to quit distributing it down the line to the retail terminals."

"Yes." Her mouth flattened, as though she'd tasted something sour. "Freedom of the press isn't what it used to be, is it?"

"Not really, no. But you can see why the talk gets so deep, back in there; Cholly never misses a chance to do some teaching on the side. When he's got 'em hooked on talk, he lets 'em start hanging out in the back room—it's got an open beer keg, and wall-to-wall books."

She nodded, looking a little dazzled. "You don't sound so 'innocent of books' yourself, come to think of it."

Dar grinned, and picked up the towrope. "Shall we go?"

They trudged down the alley and out into the plastrete street, the Hume walking beside Dar, brooding.

Finally she looked up. "But what's he doing out here? I mean, he's putting his theories into practice, that's clear—but why here? Why not on some fat planet in near Terra?"

"Well, the LORDS seem to have had something to do with that."

"That bunch of fascists! I knew they were taking over the Assembly—but I didn't know they were down on education!"

"Figure it out." Dar spread his hands. "They say they want really efficient central government; they mean totalitarianism. And one of the biggest threats to a totalitarian government is a liberal education."

"Oh." Her face clouded. "Yes, of course. So what did they do?"

"Well, Cholly won't go into much detail about it, but I gather they tried to assassinate him on Luna, and he ran for it. The assassins chased him, so he kept running—and he wound up here."

"Isn't he still worried about assassins?"

Dar flashed her a grin. "Not with Shacklar running the place. By the way, if we're going to be traveling together, we really oughta get onto a first-name basis. I'm Dar Mandra." He held out his hand.

She seemed to shrink back again, considering the offer; then, slowly, she extended her own hand, looking up at him gravely. "Samantha Bine. Call me Sam."

Dar gave her hand a shake, and her face his warmest smile. "Good to meet you, Sam. Welcome to education."

"Yes," she said slowly. "There *is* a lot here that wasn't in the reports, isn't there?"

Sam looked at the town gate as they passed through it, and frowned. "A little archaic, isn't it? I thought walled towns went out with the Middle Ages."

"Only because the attackers had cannon, which the Wolmen *didn't* have when this colony started."

"But they do now?"

"Well," Dar hedged, "let's say they're working on it."

"Hey! You, there! Halt!"

They looked back to see a corporal in impeccable battle-dress running after them.

"Here now, Dar Mandra!" he panted as he caught up with them. "You know better than to go hiking out at two o'clock!"

"Is it that late already?" Dar glanced up at the sun. "Yeah, it is. My, how the time flies!" He hauled the grav-sled around. "Come on, Sam. We've gotta get back against the wall."

"Why?" Sam came along, frowning. "What's wrong?"

"Nothing, really. It's just that it's time for one of those continual battles you mentioned."

"Time?" Sam squawked. "You mean you *schedule* these things?"

"Sure, at 8 A.M. and 2 P.M., eight hours apart. That gives everybody time to rest up, have lunch, and let it digest in between."

"*Eight* hours?" She frowned. "There's only six hours between eight and two!"

"No, eight. Wolmar's got a twenty-eight-hour day, so noon's at fourteen o'clock." He pulled the sled up against the wall and leaned back against it. "Now, whatever you do, make sure you stay right here."

"Don't worry." Sam settled herself back against the plastrete, folding her arms defiantly. "I want to get back to Terra to tell about this. I don't intend to get hit by a stray beam."

"Oh, no chance of that—but you might get trampled."

Brightly colored figures rose over the ridge, and came closer. Sam stiffened. "The natives?"

Dar nodded. "The Wolmen."

"*Purple* skin?"

"No, that's a dye they use to decorate their bodies. I think the chartreuse loincloths go rather well with it, don't you?"

The warriors drew up in a ragged line, shaking white-tipped poles at the walled town and shouting.

"Bareskins go down today! Jailers of poor natives! Wolmen break-um free today! Bareskins' Great Father lose-um papooses!"

"It's traditional," Dar explained.

"What? The way they talk?"

"No, just the threats."

"Oh." Sam frowned. "But that dialect! I can understand why they'd speak Terrese, but why the pidgin grammar and all those 'ums'?"

Dar shrugged. "Don't know, actually. There're some of us have been wondering about that for a few years now. The best we can come up with is that they copped it from some stereotyped presentation of barbarians, probably in an entertainment form. Opposition cultures tend to be pretty romantic."

The soldiers began to file out of the main gate, lining up a hundred yards away from the Wolmen in a precise line. Their bright green uniforms were immaculately clean, with knife-edge creases; their boots gleamed, and their metalwork glistened. They held their white-tipped sticks at order arms, a precise forty-five degree angle across their bodies.

"Shacklar's big on morale," Dar explained. "Each soldier gets a two-BTU bonus if his boots are polished; another two if his uniform's clean; two more if it's pressed; and so on."

The soldiers muttered among themselves out of the corners of their mouths. Dar could catch the odd phrase:

"Bloody Wolmen think they own the whole planet! Can't tell *us* what t' do! They think they c'n lord it over us, they got another think comin'!"

Sam looked up at Dar, frowning. "What's that all about? It almost sounds as though they think the Wolmen are the government!"

"They do." Dar grinned.

Sam scanned the line of troops, frowning. "Where're their weapons?"

"Weapons!" Dar stared down at her, scandalized. "What do you think we are—a bunch of savages?"

"But I thought you said this was a . . . ."

BR-R-R-R-ANK! rolled a huge gong atop the wall, and the officers shouted, "Charge!"

The Wolmen chiefs whooped, and their warriors leaped down toward the soldiers with piercing, ululating war cries.

The soldiers shouted, and charged them.

The two lines crashed together, and instantly broke into a chaotic melee, with everyone yelling and slashing about them with their sticks.

"This is civilized warfare?" Sam watched the confusion numbly.

"Very," Dar answered. "There's none of this nonsense about killing or maiming, you see. I mean, we're short enough on manpower as it is."

Sam looked up at him, unbelieving. "Then how do you tell who's won?"

"The war-sticks." Dar pointed. "They've got lumps of very soft chalk in the ends. If you manage to touch your opponent with it, it leaves a huge white blotch on him."

A soldier ran past, with a Wolman hot on his heels, whooping like a Saturday matinee. Suddenly the soldier dropped into a crouch, whirled about and slashed upward. The stick slashed across the Wolman's chest, leaving a long white streak. The Wolman skidded to a stop, staring down at his new badge, appalled. Then his face darkened, and he advanced toward the soldier, swinging his stick up.

"Every one loses his temper now and then," Dar murmured.

A whistle shrilled, and a Terran officer came running up. "All right, that'll do! You there, tribesman—you're out of the war, plain as the chalk on your chest! On your way, now, or I'll call one o' yer own officers."

"Oppressor of poor, ignorant savages!" the Wolman stormed. "We rise-um up! We beat-um you down!"

"Ayuh, well, tomorrow, maybe. Move along to the side-lines, now, there's a good chap!" The officer made shooing motions.

The Wolman stood stiffly, face dark with rebellion. Then he threw down his chalk-stick with a snarl and went stalking off toward a growing crowd of men, soldiers and Wolmen alike, standing off to the east, well clear of the "battle."

The officer nodded. "That's well done, then." And he ran off, back toward the thick of the melee.

The soldier swaggered toward Dar, grinning and twirling his stick. "Chalk up one more for the good guys, eh?"

"And another ten BTUs in your account!" Dar called back. "Well done, soldier!"

The soldier grinned, waved, and charged back into the thick of the chaos.

"Ten credits?" Sam gasped, blanching. "You don't mean your General pays a bounty?"

"No, of course not. I mean, it's not the General who let himself get chalked up, is it? It's the Wolman who pays."

"*What?*"

"Sure. After the battle's over, the officers'll transfer ten credits from that Wolman's account to the soldier's. I mean, there's got to be *some* risk involved."

"Right," she agreed. "Sure. Risk." Her eyes had glazed. "I, uh, notice the, uh, 'casualties' seem to be having a pretty good time over there."

"Mm?" Dar looked up at the group over to the east. Wolmen and soldiers were chatting amicably over tankards. A couple of privates and three warriors wove in and out through the crowd with trays of bottles and cups, dispensing cheer and collecting credits.

He turned back to Sam. "Why not? Gotta fill in the 'dead' time somehow."

"Sure," she agreed. "Why not?"

Suddenly whistles shrilled all over the field, and the frantic runners slowed to a walk, lowering their chalk sticks. Most of them looked pretty disgusted. "Cease!" bellowed one officer. "Study war no more!" echoed a Wolman chief. The combatants began to circulate; a hum of conversation swelled.

"Continual warfare," Sam muttered.

Dar leaned back against the wall and began whistling through his teeth.

Two resplendent figures stepped in from the west—an I.D.E. colonel in full dress uniform and a Wolman in a brightly patterned cloak and elaborate headdress.

"The top-ranking officers," Dar explained. "Also the peace commission."

"Referees?" Sam muttered.

"Come again?"

"I'd rather not."

Each officer singled out those of his own men who had chalk marks on them, but who hadn't retired to the sidelines. Most of them seemed genuinely surprised to find they'd been marked. A few seemed chagrined.

The officers herded them over to join the beerfest, then barked out orders, and the "casualties" lined up according to side in two ragged lines, still slurping beer. The officers walked down each other's line, counting heads, then switched and counted their own lines. Then they met and discussed the situation.

"Me count-um twenty-nine of mine, and thirty-two of yours."

"Came to the same count, old chap. Wouldn't debate it a bit."

The Wolman grinned, extending a palm. "Pay up."

The I.D.E. colonel sighed, pulled out a pad, and scribbled a voucher. The Wolman pocketed it, grinning.

A lieutenant and a minor Wolman stepped up from the battlefield, each holding out a sheaf of papers. The two chief officers took them and shuffled through, muttering to each other, comparing claims.

"That's the lot." The colonel tapped his sheaf into order, squaring it off. "Only this one discrepancy, on top here."

The Wolman nodded. "Me got same."

"Well, let's check it, then. . . . O'Schwarzkopf!"

"Sir!" A corporal stepped forward and came to attention with a click of his heels, managing not to spill his tankard in the process.

"This warrior, um, 'Xlitplox,' claims he chalked you. Valid?"

"Valid, sir."

"Xlitplox!" the Wolman officer barked.

"Me here." The Wolman stepped forward, sipping.

"O'Schwarzkopf claim-um him chalk you."

"He do-um." Xlitplox nodded.

"Could be collusion," the colonel noted.

The Wolman shrugged. "What matter? Cancel-um out, anyhow. Null score."

The colonel nodded. "They want to trade tenners, that's their business. Well!" He tapped the sheaf and saluted the Wolman with them. "I'll have these to the bank directly."

"Me go-um, too." The Wolman caught two tankards from a passing tray and dropped a chit on it. "Drink?"

"Don't mind if I do." The colonel accepted a tankard and lifted it. "To the revolution!"

"*Was hael!*" The Wolman clinked mugs with him. "We rise-um up; we break-um and bury-um corrupt colonial government!"

"And *we'll* destroy the Wolman tyranny! . . . Your health."

"Yours," the Wolman agreed, and they drank.

"What *is* this?" Sam rounded on Dar. "Who's rebelling against whom?"

"Depends on whom you ask. Makes sense, doesn't it? I mean, each side claims to be the rightful government of the whole planet—so each side also thinks it's staging a revolution."

"That's asinine! Anybody can see the Wolmen are the rightful owners of the planet."

"Why? They didn't evolve here, any more than we soldiers did."

"How do *you* know?" Sam sneered.

"Because I read a history book. The Wolmen are the descendants of the 'Tonies,' the last big opposition culture, a hundred years ago. You should hear their music—twenty-four tones. They came out here to get away from technology."

Sam shuddered, then shook her head. "That doesn't really change anything. They were here first."

"Sure, but they think we came in and took over. After all, we've got a government. Their idea of politics is everybody sitting around in a circle and arguing until they can all agree on something."

"Sounds heavenly," Sam murmured, eyes losing focus.

"Maybe, but that still leaves General Shacklar as the only government strong enough to rebel against—at least, the way the Wolmen see it. And *we* think they're trying to tell *us* what to do—so we're revolting, too."

"No argument there." Sam shrugged. "I suppose I shouldn't gripe. As 'continual wars' go, this is pretty healthy."

"Yeah, especially when you think of what it was like my first two years here."

"What? Real war—with sticks and stones?"

Dar frowned. "When you tie the stone to the end of the stick, it can kill a man—and it did. I saw a lot of soldiers lying on the ground with their heads bashed in and their blood soaking into the weeds. I saw more with stone-tipped spears and arrows in them. Our casualties were very messy."

"So what are dead Wolmen like—pretty?"

"I was beginning to think so, back then." Dar grimaced at the memory. "But dead Wolmen were almost antiseptic—just a neat little hole drilled into 'em. Not even any blood—laser wounds are cauterized."

Sam caught at his arm, looking queasy. "All right! That's . . . enough!"

Dar stared down at her. "Sorry. Didn't think I'd been all that vivid."

"I've got a good imagination." Sam pushed against him, righting herself. "How old were you then?"

"Eighteen. Yeah, it made me sick too. Everybody was."

"But they couldn't figure out how to stop it?"

"Of course not. Then Shacklar was assigned the command."

"What'd he do—talk it to death?"

Dar frowned. "How'd you guess?"

"I was kidding. You can't stop a war by talking!"

Dar shrugged. "Maybe he waved a magic wand. All I knew was that he had the Wolmen talking instead of fighting. How, I don't know—but he finally managed to get them to sign a treaty agreeing to this style of war."

"Would it surprise you to learn the man's just human?"

"It's hard to remember sometimes," Dar admitted. "As far as I'm concerned, Shacklar can do no wrong."

"I take it all the rest of the soldiers feel the same way."

Dar nodded. "Make snide comments about the Secretary of the Navy, if you want. Sneer at the General Secretary of the whole Interstellar Dominion Electorates. Maybe even joke about God. But don't you *dare* say a word against General Shacklar!"

Sam put on a nasty smile and started to say something. Then she thought better of it, her mouth still open. After a second, she closed it. "I suppose a person could really get into trouble that way here."

"What size trouble would you like? Standard measurements here are two feet wide, six feet long, and six feet down."

"No man should have that kind of power!"

"Power? He doesn't even give orders! He just asks. . . ."

"Yeah, and you soldiers fall all over each other trying to see who can obey first! That's obscene!"

Dar bridled. "Soldiers are supposed to be obscene."

"Sexual stereotype," Sam snapped. "It's absurd."

"Okay—so soldiers should be obscene and not absurd." Dar gave her a wicked grin. "But wouldn't you feel that way about a man who'd saved your life, not to mention your face?"

"My face doesn't need saving, thank you!"

Dar decided to keep his opinions to himself. "Look—there're only two ways to stop a war. Somebody can win—and that wasn't happening here. Or you can find some way to save face on both sides. Shacklar did."

"I'll take your word for it." Sam looked more convinced than she sounded. "The main point is, he's found a way to let off the steam that comes from the collision of two cultures."

Dar nodded. "His way also sublimates all sorts of drives very nicely."

Sam looked up, frowning. "Yes, it would. But you can't claim he planned it that way."

"Sure I can. Didn't you know? Shacklar's a psychiatrist."

"Psychiatrist?"

"Sure. By accident, the Navy assigned a man with the right background to be warden for a prison planet. I mean, any soldier who's sent here probably has a mental problem of some sort."

"And if he doesn't, half an hour here should do the trick. But Shackler's a masochist!"

"Who else could survive in a job like this?" Dar looked

around, surveying the "battlefield." "Things have quieted down enough. Let's go."

He shouldered the rope and trudged off across the plain. Sam stayed a moment, then followed, brooding.

She caught up with him. "I hate to admit it—but you've really scrambled my brains."

Dar looked up, surprised. "No offense taken."

"None intended. In fact, it was more like a confession."

"Oh—a compliment. You had us pegged wrong, huh?"

"Thanks for not rubbing it in," she groused. "And don't start crowing too soon. I'm not saying I was wrong, yet. But, well, let's say it's not what I expected."

"What *did* you expect?"

"The dregs of society," she snapped.

"Well, we are now. I mean, that's just a matter of definition, isn't it? If you're in prison, you're the lowest form of social life."

"But people are supposed to go to prison *because* they're the lowest of the low!"

"'Supposed to,' maybe. Might even have been that way, once. But now? You can get sent here just for being in the wrong place at the wrong time."

"Isn't that stretching it?"

"No." Dar's mouth tightened at the corners. "Believe me, it's not."

"Convince me."

"Look," Dar said evenly, "on a prison planet, one thing you don't do is ask anybody why he's there."

"I figured that much." Sam gazed at him, very intently. "I'm asking."

Dar's face went blank, and his jaw tightened. After a few seconds, he took a deep breath. "Okay. Not me, let's say—just someone I know. All right?"

"Anything you say," Sam murmured.

Dar marched along in silence for a few minutes. Then he said, "Call him George."

Sam nodded.

"George was a nice young kid. You know, good parents, lived in a nice small town with good schools, never got into any real trouble. But he got bored with school, and dropped out."

"And got drafted?"

"No—the young idiot enlisted. And, since he had absolutely no training or experience in cargo handling, bookkeeping, or stocking, of *course* he was assigned to the Quartermaster's Corps."

"Which is where you met him?"

"You could say that. Anyway, they made him a cargo handler—taught him how to pilot a small space-tug—and he had a whale of a time, jockeying cargo off shuttles and onto starships. Figured he was a hotshot Navy pilot, all that stuff."

"I thought he was in the Army."

"Even the Army has to run a few ships. Anyway, it was a great job, but after a while it got boring."

Sam closed her eyes. "He wanted a change."

"Right," Dar said sourly. "So he applied for promotion—and they made him into a stock clerk. He began to go crazy, just walking around all day, making sure the robots had put the right items into the right boxes and the right boxes into the right bins—especially since they rarely took anything *out* of those bins, or put in anything new. And he heard the stories in the mess about how even generals have to be very nice to the sergeants in charge of the routing computers, or the goods they order will 'accidently' get shipped halfway across the Sphere."

"Sounds important."

"It does, when you're a teenager. So George decided he was going to get promoted again."

"Well, that's the way it's supposed to be," Sam said quietly. "The young man's supposed to find himself in the Army, and study and work hard to make something better out of himself."

"Sure," Dar said sourly. "Well, George did. He knew a little about data processing, of course, but just the basics they make you learn in school. He'd dropped out before he'd learned anything really useful—so now he learned it. You know, night classes, studying three hours a day, the rest of it. And it worked—he passed the test, and made corporal."

"Everything's fine so far. They assign him a computer terminal?"

Dar nodded. "And for a few months, he just did what he

was told, punched in the numbers he was given. By the end of the first month, he knew the computer codes for every single Army platoon and every single Navy ship by heart. By the end of the second month, he knew all their standard locations."

"And by the end of the third month, he'd begun to realize this wasn't much better than stocking shelves?"

"You got it. Then, one day, the sergeant handed him some numbers that didn't make sense. He'd been on the job long enough to recognize them—the goods number was for a giant heating system, and the destination code was for Betelgeuse Gamma."

"Betelgeuse Gamma?" Sam frowned. "I think that one went across my desk once. Isn't it a jungle world?"

Dar nodded. "That's what George thought. He'd seen such things as insecticides and dehumidifiers shipped out there. This heating unit didn't seem to make sense. So he ran to his sergeant and reported it, just bursting with pride, figuring he'd get a promotion out of catching such an expensive mistake."

"And the sergeant told him to shut up and do what he was told?"

"You *have* worked in a bureaucracy, haven't you? Yeah, 'Ours not to question why, ours but to do and fry.' That sort of thing. But. George had a *moral* sense! And he remembered the scuttlebutt about why even generals have to treat supply sergeants nicely."

"Just offhand, I'd say his sergeant was no exception."

"Kind of looked that way, didn't it? So George did the right thing."

"He reported the sergeant?"

"He wasn't *that* stupid. After all, it was just a set of numbers. Who could prove when they'd gotten into the computer, or where from? No, nobody could've proven anything against the sergeant, but he could have made George's next few years miserable. Reporting him wouldn't do any good, so George did the next best thing. He changed the goods number to one for a giant air-cooling system."

Sam's eyes widened. "Oh, no!"

"Ah," Dar said bitterly, "I see you've been caught in the rules, too. But George was an innocent—he only knew the rules for computers, and assumed the rules for people would be just as logical."

Sam shook her head. "The poor kid. What happened to him?"

"Nothing, for a while," Dar sighed, "and there never were any complaints from Betelgeuse Gamma."

"But after a while, his sergeant started getting nasty?"

"No, and that should've tipped him off. But as I said, he didn't know the people-rules. He couldn't stand the suspense of waiting. So, after a while, he put a query through the system, to find out what happened to that shipment."

Sam squeezed her eyes shut. "Oh, no!"

"Oh, yes. Not *quite* as good as waving a signal flag to attract attention to the situation, but almost. And everything was hunky-dory on Betelgeuse Gamma; the CO there had even sent in a recommendation for a commendation for the lieutenant who had overseen the processing of the order, because that air-cooling plant had already saved several hundred lives in his base hospital. And before the day was out, the sergeant called George into his office."

"A little angry?"

"He was furious. Seems the lieutenant had raked him over the coals because the wrong order number had been filed—and against the sergeant's direct order. George tried to explain, but all that mattered to the sergeant was that he was in trouble. He told George that he was remanding him to the lieutenant's attention for disciplinary action."

"So it was the lieutenant who'd been out to get the general on Betelgeuse Gamma!"

"Or somebody in his command. Who knows? Maybe that CO had a lieutenant who'd said something nasty to George's lieutenant, back at the Academy. One way or another, the lieutenant didn't have to press charges, or initiate anything— all he had to do was act on his sergeant's recommendation. He demoted George to private and requested his transfer to Eta Cassiopeia."

"Could be worse, I suppose," Sam mused.

"Well, George heard there was a war going on there at the moment—but that wasn't the real problem. This lieutenant had charge of a computer section, remember."

"Of course—what's wrong with me? His traveling orders

came out with a different destination on 'em." Sam looked up. "Not Wolmar! Not here!"

"Oh, yes," Dar said, with a saccharine smile. "Here. And, the first time he showed his orders to an officer, the officer assumed that, if he was en route to Wolmar, he must be a convicted criminal, and clapped him in irons."

"How neat," Sam murmured, gazing into the distance. "Off to prison, without taking a chance of being exposed during a court-martial. . . . Your lieutenant was a brainy man."

"Not really—he just knew the system. So there George was, on his way here and nothing he could do about it."

"Couldn't he file a complaint?" Sam bit her lip. "No, of course not. What's wrong with me?"

"Right." Dar nodded. "He was in the brig. Besides, the complaint would've been filed into the computer, and the lieutenant knew computers. And who would let a convicted felon near a computer terminal?"

"But wouldn't the ship's commanding officer listen to him?"

"Why? Every criminal says he didn't do it. And, of course, once it's on your record that you've been sent to a prison planet, you're automatically a felon for the rest of your life."

Sam nodded slowly. "The perfect revenge. He made George hurt, he got him out of the way, and he made sure George'd never be able to get back at him." She looked up at Dar. "Or do you people get to go home when your sentence is up?"

Dar shook his head. "No such thing as a sentence ending here. They don't send you to Wolmar unless it's for life." He stopped and pointed. "This is where a life ends."

Sam turned to look.

They stood in the middle of a broad, flat plain. A few hundred yards away stood a plastrete blockhouse, with long, high fences running out from it like the sides of a funnel. The rest of the plain was scorched, barren earth, pocked with huge blackened craters, glossy and glinting.

"The spaceport." Sam nodded. "Yes, I've been here."

"Great first sight of the place, isn't it? They chose the most desolate spot on the whole planet for the new convict's first sight of his future home. Here's where George's life ended."

"And a new one began?"

Dar shook his head. "For two years he wondered if he was

in hell, with Wolmen throwing nasty, pointed things at him during the day and guards beating him up if he hiccuped during the night." He nodded toward the blockhouse again. "That was the worst thing about this place, the first time I looked at it—guards, all over. Everywhere. They were all built like gorillas, too, and they all loved pain—other people's pain."

"Yes, I was wondering about that. Where are they?"

"Gone, to wherever the computers reassigned them. When Shacklar came, the guards went."

"*What?*" Sam whirled, staring up at him. "That's impossible!"

"Oh, I dunno." Dar looked around. "See any guards?"

"Well, no, but—one uniform looks just like any other to me."

"We didn't wear uniforms when I came here. First thing they did was give me a set of gray coveralls and tell me to get into 'em." His mouth tightened at the memory. Then he shook his head and forced a smile. "But that was eleven years ago. Now *we* wear the uniforms, and the guards are gone."

"Why?"

Dar shrugged. "Shacklar thought unforms'd be good for morale. He was right, too."

"No, no! I mean, why no guards?"

"Wrong question. Look at it Shacklar's way—why have *any* guards?"

Sam frowned, thinking it over. "To keep the prisoners from escaping."

"Where to?" Dar spread his hand toward the whole vast plain. "The Wolman villages? We were already fighting them—had been, ever since this, uh, 'colony' started."

"No, no! Off-planet! Where the rest of society is! Your victims! The rest of the universe!"

"So how do you escape from a planet?"

Sam opened her mouth—and hesitated.

"If you can come up with an idea, I'll be delighted to listen." Dar's eyes glinted.

Sam shut her mouth with an angry snap. "Get going! All you have to do is get going fast enough! Escape velocity!"

"Great idea! How do I do it? Run real fast? Flap my arms?"

"Spare me the sarcasm! You hijack a spaceship, of course!"

"We *have* thought of it," Dar mused. "Of course, there's only one spaceship per month. You came in on it, so you know: Where does it go?"

"Well, it's a starship, so it can't land. It just goes into orbit. Around the . . . uh . . ."

"Moon." Dar nodded. "And a shuttle brings you down to the moon's surface, and you have to go into the terminal there through a boarding tube, because you don't have a spacesuit. And there're hidden video pickups in the shuttle, and hidden video pickups all through the terminal, so the starship's crew can make sure there aren't any escaping prisoners waiting to try to take over the shuttle."

"Hidden video pickups? What makes you think that?"

"Shacklar. He told us about them, just before he sent the guards home."

"Oh." Sam chewed it over. "What would they do if they *did* see some prisoners waiting to take over the shuttle?"

"Bleed off the air and turn off the heaters. It's a vacuum up there, you know. And the whole terminal's remote-controlled, by the starship; there isn't even a station master you can clobber and steal keys from."

Sam shuddered.

"Don't worry," Dar soothed. "We couldn't get up there, anyway."

Sam looked up. "Why not?"

Dar spread his hands. "How did you get down here?"

"The base sent up a ferry to bring us down."

Dar nodded. "Didn't you wonder why it wasn't there waiting for you when you arrived?"

"I did think it was rather inconsiderate," Sam said slowly, "but spaceline travel isn't what it used to be."

"Decadent," Dar agreed. "Did you notice when the ferry did come up?"

"Now that you mention it . . . *after* the starship left."

Dar nodded. "Just before it blasted out of orbit, the starship sent down a pulse that unlocked the ferry's engines—for twenty-four hours."

"That's long enough. If you really had any gumption, you could take over the ferry after it lands, go back up to the moon, and wait a few months for the next starship."

"Great! We could bring sandwiches, and have a picnic—a *lot* of sandwiches; they don't store any rations up there, so we'd need a few months' worth. They'd get a little stale, you know? Besides, the ferry's engines automatically relock after one round trip. But the real problem is air."

"*I* could breathe in that terminal."

"You wouldn't have if you'd stayed around for a day. The starship brings in a twenty-four-hour air supply when it comes. They send an advance crew to come in, turn it on, and wait for pressure before they call down the shuttle." Dar gazed up at the sky. "No, I don't think I'd like waiting for a ship up there, for a month. Breathing CO_2 gets to you, after a while."

"It's a gas," Sam said in a dry icy tone. "I take it Shacklar set up this darling little system when he came?"

"No, it was always here. I wouldn't be surprised if it were standard for prison planets. So, by the time Shacklar'd managed to reach the surface of Wolmar, he knew there wasn't really any need for guards."

"Except to keep you from killing each other! How many convicts were here for cold-blooded murder?"

"Not too many, really; most of the murderers were hot-blooded." He shuddered at the memory. "Very. But there were a handful of reptiles—and three of them were power-hungry, too."

"Why?" Sam looked up, frowning. "I mean, how much power could they get? Nothing that counts, if they couldn't leave the planet."

"If you'll pardon my saying so, that's a very provincial view. I mean, there's a whole *planet* here."

"But no money."

"Well, not real money, no. But I didn't say they were out to get rich; I said they were out for power."

"Power over a mud puddle? A handful of soldiers? What good is that?"

"Thanks for rubbing my nose in it," Dar snapped.

"Oh! I'm sorry." Sam's eyes widened hugely. "I just turn off other people's feelings, sometimes. I get carried away with what I'm saying."

"Don't we all?" Dar smiled bleakly, sawing his temper back. "I suppose that's how the lust for power begins."

"How—by ignoring other people's feelings?"

Dar nodded. "Only worrying about how *you* feel. I suppose if you're the boss, you feel safer, and that's all that really matters."

"Not the bosses *I've* met. They're always worrying about who's going to try to kick them out and take over—and I'm just talking about bureaucrats!" She looked up at Dar. "Would you believe it—some of them actually hire bodyguards?"

"Sure, I'd believe it! After living on a prison planet *without* guards."

"Oh. Your fellow prisoners were worse than the gorillas?"

"Much worse," Dar confirmed. "I mean, with the guards at least you knew who to watch out for—they wore uniforms. But with your friendly fellow prisoners, you never knew from one moment to the next who was going to try to slip a knife between your ribs."

"They let you have knives?"

Dar shrugged impatiently. "The Wolmen could chip flints; so could we. Who was going to stop us, with the guards gone? No, they loaded onto the ferry and lifted off; Shacklar stepped into Government House and locked himself in behind concrete and steel with triple locks and arm-thick bolts . . . and the monsters came out of the woodwork. Anybody who had a grudge hunted down his favorite enemy, and started slicing. Or got sliced up himself."

"Immoral!" Sam muttered. "How could he bring himself to do such a thing!"

Dar shrugged. "Had to be hard, I guess. Lord knows we had enough hard cases walking around. When they saw blood flowing, they started banding together to guard each other's backs. And the first thing you knew, there were little gangs roaming around, looking for people to rough up and valuables to steal."

Sam snorted. "What kind of valuables could you have had?"

"Food would do, at that point. Distribution had broken down. Why should the work-gangs work, without the guards to make them? Finally, we mobbed the warehouse and broke in—and ruined more food than we ate." He shuddered at the memory. "They started knife fights over ham hocks! That was about when I started looking for a hole to crawl into."

"Your general has no more ethics than a shark!" Sam blazed. "How could he just sit there and let it happen?"

"I expect he had a pretty good idea about how it would all come out."

"How could he? With chaos like that, it was completely unpredictable!"

"Well, not really. . . ."

"What're you talking about? You could've all killed each other off!"

"That's predictable, isn't it? But there wasn't too much chance of it, I guess. There were too many of us—half a million. That's a full society; and anarchy's an unstable condition. When the little gangs began to realize they couldn't be sure of beating the next little gang they were trying to steal from, they made a truce instead, and merged into a bigger gang that *could* be sure of winning a fight, because it was the biggest gang around."

"So other little gangs had to band together into bigger gangs too." Sam nodded. "And that meant the bigger gangs had to merge into small armies."

"Right. Only most of us didn't realize all that; we just knew there were three big gangs fighting it out, all of a sudden."

"The power-hungry boys you told me about?"

Dar nodded. "And they were pretty evenly balanced, too. So their battles didn't really decide anything; they just killed off sixty men. Which meant you had to stay way clear of *any* of 'em, or they'd draft you as a replacement."

"So two of them made a truce and ganged up on the third?"

"No, the Wolmen ganged up on all of us, first."

"Oh." Sam looked surprised, then nodded slowly. "Makes sense, of course. I mean, why should they just sit back and wait for you to get yourselves organized?"

"Right. It made a lot more sense to hit us while we were still disorganized. And we'd stopped keeping sentries on the wall, and the Wolmen knew enough to hit us at night."

Sam shuddered. "Why weren't you all killed in your beds?"

"Because the Big Three *did* have sentries, to make sure none of the *others* tried a night attack. So all of a sudden, the sirens were howling, and everybody was running around yelling—and military conditioning took over."

"Military conditioning?" Sam frowned. "I thought you were convicts!"

"Yeah, but we were still soldiers. What'd you think—the Army provided a few battalions to fight off the Wolmen for us? We had to do our *own* fighting, with our own sergeants and lieutenants. The guards just stood back and made sure we didn't try to get any big ideas . . . and handled the laser cannons."

"But how could they let you have weapons?"

Dar shrugged. "Bows and arrows, tops. That gave us a fair chance against the Wolmen. So when the sirens shrieked, we just automatically ran for the armory and grabbed our bows, and jumped any Wolman who got in our way. Then, when we had our weapons, we just naturally yelled, 'What do we do, Sarge?' I mean, he was there getting his weapons, too—if he was still alive."

"And most of them were?"

"What can I tell you? Rank has its privileges. Yeah, most of them were there, and they told us where to go."

"Sergeants usually do, I understand."

"Well, yes. But in this case, they just took us out to chop up anything that didn't wear a uniform—and look for a lieutenant to ask orders from. We pulled together into companies—and the lieutenants were already squawking into their wrist coms, demanding that Shacklar tell them what to do."

"Why would they do . . . ?" Sam broke off, her eyes widening. "I just realized something: soldiers are basically bureaucrats. Nobody wants to take a chance on getting blamed."

"It is kind of drilled into you," Dar admitted. "And as I said, when the Wolmen came over the wall, habit took over. It did for Shacklar, too, I guess. He started telling them what to do."

"Habit, my great toe! He'd been waiting for a chance like that—counting on it!"

"Looking for me to disagree with you? Anyway, he had the viewscreens, and he knew the tactics; so he started giving orders." Dar shook his head in disbelief. "If you can call them orders! 'Lieutenant Walker, there's a band of Wolmen breaking through over on the left; I really think you should run over and arrange a little surprise for them.' 'Lieutenant Able, Sergeant Dorter's squad is outnumbered two to one over on your company's right; would you send your reserves over to join him, please?' "

"Come off it! No general talks to his subordinates that way!"

Dar held up a palm. "So help me, he did it! I overheard Lieutenant Walker's communicator."

"You mean you were in that battle?"

"I had a choice?"

"But I thought you tried to find a hole to crawl into!"

"Sure. I didn't say I succeeded, did I?"

Sam turned away, glowering. "I still don't believe it. Why should he be so polite?"

"We figured it out later. In effect, he was telling us it was *our* war, and it was up to us to fight it; but he was willing to give us advice, if we wanted it."

"Good advice, I take it?"

"Oh, very good! We had the Wolmen pushed back against the wall in an hour. Then Shacklar told the lieutenants to pull back and give them a chance to get away. They all answered, basically, 'The hell with that noise! We've got a chance to wipe out the bastards!' 'Indeed you do,' Shacklar answered, 'and they all have brothers and cousins back home—six of them for every one of you. But if you *do* try to exterminate them—well, you'll manage it, but they'll kill two of your men for every one of theirs.' Well, the lieutenants allowed that he had a point, so they did what he said and pulled back; and the Wolmen, with great daring and ingenuity, managed to get back up over the wall and away."

"Then he told you to break out the laser cannon?"

"No, he'd sent the cannons home with the guards. Good thing, too; I'd hate to think what those three power-mongers would've done with them. But we *did* have hand-blasters, in the armories. Each of the power-mongers had managed to seize an armory as a power base as soon as he'd recruited a gang. They'd opened the doors and issued sidearms as soon as the sirens screamed. They weren't much good for the close fighting inside the wall; but, once the Wolmen were over the top and running, we got up on the parapet and started shooting after them, until the lieutenants yelled at us to stop wasting our charges. The Wolmen were running, and they didn't stop until morning."

"A victory," Sam said dryly.

"A bigger one than you think—because as soon as the shooting was over the three would-be warlords showed up with their henchmen, bawling, 'All right, it's all over! Turn in your guns! Go home!'"

"They *what*?"

"Well, sure." Dar shrugged. "After all, they'd opened up the armories for us, hadn't they? Shouldn't we give them their guns back now? I mean, you've got to see it from their viewpoint."

"I hope *you* didn't!"

"Of course we didn't. We just turned around grinning, and pointed the guns at *them*. But we didn't say anything; we let the lieutenants do the talking."

"*What* talking?"

"It depended. The nice ones said, 'Hands up.' The rest of them just said, 'Fire!' And we did."

Sam formed a silent O with her lips.

"It was quick and merciful," Dar pointed out. "More than they had a right to, really."

"What did you do without them? I mean, they had provided some sort of social order."

"I see you favor loose definitions. But while the ashes cooled, the lieutenants got together and did some talking."

"They elected a leader?"

"Yeah, they could all agree that they needed to. But they weren't so unanimous about who. There were four main candidates, and they wrangled and haggled, but nobody could agree on anything—I mean, not even enough to call for a vote."

"How long did they keep *that* up?"

"Long enough for it to get pretty tense, and the boys on the battlements were getting kind of edgy, eyeing each other and wondering if we were going to be ordered to start burning each other pretty soon."

"You wouldn't really have done it!"

"I dunno. That military conditioning runs pretty deep. You don't know *what* you'll do when you hear your lieutenant call, 'Fire!'"

Sam shuddered. "What are you—animals?"

"I understand the philosophers are still debating that one. My favorite is, 'Man is the animal who laughs.' Fortunately, Lieutenant Mandring thought the same way."

"Who's Lieutenant Mandring?"

"The one with the sense of humor. He nominated General Shacklar."

Sam whirled, the picture of fury. Then she developed a sudden faraway look. "You know . . ."

Dar pointed a finger at her. "*That's* just about the way all the other lieutenants reacted. They started to yell—then they realized he meant it for a joke. After they'd finished rolling around on the ground and had it throttled down to a chuckle, they started eyeing each other, and it got awfully quiet."

"But Shacklar didn't even *try* to talk them into it!"

"He didn't have to; he'd given them a taste of do-it-yourself government. So they were ready to consider a change of diet— but nobody wanted to be the first one to say it. So Lieutenant Griffin had to take it—he's the one with the talent for saving other people's faces. Too bad he can't do anything about his own. . . ."

"What *happened*?"

"Oh! Yes . . . well, all he said was, 'Why don't we ask him what *he* thinks?' And after they got done laughing again, Lieutenant Able said, 'It'd be good for a laugh.' And Lieutenant Walker said, 'Sure. I mean, we don't *have* to do what he says, you know.' Well, they could all agree on that, of course, so they put Lieutenant Walker up to it, he having spoken last, and he called the General on his wrist com, explained the situation, and asked what he'd do in their place. He said he was willing to serve, but really thought they ought to elect one of their own number."

Sam smiled. "How nice of him! What'd they do back at Square One?"

"They asked the comedian for a suggestion. He said they

ought to call out each lieutenant's name and have everybody who had confidence in him raise a hand."

"Who won?"

"Everybody; they all pulled, 'No confidence.' So Lieutenant Mandring called for a vote on General Shacklar."

"How long was the pause?"

"Long enough for everybody to realize they were getting hungry. But after a while they started raising hands, and three hundred sixty out of four hundred went up."

"This, for the man who had to hide in a fortress? What changed their minds?"

"The chaos, mostly—especially since he'd just done a good job directing them in battle. Soldiers value that kind of thing. So they called Shacklar and told him he was elected."

"I take it he was glad to hear it."

"Hard to say; he just heaved a sigh and asked them to form a parliament before they went to lunch and to start thinking about a constitution while they ate."

"Constitution! In a prison?"

"Why not? I mean, they'd just elected him, hadn't they?" Sam developed a fawaway look again. "I suppose. . . ."

"So did they. That was the turning point, you see—when we started thinking of ourselves as a colony, not a prison. When we wrote the constitution, we didn't call Shacklar 'warden'— we named him 'governor.' "

"Generous of you," Sam smirked, "considering Terra had done it already."

"Yeah, but *we* hadn't. And once he had the consent of the populace, he could govern without guards."

"That . . . makes . . . a weird kind of sense."

"Doesn't it? Only when you can make a whole planet into a prison, of course—and there's no way out. But that's the way it is here. So he *could* send the guards home, and let us fight it out for ourselves."

"Which made you realize he was better than the natural product."

"It did have that advantage. And, once his position was consolidated, he could start proposing reforms to the Council."

"Council?"

"The legislative body. The Wolmen are agitating for representation, now. But that's okay—we traders are angling for a rep at their moots. Anyway, Shacklar talked the Council into instituting pay."

"Oh, that certainly must have taken a lot of convincing!"

"It did, as it happens; a fair number of them were Communists. But pay it was—in scrip; worthless off-planet, I'm sure, but it buys a lot here—a BTU for a neat bunk, two BTUs for a clean yard, and so forth."

"Great! Where could they spend it?"

"Oh, the General talked Cholly into coming in and setting up shop, and a few of the con . . . uh, colonists, decided he had a good thing going, and . . ."

"Pretty soon, the place was lousy with capitalists."

"Just the bare necessities—a general store, a fix-it shop, and three taverns."

"That 'general store' looks more like a shopping complex."

"Just a matter of scale. Anyway, that created a driving hunger for BTUs and that meant soldiers started spiffing up, and . . ."

"Higher morale, all over," Sam muttered. "Because they *can* improve their lot."

"Right. Then Cholly started paying top dollar for pipe-leaf traders, and . . ."

"A drug baron!"

"Suppose you could call him that. But it turned out there *was* a market for it—the drug's very low-bulk after it's processed, you see; and it doesn't provide euphoria or kill pain, but it *does* retard the aging process. So Universal Pharmaceuticals was interested, and Interstellar Geriatrics, and . . ."

"I get the picture. Top money."

"But it costs a lot, too—especially at first, when it was a little on the hazardous side. But Cholly was bringing in trade goods that made glass beads just sharp-cornered gravel, so once we managed to get trade started, it mushroomed."

"And all of a sudden, the Wolmen weren't quite so hostile any more." Sam nodded.

"Aw, you peeked." Dar scuffed at the turf with his boot-toe. "And from there, of course, it was just a little fast talking to get them to agree to the chalk-fights."

Christopher Stasheff

36

"So trade is growing, and morale is growing, and you're taking the first steps toward a unified society, and everybody feels as though they've got some opportunity, and . . ." Sam broke off, shaking her head, dazzled. "I can't believe it! The central planets are mired in malaise and self-pity, and out here in the marches, you've managed to build a growing, maybe even hopeful, society! Back on Terra, everybody's living in walking despair because *nobody* feels they can make things better."

"What?" Dar was shocked. "But they've got everything! They've . . ."

"Got nothing," Sam sneered. "On Terra, you'll die doing the job your father did, and everybody knows it. You've got your rooms, your servos, and your rations. And that's it."

"But even beggars have whole houses—with furniture that makes anything here look like firewood! And they don't have to do a lick of housework, with all those servos—their free time's *all* free!"

"Free to do what—rot?"

"To do anything they want! I mean, even a rube like me has heard what's included in those rations."

Sam shrugged. "Sure, you can get drunk or stoned every night, and you can go out to a party or go to a show . . ."

Dar gave a whimpering sigh.

". . . but actually *do* something? No chance! Unless you're born into government—and even *they* can't figure out anything worth doing."

"But . . ." Dar flailed at the sky. "But there's a thousand worlds out there to conquer!"

"Why bother?" She smiled bitterly. "We've done that already—and it hasn't improved things back on Terra much."

"Hasn't improved!? But your poorest beggar lives like a medieval king!"

"Oh, does she?" Sam's eyes glittered. "Where're the servants, the musicians, the courtiers, the knights willing to fight for her smile?"

"Even a Terran reject has three or four servos! They'll even turn on the audio for him—and there's your musicians!"

"And the courtiers? The knights?" Sam shook her head.

"What made a king *royal* was being able to command other people—and there's no coin that'll buy that!"

Dar could only stare.

Then he gave his head a quick shake, pushing out a whistle. "Boy! That's *sick*!"

"Also decadent." She smiled, with Pyrrhic triumph. "They're moribund there. What I can't figure out is how you folks avoid it."

Dar shrugged. "Because we're already at the bottom? I mean, once you've landed here, there's no place to go but up!"

"There's no place to go, period!" Sam's eyes lit. "Maybe that's it—*because* it's out here in the marches! Out here, on the edge of civilization—because anything you're going to do, you're going to have to do for yourselves. Terra's too far away to send help. And too far away to really be able to run you, either. By the time they can tell you not to do something, you've already been doing it for a year! And because . . ." She clamped her mouth shut.

"Because they really don't care?" Dar grinned. "Because this place is a hole, and the only people Terra sends out here are the ones they want to forget about? I wouldn't be surprised if they even wanted to get rid of Shacklar."

"Of course; he was a threat to the ones with the *real* power. I mean, after all, he's *capable*. He was bound to make waves. Which I'm about to do too."

"I'm braced." Dar tried to hide the smile.

"You still haven't shown me how you're not really fleecing the natives."

"No, I haven't, have I. But it *does* take showing. We start trading at sundown."

2

"That's not the way to make a campfire," Sam pointed out.

"What would you know about it?" Dar blithely heaped green sticks and leaves onto the flaming kindling. "You're a city girl."

"Who says?"

"You. You said you came from Terra, and it's just one great big city."

"It is, but we've kept a few parks, like the Rockies. I do know you're supposed to use dry wood."

"Entirely correct." Dar smiled up at the roiling column of thick gray smoke turning gold in the sunset.

Sam sighed. "All right, so you're trying to attract attention. What do we use for cooking?"

"Why bother?" Dar started foraging in the foodbag. "All we've got is cheese and crackers. And raisin wine, of course."

Sam shuddered.

Darkness came down, and company came up—five Wolmen, each with a bale on his shoulder.

"Ah! Company for cordials!" Dar rubbed his hands, then reached for the bottle and the glasses.

"Get 'em drunk before they start bargaining, huh?" Sam snorted.

"That'd take more liquor than I can pack. But they count it friendly." He stepped toward the arrivals, raising the bottle. "How!"

"You not know, me not tell you," the first grunted, completing the formula. "Good seeing, Dar Mandra."

"Good to see you, too, Hirschmeir." Dar held out a handful of glasses; the Wolman took one, and so did each of his mates as they came up. Dar poured a round and lifted his glass. "To trade!"

"And profit," Hirschmeir grunted. He drank half his glass. "Ah! Good swill after long hike. And hot day gathering pipeweed."

"Yeah, I know," Dar sympathized. "And it brings so little, too."

"Five point three eight kwahers per ounce on Libra exchange," a second Wolman said promptly.

Dar looked up in surprise. "That's the fresh quote, right off today's cargo ship. Where'd you get it?"

"You sell us nice wireless last month," Hirschmeir reminded. "Tell Sergeant Walstock him run nice music service."

"Sure will." Dar pulled out a pad and scribbled a note.

"Little heavy on drums, though," another Wolman said thoughtfully.

"Gotcha, Slotmeyer." Dar scribbled again. "More booze, anybody?"

Five glasses jumped out. Dar whistled, walking around with the bottle, then picked up a bale. "Well. Let's see what we're talking about." He plopped the bale onto the front of the grav-sled.

"Twenty-seven point three two kilograms," the sled reported. "Ninety-seven percent *Organum Translucem,* with three percent grasses, leaf particles, and sundry detritus."

"The sundry's the good part." Dar hefted the bale back off the sled and set it about halfway between himself and Hirschmeir.

"You sure that thing not living?" one of the Wolmen demanded.

"Sure. But it's got a ghost in it."

"No ghost in machine." The Wolman shook his head emphatically.

Dar looked up sharply, then frowned. "Did I sell you folks that cubook series on the history of philosophy?"

"Last year," Hirschmeir grunted. "Lousy bargain. Half of tribe quote-um Locke now."

"Locke?" Dar scowled. "I would've thought Berkeley and Sartre would be more your speed."

"Old concepts," Slotmeyer snorted. "We learn at mothers' knees. You forget—our ancestors opposition culture."

"That does keep slipping my mind," Dar confessed. "Well! How about two hundred thirty-four for the bale?"

Hirschmeir shook his head. "Too far below Libra quote. Your scrip only worth eighty percent of Libran BTU today."

"I'm going to have to have a talk with Sergeant Walstock," Dar growled. "Okay, so my price is twenty percent low. But you forget—we have to pay shipping charges to get this stuff to Libra."

"And your boss Cholly also gotta pay you, and overhead," Slotmeyer added. "We not forget anything, Dar Mandra."

"Except that Cholly's gotta show *some* profit, or he can't stay in business," Dar amended. "Okay, look—how about two seventy-five?"

"Tenth of a kwaher?" Hirschmeir scoffed. He bent over and picked up his bale. "Nice talking to you, Dar Mandra."

"Okay, *okay*! Two eighty!"

"Two ninety," Slotmeyer said promptly.

"Okay, two eighty-five." Dar sighed, shaking his head. "The things I do for you guys! Well, it's not your worry if I don't come back next month. Hope you like the new man."

"No worry. We tell Cholly we only deal with soft touch." Hirschmeir grinned. "Okay. What *you* got to sell, Dar Mandra?"

"Oh, a little bit of this and a minor chunk of that." Dar turned to the sled. "Wanna give me a hand?"

Together, all six of them manhandled a huge crate onto the ground. Dar popped the catches and opened the front and the left side. The Wolmen crowded around, fingering the merchandise and muttering in excitement.

"What this red stone?" Slotmeyer demanded, holding up a machined gem. "Ruby for laser?"

Dar nodded. "Synthetically grown, but it works better than the natural ones."

"Here barrels," another Wolman pointed out.

"Same model you sold us instruction manual for?" Hirschmeir weighed a power cell in his palm.

Dar nodded. "Double-X 14. Same as the Navy uses."

"What this?" One of the Wolmen held up a bit of machined steel.

"Part of the template assembly for an automatic lathe," Dar answered.

Slotmeyer frowned. "What is 'lathe'?"

Dar grinned. "Instruction manual's only twenty-five kwahers."

"Twenty-five?" Hirschmeir bleated.

Dar's grin widened.

Hirschmeir glowered at him, then grimaced and nodded. "You highway robber, Dar Mandra."

"No, low-way," Dar corrected. "Cholly tells me I'm not ready for the highway."

"Him got high idea of low," Hirschmeir grunted. "What prices on laser parts?"

Dar slid a printed slip out of his jacket pocket and handed it to Hirschmeir. " 'Scuse me while you study that; I'll finish the weigh-in." He turned away to start hoisting bales onto the sled's scale as the Wolmen clustered around Hirschmeir, running through the price list and muttering darkly.

Sam stepped up and tapped Dar on the shoulder. "What happened to all the 'ums' on the ends of their verbs?"

"Hm?" Dar looked up. "Oh, they know me, y' see. No need to put on a show anymore."

"All right, all right!" Hirschmeir grumbled. "We take three rubies, three barrels, ten power supplies, and template assembly for lathe."

"Gotcha." Dar pressed a button on the scale, and it murmured, "Total for goods, 4235.50 BTUs."

Dar nodded. "And the total for your pipeweed is 5337.50. You can spend another 1102, Hirschmeir."

"No got any more goods we want," Slotmeyer grunted.

Hirschmeir nodded, holding out a palm. "Cash be nice."

"You could put it on deposit at the bank," Dar offered. "Cholly's starting up a new kind of account."

Hirschmeir shook his head. "Only pays lousy five percent per annum. We do better use it for stake for playing poker with soldiers."

"But this is a new kind of account," Dar reminded. "The interest is compounded quarterly."

Hirschmeir's head lifted a little, and his frown deepened. "'Interest compounded'? What that mean?"

"That means that, at the end of every five months, the interest is paid into your account, and figured as part of the principal for the next quarter."

"So for second quarter, Cholly pay interest on 1157.125?"

Dar nodded. "And for the third quarter, he'll be paying you interest on 1162.48. You're getting an effective annual yield of twenty-one and a half percent."

"Cholly go broke," Slotmeyer snapped.

"No, he'll make a profit—if enough of you open up these accounts. If he gets five thousand for capital, he can buy Bank of I.D.E. bonds that pay twenty-three percent effective."

Slotmeyer's head lifted slowly, his eyes widening.

He whirled to Hirschmeir. "Take it!"

"You sure?" Hirschmeir looked decidedly uncomfortable.

"Sure? When Cholly making profit, too? Gotta be straight deal!"

Hirschmeir looked at the ground for a few minutes; then he looked up at Dar, face firming with decision. "Right. We open new account."

"Right here." Dar whipped out the papers and handed them to Hirschmeir; but Slotmeyer intercepted them. He scanned the pages quickly, muttering to himself, then nodded and passed them on to Hirschmeir. Hirschmeir made his sign and added his signature after it in parentheses. Dar took the papers back, fed them into a slot in the sled. It chuckled to itself, then fed out a copy of the forms, and spat out a small flat blue booklet. Dar checked the passbook to make sure the deposit was recorded properly, then nodded and passed the bundle to Hirschmeir. The Wolman folded them away, straightening and grinning. "Okay, Dar Mandra. Is good doing business with you."

"Always a pleasure." Dar held up the bottle. "One for the trail?"

Sam watched the Wolman troop move off into the night, while Dar reloaded the grav-sled and fastened the tarp down again. Finally she turned back to him. "Why do they call it 'pipeweed'?"

"Hm?" Dar looked up. "Take a look at it."

Sam stepped over and fingered one of the bales. "Long, thin, hollow stems." She nodded. "Little pipes."

Dar covered the bale and fastened down the last corner of the tarp. "Good quality, too. Not a bad night's trading."

"But how can you *say* that?" Sam erupted. "You've scarcely made any profit at all!"

"About one and a half percent." Dar picked up a plastic cube and stood up. "Which is pretty good. Cholly's happy if I just break even."

"Oh, he is, huh?" Sam jammed her fists on her hips. "What is he, a philanthropist?"

"A teacher," Dar reminded, "and Shacklar's a politician. All Cholly really cares about is how much the Wolmen learn from the trading; and all Shacklar cares about is tying the Wolmen into an economic unit with the soldiers. And the good will that goes with both, of course."

"Of course," Sam echoed dryly. "And I suppose you manage to pick up a few items about Wolman culture on every trip."

"Which I faithfully report back to Cholly, who makes sure it winds up as beer-gossip." Dar grinned. "Give us ten years, and the soldiers and Wolmen'll know each other's culture almost as well as their own."

"Well, they do seem to have a pretty thorough grasp of basic finance."

"And Slotmeyer's getting some ideas about law," Dar said with a critical nod. "He's coming along nicely."

Sam frowned. "You sound like a teacher gloating over a prize pupil. . . . Oh!"

Dar gave her a wicked grin.

"Of course; I should have realized," she said dryly. "Cholly doesn't hire traders; he recruits teachers."

"Pretty much," Dar confirmed. "But we do have to have an eye for profit and loss."

"How about the loss to the Army?"

"Hm?" Dar looked up. "What loss?"

"Those laser parts—they're military issue, aren't they?"

Dar stared at her while his smile congealed.

"Come on," Sam wheedled, "you can trust me. I mean, after all, I know enough to sink you already, if I really wanted to."

Dar's smile cracked into a grin. "How? We're already sunk here."

Sam frowned, nonplussed. "But how do you know I'm not a BOA spy? Or an Army spy, trying to find out what Shacklar's *really* doing here? For all you know, when I get back to Terra, I might issue a report that would get him pulled off this planet."

Dar nodded. "Yeah. You could be."

Sam inched away from him, watching him as a mouse watches a waking cat.

"But you obviously aren't," Dar finished.

Sam frowned indignantly. "How the hell could *you* tell?"

"Well, in the first place, I don't believe *anybody* on Terra really cares about what happens out here—not in the Army, and not in BOA either."

"Shacklar *is* building a power base," Sam pointed out.

"Power to do what? He can't even conquer the Wolmen."

"But he *is* trying to weld them into one solid unit with his convicts."

Dar smiled, amused. "And just what do you think he'll do with that unit? Build a very long ladder, and *climb* to Terra?" He shook his head. "There's no way Shacklar can be a threat to anybody off this planet—and the boys on Terra don't care what kind of threat he is to anybody *on* this planet." He tossed the plastic cube in the air and caught it, grinning. "Not that I think you really are a spy. Of course, you could be a reporter, looking for a little bit of muck to rake, but why would you come all this way for it?"

"To find something to report," Sam said with a vindictive smile. "Nothing *ever* happens on Terra."

Dar shrugged. "Okay—let's say you really are that hard up. What could you actually do? Turn in a ten-minute report for a

3DT show about the horrible, crooked, scandalous doings out here on Wolmar?"

"Sure. You're far enough away to have a touch of the exotic. It might really catch on for a while. We're *really* bored on Terra."

Dar shrugged. "So we'd be a six-day wonder."

"Nine."

"Nine. And the Army would say, 'My Heavens! We didn't realize *that* was going on!' And they'd send a formal, official notice to Shacklar that would say, 'You naughty, naughty boy! How *dare* you do all these horrible things! The way you're treating your convicts is criminal!' And Shacklar, I'm sure, would give them fifty excellent reasons, and finish by saying, 'But of course, since this isn't what you want, I'll be glad to do it *your* way.' And Central HQ would say, 'Fine. You do it *our* way.' Which they would go tell the media, and the media would tell it to the people in another show, and the people would sit back with that nice, solid feeling that they'd actually managed to accomplish something. And everybody would forget about it."

"And Shacklar wouldn't actually *do* anything?"

"Oh, sure—he'd give me a week of chores for shooting off my mouth. Which is okay; it's restful to do something that doesn't involve any responsibility, now and then."

Sam sighed. "All right. Then you should just tell me about those laser parts because you *want* to—and because there's no good reason not to. . . . Is there?"

"None, except my firm conviction that you'll put the worst possible construction on anything I tell you. What *about* those laser parts?"

"They're military issue, aren't they?"

"Sure. What else would a general be able to get, that natives would want?"

"That doesn't strike you as a little bit corrupt?"

"Why? They're being used for a military purpose."

"The *Wolmen's* military purpose!" Sam exploded. "It's gunrunning!"

"I suppose you could call it that," Dar said judiciously.

"'Suppose'! Don't you realize you're signing your own death warrants?"

"Not as long as things stay peaceful," Dar pointed out. "Shacklar has more faith in trade than in firepower. It's awfully hard to fight your own customers."

"But not exactly unknown."

"True," Dar agreed. "That's why it's so important to get the two groups to understand each other, and do some socializing. You might fight your customer, but you won't fight your friend—*if* we can get them to be friends. If a real war does start, and if all the Wolman tribes ever unite against us, we're dead. They outnumber us a thousand to one. Blasters would just speed up the process, that's all."

"Then why not sell them blasters?" Sam demanded. "Why just spare parts?"

"Well, for one thing, whole blasters are a little difficult to get the Army to ship to a prison planet." Dar pressed a button in the side of the plastic cube; it started to hum. "But spare parts they'll ship us by the thousands."

Sam shook her head. "The insanities of bureaucracy!" She watched the humming cube begin to unfold and expand. "And for another thing?"

"For another thing, if we just sell them parts and instruction manuals, they have to learn how to put the dern things together." Dar smiled, a faraway look in his eyes. "And that makes 'em begin to wonder how and why it works—so they end up learning technology. Wait'll they find out what a headache that lathe's going to be! Just to get it working, they'll have to learn *so* much!"

"Something of a sadist, aren't you?"

"It goes with being a teacher." Dar watched the plastic cube finish swelling into a slant-roofed shack, ten feet on a side. " 'Bout time to turn in for the night."

Sam shook her head, looking frazzled. "If I'd known it was like this . . ."

"Hey, I never promised you a grav-bed or synthsilk sheets!"

"No, no! I mean this whole planet! The structure your General's built up! The things he's trying to do! If I'd known it was like this, I would've personally put a bomb on that new governor's ship!"

Dar froze halfway through the door.

Then he looked back over his shoulder. "Excuse me—what was that again?"

"The new governor." Sam frowned. "You know—the one that's supposed to arrive tomorrow."

Dar uncoiled back out of the door and straightened up. "No, as it happens, I didn't know. And neither does anyone else on Wolmar."

"They didn't tell you?" Sam looked startled. "Well . . . anyway, they're doing it. BOA's sending out a new governor, with power to ship Shacklar home and take over all his authority. They're kind of unhappy that the 'Wolman Question' is taking so long to resolve."

"Oh, they are?" Dar breathed. "How interesting. How'd you come by this fascinating little tidbit? Common knowledge back on Terra?"

"Well, I wouldn't exactly call it headline news. . . ."

"We're not quite that important," Dar agreed dryly.

"It was the last piece of paper to cross my desk the day I quit—arranging transportation for this man Bhelabher and his aides."

"Bhelabher, mm? What's he like?"

"Oh . . ." Sam shrugged. "You know—nothing exceptional. A career civil servant, that's all."

"Quite," Dar agreed. "Stodgy, you might say?"

"Stuffy," Sam confirmed. "Very conservative—especially about military procedure and the treatment of convicts. . . . What are you doing?"

"Packing up." Dar punched a button and watched the shack start folding itself back into a cube. "We're getting back to town."

"I said something?"

"You did—and you've got to say it again, as soon as possible. To Shacklar. We've got to make sure he knows what's coming."

3

"Whatever you do, don't let him know what's coming," Cholly advised.

"But he's gotta get ready!" Dar protested. "Repel boarders! Fire when he sees the gleam of their spaceship! Damn the triplicates, full speed ahead! Over the top!"

"Under the counter," Cholly corrected. "Whatever happens, he's got to be able to truthfully say he doesn't know anything about it."

"Oh." Dar caught the inside of his cheek between his teeth. "I forgot about that."

"Don't." Cholly began polishing the bar again. "A clean conscience and a clean record, lad."

"First rule in political lying," Dar explained to Sam. "Don't. Be able to claim somebody misunderstood you—or did it on their own."

"We'll have to do it on our own, for this one," Cholly amended. "The General's a horrible liar. Can't even claim he was misunderstood."

Dar nodded resolutely. "Right. How about a quick commando raid?"

"Illegal," Cholly pointed out.

49

"You don't think you can get rid of Bhelabher legally!" Sam exclaimed.

"Nay, but we can do it in a way that can't be *proven* illegal."

"He means we've gotta be able to claim it was an accident," Dar explained.

"Great." Sam's lips thinned. " 'Excuse me, sir, I didn't mean to slip that strychnine in your martini.' 'Oh heavens, my bomb! I *dropped* it!' "

"Effective, but impractical," Cholly said judiciously. "Very hard to ignore."

"But you've got to do *some*thing! Think of the good of the planet!"

"I do," Cholly said thoughtfully, "and personally, what I'd say this planet needs is a good customs office."

"*Real* Scotch whiskey, mind," the sergeant reminded.

Dar nodded. "Straight from Terra itself—Nova Scotia Regal. Two liters each, for you and your corporal."

"Fair enough!" The sergeant shouldered his laser rifle and came to attention. "We'll stand guard day in and day out, mate—for all day tomorrow, that is. Though why you'd want to guard this old shack is beyond my understandin'. Ain't been nothin' in there but spare parts an' waste for ten years."

"There is now." Dar peeled off the backing and reached up to press the new sign into place over the doorway of the battered geodesic. "A carpet, five chairs, two ashtrays, and a counter."

" 'Customs Office'?" The corporal squinted up at the sign. "Is this official?"

"Thoroughly," Dar assured him. "Believe me, I know—I wrote up the orders myself."

"Shacklar ordered it, hm?"

"You can't expect him to keep track of every little thing."

The sergeant let out a throttled moan and stiffened, reddening. Dar looked up at him, frowning, then followed the direction of his gaze—to see Sam coming up to him, dressed in a tight-fitting blue uniform with gold epaulets and a visored beret. Dar stiffened, too—he hadn't been sure she had a figure.

"Cholly looked up his billings and found a Wolman who'd ordered a sewing machine." She handed Dar a flat, neatly tied package, oblivious to their stares. "His wife was willing to do a rush job."

Dar shook himself. "Uh, great. What'd it cost him?"

"Four power packs, six blaster barrels, two circuit chips, and a bathtub."

"Worth every credit," the sergeant wheezed, his eyes locked on her.

"Better get to it." Sam turned to the door. "I've got to set up the terminal and the paperwork."

"Uh—right." Dar tore his eyes away from her and glanced at his watch-ring. "How much time do we have?"

"Cholly says the ferry's due to take off from your moon at thirteen o'clock," Sam said from inside the shack. "What time is it?"

"Thirteen o'clock." Dar started stripping.

"Here then, Dar Mandra!"

Dar looked up, irritated, then snatched at his uniform; it wasn't good policy for a Wolman to see soldiers naked, and the man coming up with Cholly was the shaman of the Sars tribe.

"Peace, Dar Mandra." The shaman held up a hand.

"Uh, peace, Reverend." Dar scrambled into his uniform, sealed the tunic, and held up a palm. "Honored to see you, but, uh—why're you wearing a Customs uniform?"

"Why, he's one of yer staff now, ain'cha, Reverend?" Cholly grinned. "Just to cover all bets, Dar."

"Ye-e-e-e-ah." Dar's eyes slowly widened. "Your 'hunches' might come in handy, Reverend."

"'Officer Haldane,' for the time being, Dar Mandra." The shaman wrung Dar's hand a bit awkwardly; he wasn't used to the custom. "You understand, I cannot guarantee to know the speaking of their minds."

"Yes, yes, I know the Power sends the gift when It wishes, not when we do." Dar clasped his hands behind his back and massaged his knuckles. "But I hope It'll be with us today, Rever . . . uh, Officer Haldane."

"I, too," the shaman said somberly. "Shacklar must remain with us, Dar Mandra. I have no wish to see my young men die leaning on laser beams—nor yours, either."

"Definitely not." Dar was suddenly very conscious of his age.

"And I think you had best arrange matters so I need not speak."

"Oh, I'm sure that won't be necessary, Reverend," Dar said quickly. "You speak better Terran than I do."

"It is kind of you—but I do have something of an accent."

"Less'n mine," Cholly said. "Still, the Rev has the right of it, lad—there might be an aide who knows something of Wolman."

"And though I have washed off my dye for the occasion, my nation is written in my face, for him who knows how to see it." The shaman stilled suddenly, then peered upward. "The Power favors me this day, Dar Mandra. Your enemies approach."

Dar squinted up at the sky, but couldn't detect the faintest glimmer of flame. Still . . . "Your word's good enough for me, Reverend. Shall we go look official?"

The ferry roared down, blackening the blast pit anew. Dar watched through the window as the ramp slid out and the hatch lifted. He saw the party troop out and stop in consternation at the sight of the shack. The guards glanced at each other and stepped forward; the sergeant went up to the group, holding his rifle at port arms, and had a few words with a fox-faced man in the front row. Another man elbowed his way to the fore to interrupt their conversation. He wasn't tall exactly, but he gave the impression of towering height; and he was skinny, but he had a massive presence. The longer his conversation with the sergeant went on, the more clearly Dar could hear his voice; but the sergeant remained firm and apparently soft-voiced; he just waited for a blast to blow itself out, then said a few words and leaned into the next blast. But Dar did begin to notice his rifle barrel twitching. Mentally, Dar upped the sergeant two pints of Scotch and a fifth of bourbon.

Finally, the skinny man threw his head up in exasperation and started for the shack. His entourage swept along behind him, and the sergeant followed, poker-faced.

"Get ready," Dar said softly, "customers."

The door slammed open, and the skinny man waded in. "Who is responsible for this farce?"

"I'm the senior official present, sir." Dar kept his face carefully neutral. "May I be of service?"

"Service! You can serve me admirably by dismissing this piece of asininity and conveying us immediately to your Government House!"

"Certainly, sir—as soon as we've cleared you through Customs."

"Customs! This planet has never *had* a Customs Office! I've read all the reports!"

"An innovation," Dar said truthfully. "We're constantly trying to improve conditions, sir."

The rest of the entourage had trooped in; the corporal shut the door behind them. He and the sergeant discreetly took up places at the corners of the room.

"Honorable Bhelabher . . ." The fox-faced man appeared at the skinny man's elbow. ". . . it may be that these good people are unaware of your official status." He gave Dar a glare of such intense malice that Dar felt his blood-temperature drop. Out of the corner of his eye, he noticed Reverend Haldane wince just the tiniest bit.

"Well taken, Canis, well taken," Bhelabher harrumphed. He turned back to Dar. "See here, fellow—do you know who I am?"

"Not really, sir—but I would like to find out. May I see your passport, please?" Dar decided Sam might've had the right idea after all: strychnine. "Fellow," indeed!

"Passport!" Bhelabher bellowed. "Young man, I'll have you know I'm your new governor!"

Dar paused and widened his eyes just a trifle; then he leaned forward, holding out his hand. "An interesting theory, Honorable; I'll have to validate it with Government House. I'm afraid I haven't heard anything about Governor Shacklar being replaced, though. May I see your passport, please?"

"Absurd! On a planet full of convicts, certainly *I* should be above suspicion!"

"But because this *is* a convict planet, no one can be above suspicion," Dar said smoothly. "I'm afraid I *must* insist on seeing your credentials, Honorable."

Bhelabher began to redden, making choking, gargling sounds; but the fox-faced man put a hand on his arm, and he

subsided just short of magenta. "Very well, if you must!"
Bhelabher growled. "Atavista, our credentials, please."

A skinny young woman stepped up to open a folder and lay a
set of microholos on the counter. Her clothing was skintight
and transparent which, given her figure, wasn't exactly an
advantage; but Dar found he had to focus very tightly on her
face anyway. That definitely did the trick.

Sam took the microholos and began feeding them through
the terminal. Dar noticed that the bottom wafer was a plastyrus
envelope with Shacklar's name on it.

Reverend Haldane stepped up next to Dar, collecting the
wafers as Sam handed them back. He glanced at the fox-faced
man and murmured, so softly that Dar could scarcely hear him,
"Each person has copies of all those documents in his
luggage." Dar carefully didn't let anything show in his face,
but he pressed his hand flat against the counter to show he'd
heard. He also noticed that the plastyrus envelope didn't come
back to the stack.

Sam finished and turned to murmur something to the
Reverend. He turned to Dar and murmured, "Officer Bine says
the documents bear a lock-code and will not read through our
Central."

Nice, Dar thought. He'd wondered how he was going to
justify it. Sam seemed more interesting than ever. "I'm afraid
we'll have to retain your documents, Honorable."

"*What?*"

Dar glanced up to make sure the roof was still on the shack,
then back to Bhelabher. "I'm afraid we'll have to retain your
credentials. You see, they seem to be locked under a security
code which hasn't been transmitted to our computer."

"This is outrageous!" Bhelabher stormed. "Of all the
inconceivable idiocies I've encountered, this has to be the most
imbecilic! Young man, I will not tolerate this!"

"I'm afraid *we* have no choice," Dar said regretfully. "And,
under the circumstances, I'm afraid it will be necessary to
search every item of your party's luggage."

Bhelabher began reddening and gargling again, and the fox-
faced man's glare narrowed to an ice pick.

"I appreciate that you may find this unacceptable," Dar

sympathized. "If so, the shuttle isn't quite done refueling yet; I'm sure the pilot will be glad to take you back."

Bhelabher clamped his jaw shut, his eyes bulged, and the room was very silent for a few seconds. Then he released a huge hiss of breath and snapped, "Very well. We'll begin with mine. Canis, the bags, please."

Canis glanced at him, frowning, but stepped forward and hoisted two valises onto the counter. Dar opened them and passed them to Sam and the Reverend, who each began shuffling through the stacks of paper-thin garments in a half of each bag. Dar couldn't detect anything being removed but, when Sam closed the bag, set it upright on the counter, and turned to nod to Dar, there was a very meaningful look in her eye.

Dar made a mental note that she was a sleight-of-hand artist, too, and never to play poker with her; but he also started making very definite plans to start playing some other game with her as soon as he could maneuver her into it. He opened the next suitcase and passed it on.

They were quick, she and the Reverend; but there were a lot of bags, and the time stretched out. The aides began to mutter and grumble to one another, but Bhelabher stood rock-still, legs apart, hands clasped in front of him; and Canis stood like a malevolent statue at his side—or a ventriloquist's mannequin, Dar thought. He wondered which one was really doing the talking.

Finally Sam closed the last case and gave him the nod. Dar turned to Bhelabher with a smile. "All done, Honorable."

"Thank you," Bhelabher said sourly. "I assume we now have the freedom of the planet?"

"Uh—I'm sorry, Honorable." Dar looked up in surprise. "I thought I'd made that clear."

"Clear? How so?" There was an ominous rumble under Bhelabher's voice.

"Your credentials," Dar explained. "We can't admit you officially until they've been verified with Government House. We should have them back to you in twenty-four hours, though."

"*Twenty-four hours!*"

"If General Shacklar has the lock-code for your documents. Longer, if he doesn't. But I'm sure he will."

There was a moment's silence while Bhelabher's face puffed up and passed magenta.

Dar braced himself.

Then the Honorable erupted. Dar leaned into the blast and listened closely; he was always out to improve his vocabulary. He wasn't sure what half the words meant; but he did get the impression that:

1) the Honorable was somewhat distressed by this turn of events;
2) the delay was totally unacceptable;
3) there was obviously a conspiracy afoot to prevent his assuming his rightful post; and that
4) he thought Dar's hide would make an excellent ornament for his new office, nailed to the wall and tastefully decorated with a carefully balanced pattern of intersecting whip-welts.

When Bhelabher ran down, Dar glanced at Sam, who whipped out a pad and jotted down a few lines.

"Your protest is noted," Dar said with a small, polite smile, "but I'm afraid that's all we can do about it. Regulations are regulations, Honorable. I'm sure you understand."

Bhelabher took a breath, but the sergeant cleared his throat rather loudly and transferred his blaster rifle from his left shoulder to his right. Bhelbher paused in mid-gasp, glanced at the soldier out of the corner of his eye, then slowly closed his mouth and turned back to Dar. "Of course. Quite. I trust you have accommodations for myself and my staff while we endure this outrage?"

"Not here at the port," Dar admitted. "But there are some transient facilities in town. The sergeant will show you the route—and stay nearby, in case you should need anything."

"Solely for our convenience," Bhelabher said dryly. "Surely."

He turned to survey his staff. "Well . . . there seems to be no help for it. I see now how badly this poor, benighted colony needs our ministrations, good people. However, until we have an opportunity to streamline this laughable attempt at a bureaucracy, I'm afraid we'll have to endure some inconvenience. Please be patient." He started toward the door.

The corporal stepped over and opened it for him. Bhelabher paused in the doorway to look back at Dar. "You haven't heard the last of me, young man—be sure of it."

"But you *have* heard the last of *us*," Dar said as the door closed behind the last aide, "and your credentials."

"Right here." Sam started piling wafers on the countertop.

"You're really good at that, y' know?" Dar yanked off his beret. "I didn't know BOA trained pickpockets."

"Just a difference in emphasis," Sam said. "Besides, I wouldn't have known what to do without the Reverend. He knew right where to look in each bag."

"Yeah—thanks, Reverend." Dar started peeling out of his tunic. "We couldn't have brought it off without you."

"The Power favored me," Haldane said modestly. "I wish you luck, Dar Mandra. This will be, at most, an inconvenience to him."

"Well, I'm hoping for more—but you're right; it's only a delaying tactic. And he might not be delayed very long in getting Shacklar out here." He pulled on his coverall and turned to Sam. "Better change. We've gotta get out of here, fast."

4

The glass chattered on the table, and Dar looked up. "I could swear I heard a dull boom."

"Ayuh." Cholly tilted his head to the side. "I'd almost think I had, too. Queer, ain't it?"

"Right on the borderline between hearing and feeling." Sam turned to Dar. "Either it was very soft, or very far away."

"Soldiers don't go in for target practice much." Dar turned to Cholly. "Anybody sell some Wolmen a cannon?"

"Only the parts—and they haven't got the button yet."

"Must've been a natural phenomenon." Dar tossed back the rest of his beer and set the glass down. "How long do you think it'll take 'em to realize we, ah, 'confiscated' all the copies of their credentials?"

"About as long as it takes them to find a hotel room—and I expect yer friend the sergeant'll lead 'em the long way 'round the barn."

"If I know him, he'll take 'em by way of the back pasture— which is where Bhelabher belongs, anyway. The man's got all the tact of a barbell." Dar turned to Sam. "How'd a blusterer like that get promoted to governor, anyway?"

"They couldn't fire him," she explained. "He had too much

seniority. So they had to kick him up to where he couldn't do any harm—to his bosses, anyway.''

"No *harm*? What was he beforehand, a general?"

"Chief filing clerk." Sam shrugged. "Sorry, Dar, but that's the way they see it. Gossip said he'd caused three rebellions by putting the right document in the wrong place."

"Perfect." Dar held out his glass for a refill. "Not even as important as a pile of molecudots."

"To them, you *are* a molecudot."

The door bonged, and a man in a very ornate jumpsuit came in, grinning from ear to ear.

"You're off early today, Corve." Cholly reached for a bottle and glass.

"Bit of a frumus today." Corve adjusted himself to a barstool and accepted the glass. "Boss decided to give everybody the day off and let the new guests shift fer themselves."

"That flock of civvies?" Dar managed mild interest. "Where they in from, anyway?"

"Terra, 'seems." Corve took a gulp or two. "Their boss claims he's the new governor."

"New governor?" Dar frowned. "What for? We've got Shacklar!'

"And we'd best find a way to keep him, from the looks of this one."

"Now, Corve, that's not fer you to say," Cholly reproved him. "You just holds the door at the hotel."

"Ayuh, but I'm not on duty now." Corve turned to Dar. "It's name's Bhelabher, an' its brain's in its mouth."

"Just what we need to consolidate Wolman relations," Dar said dryly. "*Is* he the new gov?"

"Dunno; he can't find his papers." Corve grinned wolfishly. "Hadn't but scarcely found his rooms when he let out a roar like a ship trying to land without jets; I swear he shook the whole hotel."

Dar looked up at Cholly. "Kind of an explosion, huh? Or a cannon? The chemical kind, I mean."

"Heard him all the way down here, eh? Well, can't say as I'm surprised. I thought of luggage-bombs, myself. But no, he came storming back into the lobby with his whole flock at his heels. 'There's thieves in this hotel!' he cries. 'They've rifled all our luggage!' Well, I don't doubt the boss was thinking of rifling him—but no, he kept his face polite, and says, 'There are no guests in this hotel today but you and yours; and as for me and mine, why, I stayed here at the desk, the maid's having her batteries charged, and the staff's there by the door, ready to hold it for you.' Well, Bhelabher, he started up some deal of nonsense about how dumb it is to have a hotel with so small a staff to blame things on, but his top aide . . . face kinda like a rat . . ."

"Fox," Dar murmured.

". . . an' he—uh . . . say again?"

"He coughed." Sam kicked Dar in the ankle. "Please go on, sir."

"Yeah, well, the rat-faced one, he says, 'Those people at the Customs Office, Honorable . . .' And Honorable, he hits his forehead with the heel of his hand—must do that a lot, I notice he's a little flat-headed—and says, 'How obvious! No wonder I overlooked it! Why, of course there'd be corruption—riddled with it! Bureaucratic piracy, without a doubt!' And he starts for the door, thundering, 'But how could they have known where to find the documents?' And the rat-faced one, he says, 'Read our minds, no doubt,' and all the rest of them, they set to wailing about how unfair it was, to have mind readers all about, and how's a decent bureaucrat going to make a living if all his little secrets are known, and what evil people mind readers are. And Honorable, he says, 'We must see the General immediately, and have those Customs people questioned,' and I pulled the door and they swirled on out, Bhelabher and his whole covey right behind him. And I closed the door and like to fell over, laughing so hard I thought I'd shake myself apart."

"No wonder." Dar managed to chuckle himself. "*Customs* office? On a *prison* planet?"

"And mind readers! Hoo!" Corve chortled. "Such a deal of nonsense! And these're *educated*?"

"Wull, knowing facts can't cure stupidity," Cholly mused, "and Shacklar's anything but stupid. I'd love to see what happens when they find him."

The door bonged, and a private stepped in, chuckling.

"I think we're about to find out." Dar turned to the new arrival. "Something go right, Cosca?"

"All depends on which end you were on." Cosca pulled himself up to a barstool. "Me, I was on the outside, listening in."

"Don't executives *any*where know better than to leave their intercoms open?" Sam demanded.

"Just the other way around," Dar corrected. "Sometimes they know better than to turn them off. What wasn't private, Cosca?"

"A complaint, chiefly." Cosca accepted his beer. "Or maybe a challenge."

"I can guess the chief who made the complaint," Corve grinned. "Who made the challenge?"

"Same as the complainer—this Terran bigwig, Beelubber . . ."

"Bhelabher," Dar and Corve both corrected.

"Who's telling this story, anyway? All right, Bhelabher. Honorable high huckster from Terra—he says. He comes sailing in without so much as a by-your-leave, roars, 'Where's the governor?' and goes slamming into Shacklar's office afore a one of us could say a word. Matter of fact, we couldn't even hear ourselves, his gang was making so much noise, chattering about how telepaths was undermining the foundations of society. . . ."

"Telepaths?" Dar frowned.

"Mind readers," Corve explained. "Gotta hand it to 'em—they keep to a line of thought. How'd the General take it, Cosca?"

"Well, he was in conference at the time. . . ."

"With his cat-o'-nine-tails, or a patient?"

"Patient. As long as we can keep the troubled ones coming, it keeps him away from the cat. Analysis, it was—with Rogoure."

"Rogoure?" Dar stiffened. "Isn't he that private who almost chopped a Wolman in Monday's battle?"

"The same. An' you know how Shacklar is—he wouldn't ask the man to leave his knife outside. Well, I'd guess that Rogoure's paranoid."

Dar started to grin.

"And they were deep into his childhood when Bhelabher charged in?" Cholly guessed.

"I'd say—but all I know is, Rogoure bellows, 'They've come to get me!' and jumps up with that knife out. . . ."

"Good reflexes," Dar noted.

Corve nodded. "He'd make a top-notch soldier. Well! I don't need to tell you. It got somewhat furry for a while there."

"Meaning Bhelabher was screaming, and Rogoure was shouting war cries, and Shacklar was trying to bellow them both into order?"

"Something of the sort. Well, the General, he did manage to get Rogoure calmed down, and apologized for the interruption. 'But you know how it is,' he says, 'when one's involved in government. Any Johnny in the street thinks he's got the right to bust in to see you at all odd hours of the day and night.' 'Well, I can comp that,' Rogoure, he answers. 'I'd likely do the same if I felt I really had a gripe.' He'd made progress already, that one. 'I hope you will,' says Shacklar. 'Take it out on me, not on the Wolmen. Will you, Private?' 'My word upon it, sir,' says Rogoure. 'Next time I'm feeling homicidal, I'll come for you.' 'Good chap!' says Shacklar. 'But if you do stay calm, I'll see you at this time tomorrow?' 'That you will, sir.' And Rogoure, he salutes. 'Well enough,' says Shacklar, saluting back. 'Dismissed!' And Rogoure clicks his heels, about-faces on the mark, and marches out."

"And this time last week, you couldn't've gotten him to come to parade rest." Dar shook his head. "Shacklar's amazing."

"Bhelabher didn't think so. Rogoure was barely out before the Honorable pulled himself together enough to bellow, 'What is this place—a lion's den?' 'So it would seem,' says Shacklar, 'when the folk who come don't even have the manners of a flea. I thought civilians still abided by the old quaint custom of requesting admittance when the door was closed.'"

Even Sam smiled. "He sounds a little miffed."

"Oh, his tone was fresh dry ice! 'That's a rather poor reception,' Bhelabher says, 'for the new governor of this planet.' Well. I tell you, Shackler all but froze."

"I should think the news would've come as a bit of a shock, yes."

"Oh, the General's used to delusions of grandeur. You could almost see it going through his mind. 'I understand a cargo ship came down today,' he says. Bhelabher nods. 'Myself was on it, and my whole staff.' Well, if you knew the General, you could see he didn't think that ruled out aberrations. 'You've come from Terra?' 'We have,' says Bhelabher, 'sent out by the BOA to take charge of this planet and rid it of corruption and of vice.' Shacklar, he sat down at his desk and made a note or two. 'I assume you have got credentials to support your claim?' 'I *had*,' Bhelabher says, like it was an accusation, 'but the officials at your Customs Office confiscated not only the originals, but all the copies, too.' "

Corve chuckled.

Cosca nodded. "I expect Shacklar thought so, too—but he didn't show it, of course. Bhelabher bellows, 'You must find those scoundrels!' And Shacklar answers, 'It would be rather surprising if we could. In fact, it's amazing that you managed to find our Customs Office, since we don't have one!' 'Come, sir,'' Bhelabher says. 'Surely you at least know the departments of your own administration.' 'I do,' says Shacklar, 'and I tell you, there's no Customs Office. Where did you find it, by the way?' 'Right at the spaceport,' says Bhelabher. 'A small plastrete structure, about twenty feet square.' 'One of the storage sheds,' Shacklar says, nodding. 'What did it have by way of personnel?' 'Two men and a woman,' answers Bhelabher. 'Surely you know of them!' 'I'm afraid not,' says Shacklar, 'though it shouldn't be too difficult discovering who the woman was; there're only about seventy of them in the settlement.' Well, then you could begin to hear it in Bhelabher's voice; he'd begun to figure it out for himself. 'Do you imply that these personnel were not official?' 'Not really,' says Shacklar. 'I'm sure they appointed themselves properly before they took office.' Well, Bhelabher was quiet then, but his face turned a very interesting color. . . ."

"Mauve," Dar supplied.

"Magenta," Corve corrected.

"Closer to maroon, I'd say. Then he explodes: 'I have been deceived!' 'I believe "conned" is the old term,' Shacklar agreed. 'Certainly someone has played on your gullibility.' Bhelabher rumbles, 'I don't quite think . . .' 'Quite,' says

Shacklar. 'At any rate, this puts us both in a rather delicate position, Honorable.' Bhelabher says slowly, 'Yes, I can understand that,' which I, for one, found surprising. 'Your claims may be quite legitimate,' Shacklar goes on. 'BOA may have sent you out here to assume the administration of this colony.' 'Indeed they have!' snaps Bhelabher. 'But you have no credentials to verify that statement,' Shacklar points out. 'I have witnesses!' Bhelabher huffs. 'My whole staff will testify in support of this robbery!' 'I'm sure they will,' Shacklar says, and his voice was vermouth. 'But you'll pardon me, Honorable, if I can not quite accept their testimony as totally impartial.' Bhelabher says nothing, and Shacklar gets gentle. 'I'm sure you must see that I cannot cede administration of this colony to you merely on your say-so.' 'But this is intolerable!' Bhelabher cries. 'My appointment is totally legitimate!' which was more than I could say for himself. 'As well it may be,' says Shacklar, getting hard again, 'but it *could* also be a scheme of deception on a very large scale.' 'Sir,' Bhelabher rumbles, 'do I understand you to say that *I* am a confidence swindler?' 'You do not,' Shacklar answers, 'but since you wish to say it, you may. Certainly I must assume as much, since you lack proof of your claim.' 'But this is intolerable,' Bhelabher explodes again, 'Especially since it is far more likely that *you*, sir, are the schemer! You have absolute control of this settlement; how could a few of its inhabitants mount such a ruse without your consent, nay, your command? Is it not logical that you would so seek to maintain your own . . .' Well, sirs and madam, that's just about when the General turned 'round and slammed the door, and we had to content ourselves with what we could hear through the wall."

"Which was?" Corve demanded.

"Oh, a deal of shouting and bellowing, and the odd low mutter from Shackler, but nothing you could make out in words. It slackened, though, got softer and softer, till we couldn't hear nothing at all. And that's just about when we thought to see if the General'd maybe been careless with his intercom again."

"You just checked it, of course."

"Of course; I doubt that we listened for a full thirty seconds."

Dar coughed delicately. "We, uh, certainly wouldn't want you to violate a confidence or anything, but . . ."

"No fear. Not much we could violate, anyway; 'bout all we heard was, when we pressed the button, the Honorable saying, '. . . started when I was four. That's when my mother became involved with the amateur holovision programming club, you see, and of course it demanded a great deal of time. Our district child-care center was very nice, really, but most of the children were older than I was, and looking back on it, I see that they all must have been rather disturbed. . . .' Shacklar murmured something sympathetic, but that's just about when the rat-faced aide noticed us and started saying something about telepaths' eavesdropping couldn't be avoided, but . . . Well, we decided the intercom was working, and switched it off."

"The ethical thing to do," Dar agreed. "How long ago was that?"

Cosca glanced at his ring. " 'Bout half an hour. I'd expect that by this time he's into the traumas of grade school."

"Ever Shacklar's way," Cholly grinned. " 'If you can't beat 'em, analyze 'em.' What were his henchmen doing, Cosca?"

"Oh, the usual—sitting around waiting, and bothering us for coffee, and wondering how the psi who'd swiped their credentials had known they was comin'. I mean, he'd've had to, wouldn't he, to've been able to set up a fake Customs Office in time to catch 'em comin' off the ferry?"

"Makes sense," Dar said judiciously. "Did they?"

"Not a bit." Cosca shook his head. "The rat-faced one, he said this proved there must be a conspiracy of psis, all the way from Terra to here, 'cause that was the only way word could've come out faster than an FTL starship could carry it—at the speed of thought, which he claimed to be faster than the speed of light. . . ."

"Ridiculous," Sam snorted.

"Isn't it just? There's nothing so unbeatable as wanting to stay ignorant. But even Ratty wasn't about to believe one single telepath could hear thoughts on Terra from all the way out here on Wolmar; so, he claimed, there must've been a network of psis, each one relayin' the message, till a telepath here picked it up and set up a reception for 'em. He didn't quite *say* Shacklar was a part of the conspiracy, and a telepath, too, but . . ."

"But that's when you decided you'd best take a beer break and cool off under the collar, hey?" Cholly guessed.

Cosca nodded. "Got my perspective back on the way over, though, and got to seeing the humorous side of it. Well! I'm recovered, and I'd best get back to the office."

"And let one of your mates come out and cool off?"

Cosca nodded. "And hope there's no mayhem been done while I've been gone. Well! Ta, chaps!" He headed for the door.

"And to yerself, Cosca." Cholly waved. "Corve, would you mind the store for a bit? Dar and Sam and me got to talk over their list for the next trading trek."

"Eh? Eh, surely now, Cholly!" Corve heaved himself up, ambled round behind the bar, and began whistling through his teeth as he poured himself another mugful.

Dar looked up at Cholly, already halfway to the back room, and frowned. Then he nodded to Sam and followed.

"What's this all about?" she muttered as she caught up with him.

"Don't know," Dar answered softly, "but something's gone wrong. I wasn't supposed to go trading so soon."

They stepped into the back room, and Sam stared.

Books. All around. Ceiling to floor, and the ceiling was high. Books bound, micro-books, molecue-books, holotapes, and readers for everything. Even some antique paper books.

"Just your average hole-in-the-wall tavern," Dar said cheerfully. "What's up, boss?"

"Sit down, lad, sit down." Cholly pulled a large box from a drawer and set it on the table. Dar sat down, looking wary. "The problem is," Cholly said, shaking out a large white cloth and fastening it around Dar's neck, "that the General's likely to give the Honorable and his troop the freedom of the planet."

Dar blanched. "I hadn't thought of that."

"No, nor did I. Understandable lack, I'm sure, in view of the rush we were under; still, there it is. So you two've got choices: to hole up till it all blows over, or to go in disguise while they're here."

"We can't be so well disguised that they won't recognize us," Sam blurted.

Cholly held up a hand. "Have faith. I had occasion, one time, to travel with a group of wandering actors . . ."

"The cops were after him," Dar explained.

"Be that as it may, be that as it may." Cholly took some putty out of a can and started kneading it. "Took a small part now and again, myself, and didn't do badly, if I do say so. . . . Well. The long and the short of it is, I became reasonably good with theatrical makeup, and accumulated a trunkful."

"Which we are now about to get the benefit of," Dar interpreted.

"Close yer mouth, now; you don't need no prosthesis on yer tongue." Cholly pressed the lump of putty to Dar's nose and began shaping it into a startlingly natural hook. " 'Robex,' this is—best way of changing the shape of the face that the theater ever came up with. Beautiful, 'tis—just knead it till it gets soft, set it on cartilage, shape it, and it'll adhere as tight as yer natural-born skin."

"How do I get it off?" Dar muttered.

"With the solvent—and it tastes terrible, so close yer great gape of a mouth. Then it dries as hard as cartilage, this being Robex # 1."

"It's changing color," Sam pointed out.

Cholly nodded. "That's part of the beauty of it, don't yer see—it starts out pasty-gray, but takes on the color of the flesh it's on. Now, back in the old days, you'd've had to choose the premixed sort of base that came closest to yer natural skin tone and baste it on all over yer flesh—you would've had 'Dark Egyptian,' lad. But with Robex, you see, all you do is blend it into yer skin, and it does the rest. No need for base."

"That's great for cartilage. But if it hardens that way, won't it be just a teeny bit obvious if I use it to shape my cheeks?"

"Oh, we use Robex # 2 for that—dries to the consistency of whatever flesh it's on." Cholly opened another can and scooped out a lump of dough. "Yer own mother'll never know ye when I'm done with you, lad."

"My own mother," Dar mumbled, "never wanted to know me at all."

About an hour later, the door opened, and Corve stuck his

head in. "Uh, Cholly, I believe as how ya might want to be out here."

"Do I indeed, do I indeed!" Cholly whisked the cloth off Sam and over his makeup chest. "Ayuh, Corve, certainly."

"Who's the strangers, Cholly?" Corve frowned dubiously.

"Why, this here's Enib Mas, Corve." Cholly gave Sam a pat on the head, incidentally setting the roots of her wig into the adhesive. "And that there's Ardnam Rod. Just in off the freighter. Turns out Enib's had a year of college, and Ard's had two, so I thought they'd like a look back here."

"Oh! Welcome, welcome!" Corve bustled in, holding out a hand. "What ya up for?"

"Rather not say," Dar rumbled in his deepest voice. He pumped Corve's hand. "Pleased to meet you."

"Me, too," Sam said in a high, nasal tone. "Do you ever get used to this place?"

"Quick enough, quick enough." Corve shook her hand. "You don't look too well, lad—but don't worry, Wolmar'll put meat on yer bones. Well! Afraid I gotta be off, Cholly—if I know the boss, he'll've got over his miff, and be open for business again."

"Best to be sure, best to be sure." Cholly took Corve by the arm and guided him out. "See you this evening, Corve."

"That ya will, that ya will. Here's yer company, Cholly. Good day to you." And Corve headed out the door, leaving Cholly to face General Shacklar and Bhelabher.

"Had him totally fooled, didn't we?" Sam murmured.

"Not for a second," Dar muttered back. "Why do you think he was so over-polite? And didn't ask where Dar and Sam were?"

Sam said nothing, but her eyes were wide.

". . . nothing exceptional to look at," Shacklar was saying as Cholly bustled over behind the bar, "but the drink's as good as you can get out here, and the food's excellent. Most importantly, though, this is really our community center. Groups meet here to discuss anything and everything, to socialize, and to work out personal problems into a sympathetic ear."

"Hello, Sympathetic Ear!" Bhelabher reached out a tentative hand and smiled at Cholly with genuine, if confused, warmth.

Cholly accepted the hand as Shacklar murmured, "The Honorable Vincent Bhelabher, of the Bureau of Otherworldly Activities."

"Pleased," Cholly affirmed, with an eye on the General. Dar choked in his beer.

"Yes . . . " Bhelabher murmured. "The General had mentioned something about your commercial enterprise. . . ." He seemed rather bemused.

"Enterprising it is, enterprising it is." Cholly nodded. "Though lately, it's not been too commercial. . . ."

"Well, I'm, sure there're slack periods in any line of commerce. But the General seems to feel that this particular line of exchange offers his only real hope of any lasting peace with the natives."

"The General's too kind," Cholly demurred. "Has he told you of his war games?"

"Only a stopgap, Charles," Shacklar murmured. "I was speaking of hopes for a permanent peace, which must be founded on mutual understanding."

"I'm sure, I'm sure." Bhelabher nodded genially. "Still, I'd like to witness one of these, ah, 'games.' "

"As indeed you shall. I regret that I won't be able to conduct you, myself, due to the press of business; will you excuse me, Honorable?"

"Eh? . . . Yes, of course, of course!" Bhelabher seized Shacklar's hand and pumped it. "No need even to explain, of course, old chap; I've had responsibility for major administrative sectors myself. Of course I understand!"

"I hoped you would." Shacklar's smile seemed real. "Charles, I trust you'll be able to spare the Honorable your best trader for a guide during his stay here."

"Oh, of course!" With a wicked grin, Cholly slapped Dar on the back. "None but the best, General! Ard here, he's yer man!"

This time Dar managed to at least get the beer down the right pipe, and lifted his head to give Cholly his best gimlet-glare. But Cholly just kept grinning, as though he hadn't a care in the world, which *he* hadn't.

"Ard will see you get a thorough look at our piece of this planet, and a good bit of what's outside the wall then," Shacklar said. "In the meantime, please be assured we'll do all we can to recover your credentials."

"Not unless they're awfully good at reconstructing ashes," Dar murmured to Sam. She kicked him.

"I very much appreciate it," Bhelabher said earnestly. "For my part, I've seen to it that the shuttle pilot carried back a note to BOA, an official dispatch, of course."

"And the liner should be bound back inward in a week." Shacklar nodded. "But I'm afraid I'll have to ask your indulgence there, Honorable—after all, it *is* a two-month journey to Terra."

"Oh, I quite understand! But if all goes well, we should receive a reply in half a year, Standard Terran. Still, I have hopes we'll recover our credentials before then."

"I'm sure we'll manage to conclude the manner in *some* fashion," Shacklar assured him. Something beeped at his hand, and his brow netted. "Can't they get by without me for a short hour? Yes, Fordstam, what is it?" he murmured into his ring, then held it to his ear. After a moment, he sighed and spoke into it again. "Yes, yes, I'm on my way. . . . You'll excuse me, Honorable, but it seems one of my soldiers has been making decent proposals to a Wolman girl, and the tribe's mayor's concerned. Indecent proposals they're used to, but they don't know quite what to make of this one."

"Well . . . I'm sure it had to happen sooner or later," Bhelabher mused. "What's your policy on intermarriage?"

"None at all, at the moment," Shacklar confessed. "But I hope to have one by the time I get back to HQ. Will you excuse me?" The General went out the door.

Dar counted mentally, ticking off seconds on his fingers. When he got to five, a joyful whoop resounded from the street outside. Bhelabher looked up, blinking, but Dar nodded. Shacklar'd been waiting a long time for this "incident." He might not have had the policy, but he sure had it ready.

"Do your people always express themselves so exuberantly?" Bhelabher seemed smaller, somewhat lost, with Shacklar's departure.

"Not always," Cholly admitted. "They're often depressed.

Still, there's no sense just telling you—take the good man and show him, Ard."

"Mm?" It only took Sam's elbow in his ribs to make Dar react to his new name. "Oh, yes! Yes. . . ." He heaved himself to his feet with a sigh. "Yes, if we hurry, we can just make the two o'clock war. See you later, Cholly." It was more of a threat than a promise.

5

Dar lifted a glass in a trembling hand and drank deeply. "I tell you, I don't know if I can last it out."

"What for?" Cholly twisted the empty out of his hand and replaced it with a full one. "There's never a chance that he'd recognize yer."

"Yeah, but I'm running out of things to show him." Dar started to sip, then stared at the glass. "I just emptied this."

"And he just refilled it." Sam shook her head. "You *are* in bad shape."

"Come, now!" Cholly cajoled. "A whole planetful of marvels, and you can't find a week's tour? Come, indeed! What've you shown him?"

"Well, let me see." Dar started ticking them off on his fingers. "The Wall—all—all thirty miles of it. The Two-O'Clock War. A Wolman village. The Eight-O'Clock War. He had a conference with Shacklar. The Two-O'Clock war. The enlisted men's recreation complex and organic market. The officers' recreation complex and fixed market. The Eight-O'Clock War. Conference with Schacklar. The Two-O'Clock War. A Wolman trading session. A Wolman information-barter . . ."

"Adult school," Cholly murmured.

"That, too. . . . A Wolman workshop. The Eight-O'Clock War. Conference with Shacklar. The Two-O'Clock War. He likes wars."

"I was beginning to get that impression," Sam agreed.

"You still haven't shown him the parade ground. Or the gaol."

Dar shook his head. "Depressing."

"Or the Little Theater. The Concert Hall."

"Boring."

"How do you know? Could be he *likes* amateurs. Then there's the radio studio, the 3DT studio, the barracks . . ."

"All the high spots, huh?"

Cholly shrugged. "Nobody said you had to entertain the man—just to guide him. You wouldn't want him to get a false impression of us, would you?"

"Yes," Dar snapped. "Definitely."

Cholly straightened up with a sigh. "Then ye've nought but yourself to blame if he's hard to get along with."

"That's the strange part." Dar's brow knit. "He's not."

" 'Course he would be. You'd be, too, if . . . how's that again?"

"He's not," Dar repeated. "He's not tough to get along with at all. He's been getting more and more pleasant every day. In fact, today he was a real nice guy. I'm amazed at how wrong my first impression of him was."

"I'm amazed at how good a psychiatrist the General is," Cholly grunted.

Something beeped in the back corner, and kept on beeping.

Sam looked up. "A holophone? Here?"

"Why not?" Dar smiled. "Radio waves don't *have* to have plastrete buildings around them, you know."

Cholly ambled back to the phone and pressed the "receive" button. "Cholly's Hash House, Bar, an' Natural Food Emporium. . . . Oh, it's yerself, General! . . . Who? . . . Oh, yes, he's here! You want to . . . You don't want to. . . . You want to see him? Right now? Begging yer pardon, General, but—what's he done? . . . Oh? Oh, I see. Yes, yes, right away. . . . Same to you, General. . . . Right." He switched off and ambled back to Dar. "Well, well, my boy, seems you've attracted notice."

Dar's mouth went dry. "What'd I do now?"

"Nothin', it seems, except maybe a good job. He says it's not what you have done, but what you *will* do, if you follow me."

"I don't."

"Neither do I. But that's what he said, and if you've any hopes of our scheme working out, I think ye'd best get over there. Hop to it now, Dar! Lick-split!"

Dar hopped.

"Yes, I really must thank you," Bhelabher agreed. "Seeing the way this colony's been organized has been a revelation to me."

"My thanks," Shacklar murmured. "Still, it's scarcely in the same category as changing wine into water."

"It certainly seems not far less." Bhelabher beamed at Dar with owlish enthusiasm. "Do you realize what this man has managed to induce here? Hope! Optimism! An atmosphere of opportunity! A growing, progressing society!"

"Well, yes, I had sort of realized something of the sort." Dar wondered if he was missing something. "And it sure is darn near a miracle, compared to the ball-and-chain world this place was when I came."

"Compared to Terra! To the Proxima Centauri Electorate! To any of the Central Worlds! Do you *realize* what a paradise this is?"

Dar stared. "You *like* outdoor plumbing?"

"I'll take it any day over the spiritual septic tank the Central Worlds have become! We've become stratified there, young man, stratified! Do you know what that means?"

"Uh-h-h-h-h . . ." Dar rewound his memories to a conversation with Cholly, six years ago, about the nature of tyranny. "Yeah. It means you're either a subject or a ruler, and there's no way to change it."

Bhelabher looked startled for a moment; then he nodded. "Well put, well put!" He turned to Shacklar. "Isn't it amazing how the simpler way of stating something so often catches the essence of it?" He turned back to Dar. "But you're quite right, young man, quite right—no one can move up. So the vast majority live out their lives in dull, repetitious desk jobs, with only 3DT, euphorics, and cabaret passes for pleasures."

"Sounds wonderful," Dar sighed. "When do I get a chance to be bored?"

"I'm sure any of our Terran slaves would be delighted to trade places with you if they really had the slightest inkling of what you have here. And our 'fortunate few' would be even more eager—they can have anything they want, but find nothing worth having. Still, they're convinced there must be *some* job worth having—so they spend their lives in pursuit of some meaning in pleasure."

"I'll find it." Dar raised a hand. "Won't take me long, either."

"I'm sure you would. The pleasures of the senses only seem to have meaning when they're rare. So our poor privileged ones never *can* find the purpose they're seeking—but they keep looking for it."

Dar frowned. "Are you trying to tell me that the only real difference between the classes and the masses is that the classes' desperation is noisy, and the masses' desperation is quiet?"

"No, I'm trying to tell you that the only difference that matters is between them and yourself—or, more accurately, between Terra and Wolmar. Here, a mere private has as good a chance as the General of getting whatever pleasures *are* available—that is, if he earns his points and saves his credits."

Dar nodded. "I do. And now that you mention it, we all do have pretty much the same, ah, forms of recreation . . ."

Shacklar nodded. "The advantage of having very few pleasures."

". . . and Cholly and the General, between them, keep opening up more upper-level jobs, such as . . ." Dar swallowed ". . . trading."

"The advantage of an expanding economy." Shacklar leaned back, locking his fingers across his chest. "Fortunately for us, the Wolmen had a very unsophisticated technology."

"True, you found all the elements here when you came," Bhelabher admitted. "But you also had the wisdom and ability to combine them!" Bhelabher's smile saddened. "Such traits are rare. I, for example, lack both."

"You're wise to realize your limitations." Shacklar picked up a data cube and rolled it between his fingers. "But I wonder—do you have as sure a grasp of your strengths?"

"Oh, I think that I do." Bhelabher fairly beamed. "That cube you're playing with, now—give me a million of them, and the tools of my trade, and I'll set them up for you so that I can have any of their septillions of bits for you within thirty seconds of your asking for it."

Dar developed a faraway look. "General, excuse me—we have the complete military personnel records on cube, don't we?"

"Not for personal use," Shacklar said dryly. "And I'm sure the Honorable Bhelabher understands the importance of confidentiality."

"That's what I was hoping. . . ."

"I don't think you appreciate how great a benefit the computer can be, for all humankind."

Bhelabher nodded. "Quite true, really. If the sum total of human knowledge holds the answer to a question, the computer will find it for you."

"Quite enviable, really." Shacklar toyed with the cube again. "Myself, I have no ability to organize data. I have to keep everything in my head—and it goes without saying that, far too often, I fail to find the solution, because the one vital bit of information is *not* in my head."

"Well, that won't happen again." Bhelabher's eyes gleamed. "I'll revamp your data banks so that you'll be amazed at the myriads of facts that you didn't know were there."

Dar stiffened. That had an unpleasantly definite ring to it.

Bhelabher turned to him, beaming, to confirm it. "The General has accepted my application, you see. I'm going to stay here on Wolmar, and set up an information storage-and-retrieval system."

"And streamline our bureaucracy a bit," Shacklar added. "You'd be amazed at all the points of inefficiency he's noticed already. The Honorable Bhelabher has been gracious enough to place his considerable talents at our disposal."

"And gracious of you it is to say so." Bhelabher gave Shacklar a polite nod that bordered on a bow.

Privately, Dar shuddered, and wished he *weren't* going to be staying. He had an idea that living under Bhelabher's streamlining wasn't going to be much fun.

But then, he'd figured without Shacklar's restraining influence. Certainly the General had worked wonders in the Honorable already.

"But I do realize that I'm not the man for any more of a job than that here," Bhelabher explained to Dar. "So I'm sending my resignation back to Terra."

Dar's eyes widened. It was too good to be true. Even if it *was* sort of what Cholly had figured would happen. . . .

"And my staff will be staying here with me," Bhelabher went on. "The General assures me they're needed."

That, Dar could believe. Most of Bhelabher's staff were female.

"This, however, leaves me without someone to carry my resignation back to Terra," Bhelabher noted.

Dar suddenly felt very wary.

"Would you like to see Terra, Ardnam?" Shacklar murmured.

Dar held onto his chair while the blood roared in his ears and the world seemed to grow insubstantial. Escape! And to Terra!

"I'm afraid you must decide rather quickly," Shacklar went on. "The courier ship that brought the Honorable is scheduled to blast out of orbit in three hours, bound for the colonial branch government on Haldane IV. From there, you'll have to arrange transportation to Terra, and I don't doubt it'll take quite a few transfers. There's very little direct traffic to or from the Central Worlds."

Dar's mouth went dry. "Don't get me wrong, I'd love to do it—but I don't have much experience at that kind of traveling."

"No, nor do you know how to work your way through the web of the I.D.E. bureaucracy on Terra—but I understand there's a young lady, just in from the home planet, who's been in your company lately . . ."

"Sam Bine," Dar croaked.

"Yes, a Ms. Bine. I know it's beastly to ask her to leave so soon after she's arrived; but, in view of the importance of the matter . . ."

"She was just leaving, anyway." Better and better! Escape

to Terra, and with a female traveling companion! "Or should I say, I think I can talk her into it."

"Please do." Shacklar picked up a pen and made a note. "With luck, the two of you might reach BOA about the same time as my request for clarification of the Honorable Bhelabher's credentials."

"You could cancel that, you know," Bhelabher pointed out.

Shacklar looked up, his face a total blank. Then the light slowly dawned. "Do you know, I believe you're right."

"You see?" Bhelabher beamed at Dar. "There's so much I can *do* here!"

"True," Dar agreed—but he wondered how long Shacklar could keep up such high-quality acting.

Long enough for Bhelabher's resignation to reach Terra, at least.

"You'll have an official pardon, of course," Shacklar added.

"I'll do it! But, uh—just one question. . . ."

"Yes?" Shacklar blinked mildly.

"Why'll it be so hard to find the right person in the BOA bureaucracy to give your resignation to?"

"Because," said Bhelabher, "my appointment to Wolmar was a very highly classified secret."

Dar managed not to look startled.

6

"But if it was such a deep dark secret, how did you find out about it?" Dar demanded.

Sam's lips thinned. "Oh, all right! If you really have to know—I was a clerk in the classified division, with a top-level security clearance."

"Oh." Dar's lower lip thrust out as he nodded slowly. "Yeah, that makes sense. Weren't your bosses a little, ah, taken aback, when you resigned?"

"Very," Sam said grimly, "especially when they found out I'd turned into a Hume. I had a very difficult time getting a passport."

"How *did* you manage it?"

Sam shrugged. "Very involved. Let's just say I know how to handle a bureaucracy."

"Uh, yeah, I don't think I really want to know the details." Dar pressed a hand over his eyes. "But you did get away. That's what counts."

"Not all that much," Sam answered with a grim smile. "There was a commercial traveler outbound from Terra on the same liner I was on, and he made every transfer I did, up until the last leg from Haldane IV to here."

"Agent, following you?" Cholly grunted.

Sam nodded, and held out her glass for a refill. "You sound as though you recognize the symptoms."

"In a manner of speaking." Cholly poured. "Now, I'm certain it's just my nasty, suspicious mind, but—I do believe that nice young blond man from Bhelabher's staff's been keeping an eye on you."

"Just my glamor and magnetic personality, I'm sure," Sam said dryly. "I've noticed him, too. In fact, I'd've had to've been blind not to."

"Well, every secret agent has to learn his trade sometime."

"I know a way to ditch him," Dar ventured.

"So do I," she said sourly. "Leave Wolmar."

Dar stared. "How'd you know?"

Sam's head lifted. "You mean you were seriously going to recommend that? What's the matter, am I getting to be an embarrassment?"

"No, no, just the other way around!" Dar said quickly. "You see, I've got this great offer to leave, but I have to take somebody with me who knows the ropes in the Terran bureaucracy."

The silence stretched out while Sam's lower lip slowly protruded. "So. They made you an offer you couldn't refuse."

"Well, I wouldn't say *couldn't*—but I wasn't about to. How about it?"

Sam frowned. "The idea's got its appeal—I've learned what I wanted to here. But this place has a lot of advantages over Terra, if you know what I mean."

"No," Dar said promptly. "I can't imagine how *any* place could have an advantage over Terra—especially a backwater like this."

Cholly turned away to put glasses back on shelves, whistling tunelessly between his teeth.

"Don't worry," Sam said bitterly, "you will. And, although I wouldn't mind a return visit to Terra, I have a notion I'd very quickly find myself looking back to this place with nostalgia. How do I get back here if I want to? It took me ten years of saving, just to get the fare out here in the first place."

"Well, I think Shacklar might be induced to guarantee your return fare," Dar said judiciously. "He seemed awfully anxious to get me to leave."

"Sheriff trouble?"

"No, no! I'm taking Bhelabher's resignation back to Terra!"

Cholly dropped a glass and spun around. "That's all I need to hear. You're going. An' so're you." He aimed a finger at Sam. "Can't leave this poor, innocent lamb to the mercy of them Terran wolves. *I'll* guarantee yer return fare, if it comes to it."

"Done!" Sam slapped the bar. "I'm off on the road back to Terra! But why can't Bhelabher take it back himself?"

"Because he's staying here."

Cholly dropped another glass.

"Oh." Sam chewed that one over. "How about his staff?"

"They're staying too. Seems we'll be needing 'em."

"No, don't tell me—you're cutting into me glassware." Cholly held up a hand. "Shacklar's giving 'em all jobs."

Dar nodded. "Bhelabher's going to revise the filing system and streamline the bureaucracy."

"Well, there goes private enterprise," Cholly sighed.

"No, Bhelabher's not that bad," Sam said judiciously. "He did a fine job as long as he was only in charge of the records for Terra. It was when they put him in charge of the records for the whole I.D.E. that he ran into trouble."

"Oh?" Cholly looked up, with a glimmer of hope. "He had the ability, but couldn't handle responsibility, heh?"

Sam nodded. "Something like that. As long as he was able to take orders, he was fine. It was being top man that stymied him."

"Better 'n better." Cholly nodded. "Then no doubt he'll take Shacklar's orders to leave some glitches in the bureaucracy."

Sam frowned. "Why?"

"It makes for flexibility, lass. If the bureaucracy's too efficient, it gives the central government too much power, and they control every aspect of life. But a little inefficiency . . . now, that leaves some room for a man to beat the system. . . . Well! You'll only have one problem, then, Dar."

Dar looked up, startled. "What's that?"

"Shacklar thinks you're Ardnam Rod now, and all yer papers'll be made out to him."

"Oh." Dar pursed his lips. "That will be a problem, won't it?"

"But not much of one." Sam patted his arm reassuringly. "Trust your traveling bureaucrat."

Dar frowned. "Where's *he* going?"

"Who?" Sam pressed up to the window, craning her neck. "That guy in the coverall, going over to the control shed?"

"Yeah—he's the pilot! Who's going to fly the ferry up to the courier ship?"

Sam shrugged. "His relief, I suppose. No doubt he's taking a planet-side leave."

"He's just had a week's worth—or, no, I can't really say that, can I?"

"Right. For all you know, he's run daily missions since Bhelabher came in."

"But I didn't know we had a relief pilot down here."

"Is it your job to know the duty roster?"

Dar turned to her. "You know, as a traveling companion, you might get to be a bit difficult."

Sam shrugged. "You're free to choose any other BOA clerk you can find here."

"Well, I suppose I could talk to one of Bhelabher's people." Dar turned back to the window. "But somehow, I think you'd be a little more . . ."

"Dependable, I assure you," murmured an approaching voice.

Dar stiffened. "Company."

". . . Oh, I have no doubt of that," Bhelabher was saying hurriedly. "But the situation is not. I am concerned that our courier might be delayed."

Dar and Sam turned around slowly as Bhelabher and Shacklar came toward them. "I suggest you have a word with him yourself, and warn him of the pitfalls of the journey." Shacklar looked up. "Well, Ardnam! This will be 'bon voyage,' then." He clasped Dar's hand tightly and gave it a shake. "You've been a credit to my command here, young man. I'll be sorry to lose you—but do remember how great a service you'll be performing, for all of us who remain here on Wolmar."

"It's a pleasure to do my duty, sir." Dar took Shacklar's commendation with a grain of salt, since "Ardnam" had only been under Shacklar's command for a week.

Shacklar released his hand and stepped back. "I believe the Honorable has a word for you, too." Bhelabher pressed in, and Shacklar turned away to Sam.

"Be careful, young man, do be careful," Bhelabher said loudly, drawing Dar further away from Shacklar and Sam. He dropped his voice to a low rumble. "Now, I hadn't wanted to mention this to the general; after all, there's no need to worry him with something over which he has no control."

Dar instantly felt a need to worry. "Uh . . . such as?"

"When I was back on Terra, and in an office of some influence, some members of the LORDS party approached me—you know of them?"

"Uh, yeah." Dar wet his lips. "They're the arch-conservatives in the assembly, aren't they?"

"I wouldn't have used the 'arch' a week ago. I do now, though." Bhelabher shook his head in wonder. "What an amazing planet this is!"

"About the LORDS," Dar prompted.

"Indeed. They approached me, to see if I would be interested in joining in a scheme to overthrow the Secretary-General and establish a temporary LORDS junta, to govern while the I.D.E. government could be restructured along more efficient lines."

Dar stood rigid, feeling like a resistor in a high-voltage circuit. "You're . . . talking about a dictatorship."

"Certainly; it's the most efficient form of government there is!"

"Oh, sure." Dar passed a dry tongue over drier lips. "Of course it's efficient. It just wipes out all those silly time-wasters—you know, parliamentary debate, public input, elections, trial by jury. All those silly, inefficient boondoggles."

"Indeed it does. And as an administrator, I can assure you—they *do* take a great deal of time. They also encumber an amazing number of people, keeping them from tasks in production."

Dar nodded sardonically. "And all you get for all that time

and trouble are little, unnecessary luxuries, such as liberty and justice."

"Make no mistake; they are luxuries." Bhelabher smiled with sudden, amazing warmth. "But they seem much more important out here, where they help people to actually *do* something!"

"Kind of makes up for the cost?"

"Well worth it, well worth it! In fact, I've a suspicion liberty is actually cost-efficient, in a growing society."

"But you couldn't prove it, to the LORDS?"

Bhelabher smiled sadly. "Would they even listen?"

"I'd think so." Dar frowned. "Even a conservative can have an open mind."

"Not if he's in power. Efficiency matters far more to those who give orders than to those who take them." Bhelabher held up a forefinger. "Take the Minister of the Exchequer, now—his purpose is to keep the economy of the whole I.D.E. family of planets as high as possible."

"Uh, with respect, Honorable—isn't the correct word 'profitable'?"

"No, it certainly isn't—but the Minister very quickly comes to believe that it is. Consequently, he tends to frown on anything that costs more than it makes."

Dar frowned. "Such as?"

"Such as trade to the outlying planets—for example, Wolmar."

"Now, hold on!" Dar was amazed to realize he was getting angry; he fought down his temper, and went on. "We always ship out a lot of pipeweed."

"Indeed you do—but I've seen the trade reports, and the goods I.D.E. sends to you cost far more than your pipeweed brings—not even counting the shipping cost. No, I.D.E. shows a definite loss on you."

"Well, you'll pardon me if I think we're worth it!"

"Of course—more than worth it. But how do you explain that to the Minister of the Exchequer?"

"Hm." Dar frowned. "I see the problem. And there're a lot of planets like ours, aren't there?"

"Upwards of thirty." Bhelabher nodded. "Thirty frontier worlds, and the Minister shows a loss for each of them—thirty or forty billion BTUs apiece. It adds up to a very substantial drain on the economy."

"It'll pay off, though—someday!" Dar's temper kindled again. "Give us time, and we'll be sending out more than we bring in!" A sudden thought nudged Dar's brain. He cocked his head to the side, gazing at Bhelabher through slitted eyes. "It's no accident that you mentioned the Minister of the Exchequer, is it?"

Bhelabher stared at him in surprise. Then he smiled sheepishly. "Indeed it's not. Yes, the Exchequer was the LORD who came to call on me. And his argument was very persuasive—very persuasive, indeed! And once he had me believing that the outlying planets *should* be cut off and left to their own devices, he arranged my appointment as governor."

"So . . . that's . . . why!" Then another sudden hunch hit, and Dar frowned. "You wouldn't be telling me this if you didn't think I could do something about it."

"I don't know if you can or not," Bhelabher said earnestly, "but you must try. It isn't easy to gain an appointment with the Secretary-General, young man, but if you can, you must tell him that Electors Boundbridge and Satrap are leaguing with General Forcemain to attempt a coup d'etat. Can you remember those names?"

"Boundbridge, Satrap, and Forcemain." Dar nodded, repeating them silently in his head, getting the meter down. "Boundbridge, Satrap, and Forcemain . . . yeah, I'll remember. But this is the top man in all of human civilization we're talking about, Honorable. He's not going to believe the ordinary young punk off the street without some pretty powerful evidence!"

"He shall have it." Bhelabher pressed a slip of paper into Dar's hand. "Memorize that set of numbers, young man, and when you've done so, burn the paper. The Secretary-General has only to put them into the nearest computer terminal, and the screen will display an excellent little collection of documents, complete with signatures."

Dar stared at the slip of paper. "But . . . but how did you . . . ?"

"Find them?" Bhelabher smiled. "I do give myself some credit, young man; and I know that I am an expert on data

storage and retrieval. When I'd spoken with Minister Boundbridge, I was thoroughly convinced; but my bureaucrat's
instincts still functioned, almost by themselves. I was determined to aid the LORDS' coup; but I was also determined that
I would not be made a scapegoat if anything went wrong."

Dar's eyes widened. "My lord! Is human trust *that* far gone
on Terra?"

Bhelabher waved the objection away, irritated. "It has been
for centuries, young man—probably ever since the Chinese
invented bureaucracy. One of the first rules you learn in an
office is, 'Get the directive in writing—and keep a copy.' And
if I knew that, certainly Satrap and Forcemain did, too, plus
whomever else was involved in the conspiracy. I knew they'd
each have saved their own bits of evidence."

"But how could you find it?"

Bhelabher smiled, preening. "People don't hide things in
chests with false bottoms, or secret rooms, anymore, young
man. They hide them in computers, with secret activation
codes. But whatever code one man can think up, another can
deduce—especially if he has his own computer to do the
donkey-work of searching. I *am* an expert, after all—and I did
have some time."

Dar stared. "You mean you actually managed to break each
of their personal codes?"

"Only Satrap's and Boundbridge's; General Forcemain held
his inside the military computer, which is somewhat better
protected against even expert pilfering. But the Electors'
dossiers sufficed—especially since they directed me to several
others. No, young man, that code I've given you will reveal
enough documented evidence to convince even the Secretary-
General."

The slip of paper suddenly seemed to burn Dar's fingers. He
held onto it resolutely, the numbers fairly searing his retinas.
"Somehow I don't think I'll have any trouble remembering
these numbers now, Honorable."

"Stout fellow!" Bhelabher clasped his arm and pumped his
hand. "I'll be eternally indebted to you—and so will quadril-
lions of other persons, most of whom have not even been born
yet!"

"I'll collect when they've grown, and the interest has, too."

Dar forced a smile. "Don't worry, Honorable—I'll do my best."

"More than that, no man can ask." Bhelabher looked up. "Except possibly your commander; I see he wants another word with you." He stepped aside, and Shacklar stepped up. "It's about time to depart, Ardnam."

A high-pitched whine hit their ears as the ferry's coolant pumps started up. Sam pushed her way through the door and strode over to the small ship.

"Allow me to escort you," Shacklar murmured, taking Dar by the elbow and steering him out the door.

Once outside, he raised his voice to be heard over the beginning rumbles of superheated steam. "You do realize the importance of the mission you're undertaking?"

"Yeah, to make sure BOA leaves us alone," Dar called back. "Uh, General . . ."

Shacklar gave him an inquiring blink.

"The Honorable just told me about a coup the LORDS're planning, back on Terra. Think I should take him seriously?"

"Oh, very seriously. I've been sure it would happen for quite some time now."

Dar whirled to stare to him, appalled. "You *knew*?"

"Well, not 'knew,' really. I can't tell you the date of its beginning, nor who will be behind it—but I do see the general shape of it. Any man who's read a bit of history can see it coming. On the inner worlds, it's all about you, the signs of a dying democracy. I'd been watching it happen for twenty years, before I came out here."

"And that's *why* you came out here?"

Shacklar nodded, pleased. "You're perceptive, young fellow. Yes. If democracy is doomed on the interstellar scale, it can at least be kept alive on individual planets."

"Especially one that's far enough away from Terra so that whatever dictatorship replaces the I.D.E. will just forget about it," Dar inferred.

Shacklar nodded again. "Because it's too costly to maintain communication with it. Yes. By the end of the century, I expect we'll be left quite thoroughly to our own devices."

"Not a pleasant picture," Dar said, brooding, "but better

than being ruled by a dictator on Terra. So what should I do about it?"

"Do?" Shacklar repeated, surprised. "Why, there's nothing you *can* do, really—except to make the quixotic gesture: inform the media, if you like, or the Secretary-General, or something of the sort."

"You can't mean it," Dar said, shocked. "We can't let democracy go down without a fight!"

"But it already *has* gone down, don't you see? And all you can gain by a dramatic flourish is, perhaps, another decade or so of life for the forms of it—the Assembly, and the Cabinet, and so forth. But that won't change the reality—that the frontier worlds have already begun to govern themselves, and that Terra and the other Central Worlds are already living under a dictatorship, for all practical purposes. Ask anyone who's lived there, if you doubt me."

Dar thought of Sam's disgust and despair, and saw Shacklar's point. "Are you saying democracy isn't worth fighting for?"

"Not at all—but I am saying that all such fighting will get you is a lifelong prison sentence in a real, Terrestrial prison, perhaps for a very short life. The press of social forces is simply too great for anyone to stop. If you really want to do something, try to change those social forces."

Dar frowned. "How can you do that?"

Shacklar shrugged. "Invent faster-than-light radio, or a way of educating the vast majority to skepticism and inquiring thought—but don't expect to see the effects of it within your lifetime. You can start it—but it'll take a century or two before it begins to have an effect."

"Well, that's great for my grandchildren—but what do I do about the rest of my life?"

Shacklar sighed. "Try to find a nice, quiet little out-of-the-way planet that the new dictators are apt to overlook, and do your best to make it a pocket of freedom for the next few centuries, and live out your life there in whatever tranquility you can manage."

"Which is what you've done," Dar said softly.

Shacklar flashed him a smile. "Well, it's still in process, of course."

"It always will be, for the rest of your life. Which is how

you're going to maintain your illusion of meaning in your life."

"Quite so," Shacklar said, grinning, "and can you be certain it *is* an illusion?"

"Not at all," Dar breathed. "If I could, it wouldn't work. But that line of thought is supposed to induce despair."

"Only if you take it as proof that there is no purpose in life—which your mind may believe, but your heart won't. Not once you're actually involved in it. It's a matter of making unprovability work *for* you, you see."

"I think I begin to." Dar gave his head a quick shake. "Dunno if I'm up to making that little 'pocket of freedom,' though."

"You'll always be welcome back here, of course," Shacklar murmured.

"Two minutes till lift-off," declared a brazen voice from the ship.

"You'd better run." Shacklar pressed a thick envelope into Dar's hand. "You'll find all the credentials you'll need in there, including a draft on the Bank of Wolmar for two first-class, round-trip fares from Wolmar to Terra." He slapped Dar on the shoulder. "Good luck, and remember—don't be a hero."

Dar started to ask what he meant, but Shacklar was already turning away, and the ship rumbled threateningly deep in its belly, so Dar had to turn and run.

"Took you long enough," Sam groused as he dropped into the acceleration couch beside her and stretched the shock webbing across his body. "What was that high-level conference all about?"

"About why I should flow with the social tide."

"Hm." Sam pursed her lips, and nodded slowly. "Quite a man, your General."

"Yeah. I really feel badly about deceiving him." Dar rolled back the envelope flap.

"What's that?" Sam demanded.

Dar didn't answer. He was too busy staring.

"Hi, there!" Sam waved. "Remember me? What *have* you got there?"

"My credentials," Dar said slowly.

"What's the matter? Aren't they in order?"

"Very. They're all for 'Dar Mandra.'"

"Oh." Sam sat quietly for a few minutes, digesting that. Then she sighed and leaned back in her couch. "Well. Your General . . . perceptive, too, huh?"

7

The courier ship had room for ten passengers. Dar and Sam were the only ones. After five days, they'd both tried all ten seats at least twice.

"No, really, I do think it looks better from back here," Dar said from the seat just in front of the aft bulkhead. "You get more of a feeling of depth—and it's definitely more aesthetic to feel the force of acceleration on your back."

"*What* force of acceleration? This ship could be in free-fall, for all we feel. Built-in acceleration compensators, remember? This cabin's got its own gravity unit."

"Luxury craft," Dar griped, "absolutely destroys all sense of motion."

"Which makes it far more aesthetic to sit in the middle of the cabin," Sam opined. "You get the sense of the environment this way." She spread her arms. "The feeling of *space*— limited, but space. You're immersed in it."

"Yeah, but who wants to be immersed in molded-plastic seats and creon upholstery?"

"If your accommodations bother you, sir . . ."

Dar looked up at the stewardess in annoyance. "I know: I don't have any choice about it."

"Not at all, sir. I can offer you a variety of other realms of reality." The stewardess's chest slid open, revealing several shelves crammed with pill bottles. "All guaranteed to make you forget where you are, sir, and make the time fly."

"And my brain with it. No, thank you—I'll stick with the old-fashioned narcotics."

A plastic tumbler rammed into his palm; the stewardess's finger turned into a spigot, and splashed amber-colored fluid and crushed ice into his tumbler. "One old-fashioned, sir."

"I had in mind a martini," Dar grumbled. "But thanks, anyway."

"It is unnecessary to thank me, sir. I am merely . . ."

"A machine, yes. But it keeps me from getting into bad habits. When do we get to Haldane IV?"

"That's got to be the twelfth time you've asked that question," Sam sighed, "and I told you as soon as we'd boarded—Bhelabher said it'd take us five days!"

"I know, I know," Dar griped, "but I like to hear *her* say it. When do we get to Haldane IV, stewardess?"

"Experienced space travelers never ask 'when,' sir," the stewardess answered, a bit primly.

"I love the programmed response." Dar leaned back, grinning.

"Look at it this way—it's a faster trip then I had on the way out," Sam offered. "That took a week and a half."

"I believe the ship transporting you on the outbound swing was a common freighter, sir. . . ."

"Miz!"

"Oh, really? But I believe you'll find that an I.D.E. courier ship is a bit faster than your earlier conveyance. In fact, we're approaching breakout now. Stretch webbing, please." And the stewardess rolled into her closet, clicking the door shut behind her.

"Talk about bad habits!" Sam snorted. "Or didn't you realize you were making fun of her?"

"I know, I know," Dar growled. "But I have definitely taken a dislike to that machine."

"Programmed by a snob," Sam agreed. "Come on, we'd better get ready."

"Approaching breakout," the resonant PA ship's voice informed them.

"I don't know why we bother." Dar stretched his shock webbing across his body. "What could happen when you break out of H-space, anyway?"

"Y'know, you're getting to be a pretty surly bird."

"So, I'll get a worm. You've got to admit, there isn't even a jar when you break out into normal space."

"Not unless they've got you bottled up."

Dar frowned. "What's that supposed to mean?"

Sam sighed. "It's a holdover from the pre-I.D.E. days, when there wasn't any central government and things were pretty chaotic outside the Sol system. Pirates used to lie in wait for ships at the breakout points. They couldn't touch a freighter while it was in H-space, but they *could* jump it as soon as it broke out."

"Oh." Dar felt a slight chill of apprehension. "Uh—the central government isn't too effective, these days. . . ."

"Breaking out," the ship's voice informed them. "We will be without interior power for a few seconds."

The lights went out as all the ship's power was channeled into the isomorpher, translating them back into normal space. A surge of dizziness washed over Dar, and objective reality became a little subjective for a second or two—in fact, it seemed to go away altogether. Then it came back, and the lights came on again. Dar blinked and turned his head from side to side, to see if it still worked. "On second thought, maybe the webbing isn't such a bad idea."

"Please maintain your position," the ship's voice advised. "There is an unidentified craft in pursuit."

Dar looked over at Sam. "What were you saying about pirates?"

"Not in this day and age, certainly." But she looked a little pale.

"I think they said something like that in the early 1800s, to a man named Jean Laffite." Dar turned to stare out the porthole. "You know, you can actually see something out there now."

"Of course—stars. We're back in normal space, remember? So what did he answer?"

"That one's got a discernible disk; must be Haldane. . . . Who?"

"This Jean Laffite."

"Oh—'Stand and deliver.'" Dar peered through the porthole. "There was more; I forget the exact wording, but it had something to do with the ownership of a place called 'the Caribbean. . . .' Wow!"

An orange glare lit up the cabin.

"That was *close!*" Sam said through the afterimages.

"I think that's what they used to call a 'shot across the bow.'"

"This is *serious!*" Sam yelped. "Where's the Navy when you need it?"

"Ask the pirates—I'm sure they know."

"So do I; I got one of the Navy data operators drunk one night, just before I quit, and got the access code out of him."

Dar frowned. "Why'd you do that?"

"I wanted to make sure I was going to be safe on my trip out here. And I found out I would be; there wasn't supposed to be a sailor for fifty parsecs. The nearest fleet's a hundred seventy-five light-years away, over toward Aldebaran, sitting on their thumbs and polishing the brightwork."

"What're they doing there?"

"Somebody called 'em, about a year ago, to come take care of some pirates."

"So, while they were on their way out, the pirates were coming back here! Great!" Dar said.

Sam took a deep breath. "Now, wait a minute. Wait a minute. We're getting carried away here. For all we know, those aren't pirates out there."

"Sure, maybe it *is* the Navy—and for all *they* know, *we're* pirates. If you'll pardon my saying so . . ."

A brilliant flare lit up the cabin. Sam shrieked. "I'm convinced! It's pirates!"

Dar shrugged. "Pirates or Navy—after we've been turned into an expanding cloud of hydrogen atoms, I'm afraid I won't really care much about distinctions."

"You're right." Sam loosed her shock webbing. "Whoever it is, we've gotta get out of here."

Dar's head snapped up, startled. Then he waved an airy hand toward the porthole. "Sure—be my guest. It's a great day outside, if you face sunwards. Of course, the night on your backside gets a teeny bit chilly."

"Credit me with *some* sense," she snorted. "This ship *must* have some kind of lifeboat!"

But Dar was looking out the porthole. "Get down!"

Startled, Sam obeyed. A rending crash shot through the ship, and she slammed back against the cabin wall. Dar bounced out against his webbing.

"What in Ceres' name was *that*?" Sam gasped.

"They got tired of playing games." Dar yanked his webbing loose and struggled to his feet, bracing himself against the pull of acceleration. "They shot to maim this time, and they had some luck. They got our gravity generator. Where'd you say the lifeboat was?"

"It'd make sense to put it between the pilot's bridge and the passenger cabin, wouldn't it?"

"Right." Dar turned aft. "Since that makes sense, it'll obviously be between the cabin and the cargo space. Let's go."

Sam started to protest, then shut up and followed.

The ship bucked and heaved. Dar caught the tops of the seats on either side, bracing himself. Sam slammed into his back. "Near miss," he grated. "We got hit by a wave of exploding gas. Wish I had time to watch; this pilot's doing one hell of a job of dodging."

"Is that why my body keeps trying to go through the wall?"

"Yeah, and why it keeps changing its mind as to which wall. Come on."

They wallowed through a morass of acceleration-pull to the aft hatch. Dar turned to a small closet beside the hatch, and yanked it open. "Two on this side; there'll be three on the other side, I suppose." He took down a slack length of silver fabric with a plastic bulb on top. "Here, scramble into it."

Sam started struggling into the space suit. "Little flimsy, isn't it?"

Dar nodded. "It won't stop anything sharper than a cheese wedge. It's not supposed to; the lifeboat'll take care of that. The suit's just to hold in air."

The ship bucked to the side with a rending crash, slamming Sam up against him. Jumpsuit or not, he realized dizzily, she was *very* definitely female. Somehow, this didn't seem like the time to mention it.

She scrambled back from him, and kept on scrambling, into her suit. "They're getting closer! *Hurry!*"

Dar stretched the suit on and pressed the seal-seam shut, being careful to keep it flat. Sam copied him. Then he braced himself and touched his helmet against hers, to let his voice conduct through the plastic. "Okay, turn around so I can turn on your air supply and check your connections."

Sam turned her back to him. Dar checked her connections, then turned on her air supply. When the meter read in the blue, he tapped her shoulder and turned his back. He could feel her hands fumbling over him; then air hissed in his helmet. He took a breath and nodded, then turned to the hatch, wrenched it open, and waved Sam in. She stepped through; he followed, and pulled the door closed behind them, wrenching it down. Sam had already pushed the cycle button. When the air had been pumped back into the reserve tank, the green light lit up over the side hatch. Dar leaned on the handle and hauled back; the three-foot circle swung open. Sam stepped through, and Dar stepped after her.

He sat down, stretching the web over his body. Sam leaned over to touch helmets. "How about the pilot?"

"He's on his own—got his own lifeboat if he wants it." Dar punched the power button, and the control panel lit up.

"You know how to drive this thing?"

"Sure; besides, how can you go wrong, with two buttons, two pedals, and a steering wheel?"

"I could think of a few ways."

Dar shrugged. "So I'm not creative. Here goes." The "READY" light was blinking; he stabbed at the "EJECT" button.

A five-hundred-pound masseur slammed him in the chest, and went to work on the rest of his body. Then the steamroller lightened to a flatiron, and Dar could breathe again. He sat up against the push of slackening acceleration and looked around through the bubble-dome. It had darkened to his right, where a sun was close enough to show a small disk and kick out some lethal radiation. But that didn't matter; the silver slab of pirate ship filled most of the starboard sky. "Way too close," Dar muttered, and pressed down on the acceleration pedal. The flatiron pressed down on him again, expanding into a printing press. He glanced behind him, once, at the silver-baseball courier ship, then turned back to the emptiness before him.

Sam struggled forward against the pull of acceleration. "Any chance they haven't spotted us?"

Dar shrugged. "Hard to say. We'll show up on their detectors; but they might not pay attention to anything this small."

Then the silver slab began to slide toward them.

"Do they have to be so damn observant?" Dar adjusted his chair upright and tromped down on the acceleration pedal. The masseur dumped the steamroller on him again, shoving him back into the chair; he could just barely stretch his arms enough to hold onto the wheel.

The silver slab picked up speed.

"Somehow, I don't think we can outrun them." Dar turned the wheel left; the port-attitude jets slackened, then died, as the starboard jets boosted their mutter to a roar, and the lifeboat turned in a graceful U, throwing Dar over against Sam. She sat huddled back in her chair, face pale, eyes huge.

No wonder, Dar thought. He'd feel the same way if he were a passenger in a boat he was driving. He straightened out the wheel and held the pedal down, sending the little ship arrowing back toward the courier ship, which was taking advantage of the pirates' preoccupation to try to sneak away.

Sam struggled forward, adjusting her chair upright, and laid her helmet against his. "Shouldn't we be going *away* from them?"

Dar shook his head. "They'd have about as much trouble catching us as a lean cat would have with a fat mouse. Our only chance is to hide."

"Hide? Behind *what*? There's nothing out here!"

A bright red energy-bolt exploded just behind them and a little to their right.

"YEOW!" Sam shrank down inside her suit. "Hide behind *something*! Fast!"

"As fast as I can." Dar threw the wheel hard over. Sam slammed hard against his side.

"What're you *doing*?"

"Evasive action. They might get smart and hook that cannon up to a ballistic computer." And Dar proceeded to lay a course that would have given a triple-jointed snake double lumbago. They rattled around inside the lifeboat like dice in a cup.

"We're winning," Dar grated. "We've got it confused."

A fireball exploded right under their tail.

"YEOW! Learns fast, doesn't it?" Dar tromped hard on the accelerator and pushed on the wheel. They dived, and a great gleaming curve slid by overhead. Then they were out, with open space before them. Dar pressed down on the deceleration pedal, and threw himself and Sam forward against their webbing.

Her helmet cracked against his. "Why don't you keep on running?"

" 'Cause they'd catch us." Dar turned the boat, sent it racing back toward the silver sphere and the slab that loomed over it like a tombstone.

Sam stiffened in her seat. "Don't ram it!"

"No fear."

Blue sparks spattered up all around the courier. "I think they just mistook it for us." Then Dar pushed on the wheel again. The lifeboat dived, and the bottom of the silver sphere swam by overhead again.

"*Why?*" Sam fairly shrieked.

"Because."

The little ship spat out from under the courier, darting across the gap toward the silver slab.

Sam took a deep breath. "Correct me if I'm wrong—but aren't we supposed to be trying to get *away* from them?"

"Yes—and we are." The silver slab loomed right above them, so close it seemed they could almost touch it. Dar shoved on the deceleration pedal again, slowing the lifeboat by deft touches till the pitted silver plates above them were almost motionless. "There!" He sat back and relaxed. "We've matched velocities. With any luck, they won't have noticed us jumping under them; they'll have been too busy taking potshots at the courier."

"Why wouldn't they notice us?"

"Because it would make a lot more sense for us to be still hiding behind our mother ship."

"Definitely." Sam glanced up at the pirate with apprehension.

"Even if they do start looking for us, they're apt to *over*look us—unless they've got their ventral detectors on."

"Which they probably have."

"With our luck, of course. But even if they do, they probably won't see us—we're too close to their skin, in their detectors' 'shadow.'"

"Nice theory." Sam settled back. "What happens if you're wrong?"

"Well, in that case, they shoot away from us faster than we can go, leave us sitting here, and play skeet shoot."

"Now I know why I always sympathized with the clay pigeons." Sam shivered. "What're they doing?"

Dar turned around, looking out over the tail. "Still trying to shoot through the courier . . . whup!"

"'Whup,' what?" Sam asked with foreboding.

"The courier's moving away—'streaking' would be more likely. Brace yourself—the pirates're going after him, and fast! Even damaged, that courier's *quick!*"

Sam frowned. "Then how'd the pirates catch 'em in the first place?"

"Lurking in ambush."

"Lurking *where*? There's no cover bigger than a hydrogen atom out here!"

"Whup! There they go!" Dar spun around and set himself as the silver slab slid away toward their rear. Dar pushed down the acceleration pedal, heading sunwards.

"We . . . can't . . . possibly outrun . . . them," Sam grated against the pull of acceleration.

"Not if they're going . . . our way," Dar answered. "But at the moment . . . they're going . . . out, and we're going . . . in."

"Why bother?" Sam spoke more easily. "As soon as they're done with the courier, they'll come after us."

"Assuming we're big enough to bother with. But by that time, maybe we can find a place to hide."

"Hide? *Where?*"

"Wherever they did, while they were lurking . . . *there!*" Dar's forefinger stabbed out, pointing ahead, at a string of pierced diamonds backlit by the sun. "Asteroids! They confused the ship's detection system; it thought the pirates' ship was just a large rock, closer than the others!"

Sam stared. "What're they doing here?"

"This is *not* the time to ask questions." Dar craned around, looking aft. "They're still going after the courier . . . they've overhauled it, they're gonna fire a warning shot. . . . NO! They're starting to slow and turn!"

Sam stared. "Why?"

"Because they're not interested in the courier, obviously! They just took a peek, saw our boat's pod was still empty and we were nowhere in sight, and started scanning for us!"

Sam frowned, shaking her head. "I don't get it. You make it sound as though they want *us*."

"Guess what?" Dar said dryly. "What I'd like to know is how they knew we were aboard?"

"Maybe they didn't," Sam said hopefully. "Maybe they think we're somebody else."

"You'll pardon me if I don't stay around to find out." Dar swerved and jammed the deceleration pedal; the ship bucked as the nose rockets spewed superheated steam, slamming them into their webbing. The shiplet danced and curvetted as Dar tried to avoid the smaller chunks of stone and metal. The ship rang like a cymbal in a percussion solo, but nothing holed them. Dar managed to match velocity with an asteroid a little larger than the lifeboat. The ringing diminished to an occasional dong.

"So far, we're fantastically lucky." Dar killed all power. "As long as we don't run into a really fast-moving pebble astern, or a slow-moving one ahead, we're okay. This lifeboat's got enough armor to take care of most of the debris."

Sam released a long, shaky breath. "Taking a bit of a chance, weren't you?"

Dar shrugged. "I had a choice? Now, as long as we don't get our engines smashed, we're okay."

"And if we do?"

"So, which would you rather be—a prisoner, or an asteroid?"

Sam frowned. "Let me think it over."

"Sure." Dar leaned back, folding his arms. "You'll have plenty of time."

The asteroid's path had carried them considerably out of the pirates' path; the huge silver slab flashed by overhead and well behind them.

"Just like that?" Sam looked about her, puzzled. "They just go by and leave us?"

"Wrong," Dar said grimly. "They saw us curve off and join the asteroids, you can bet on it. But they couldn't decelerate fast enough to follow us—we *do* have an edge in maneuverability. They'll be back, though, don't worry."

"Thanks for the reassurance." Sam sat very still. "Why'd you kill the power?"

"Because at least one of their detectors searches for it. Right now, that's the only thing that makes us different from an asteroid, unless they happen to get close enough to eyeball us."

"Don't we reflect a lot more light?"

"I chose a bright asteroid to hide next to."

"Here they come!" Sam yelped.

Dar poised a finger over the power button.

The pirates couldn't hear them, of course, and they both knew it—but the rabbit reflex took over, and they both sat rock-still as the silver tombstone drifted slowly over them in a prowling zigzag. It cruised closer, closer, and Dar felt an urge to shove his tiny boat to starboard, to nestle up against the comforting bulk of the asteroid. The pirate zagged to the right—and, as it zigged past them, it was out beyond their covering asteroid. It loomed closer and closer, but slanting away now. It crossed their path a good half-mile in front of them, and kept on going.

Sam collapsed back against her chair with a sigh. "Thank heaven."

"Yeah." Dar felt himself beginning to tremble as he lowered his finger from the power button. "I never thought I'd be so glad to be inconspicuous."

"As long as it worked." Sam eyed him with dawning respect.

Dar felt his pulse quicken—after all, she *was* the only woman for several million miles. Sam stiffened, pointing ahead. "Look! What're they doing?"

Dar stared. A giant hatch had opened in the stomach of the silver tombstone.

"They're gonna send down their scout boat for a closer look!" Dar lunged at the power button.

Sam caught his arm. "No! You said that was a dead giveaway!"

Dar paused, his eyes on the pirate ship. "Wait a minute! They're thinking it over."

A shuttle hung halfway out the huge hatchway, motionless. Then it started to rise back up into the mother ship, and the huge doors swung shut.

"But *why*?" Dar bleated. "They had us dead cold!"

"*That's* why!" Sam jabbed a finger toward the back window.

A huge, truncated pyramid came hurtling toward them. A vast eye seemed to float above it. The pirate ship slid into motion, gathering speed, and streaked away.

Dar winced in sympathy. "I'd've hated to've taken *that* slap of acceleration. . . . But they didn't have much choice, did they?"

"Why not?" Sam stared at the approaching pyramid. "What *is* that megalith?"

"The cops." Dar shrugged. "Which ones, I'm not sure—but it comes out to the same thing. For once, I'm glad to see them."

"Yo! Over here! Whoa! Help!" Sam tried to stand up, waving her arms frantically. "Damn! Don't they *hear* us?"

"Sound waves don't travel too well through vacuum," Dar pointed out.

"I know, I know," Sam groused, dropping back into her seat. "Just carried away by the heat of the moment."

"So are they," Dar noted, watching the police ship zip by.

"*Now* what do we do? Get out and walk?"

"Well, presumably we're in the Haldane system, since that's where we were going. And at our top speed, it can't be more than three or four months to the nearest habitable planet."

"I don't think I can wait that long for lunch."

"Oh, I'm sure there're some rations tucked away around here somewhere. But I don't think we'll have to wait that long. I expect the police ship to be coming back this way pretty soon."

"Why?" Sam frowned. "For reinforcements?"

"Oh, they don't need any. Did you see that 'eye' on top of their ship? It is one *very* powerful blaster."

"Oh." Sam chewed that one over. "That why the pirates ran?"

Dar nodded. "With that 'eye,' the police have the pirates out-ranged, no matter *how* many guns they mount."

"So why'll the police be coming back?"

"Because the pirate ship also mounts an isomorpher, and I strongly suspect that police ship is purely local. As soon as the pirate goes into H-space, the police'll be homeward bound."

"Oh." Sam thought it over. "But couldn't the police catch the pirates before they isomorph?"

"They could," Dar said judiciously, "but I don't think they will. Those pirates're going to be very good at running. If they're not, they lose profits. So they'll take risks the police won't."

"Like going into H-space too soon?"

"That's possible. If you see a big explosion, you'll know they tried it."

They waited, staring ahead, where the police ship had dwindled to a glint of light.

After a while, Sam ventured, "I don't think they tried it."

A speck of light glinted in the distance. Dar's finger sprang out to the power button again.

"Not yet!" Sam cried. "We don't know who won!"

"I bet we're gonna find out, though." Dar waited, tense.

The glint grew into a dot, and kept growing.

It became a triangular dot.

"*Victory!*" Dar stabbed the button, and the engine roared into life. "Let's hear it for the good guys!" He hauled back on the wheel, and the boat sprang up out of the plane of the ecliptic, toward the police ship.

"Shouldn't we identify ourselves? So they don't think we're attacking?"

"Not as ridiculous as it sounds," Dar said soberly. "For all they know, we could be a torpedo. There oughta be some kinda distress beacon around here. See if you can find it, will ya?"

It was labeled "Distress Beacon," and it only had one button. Sam pressed it, and waited.

"How do we know if it's working?" she said finally.

"How do you know God listens?" Dar retorted. "It's got radio; we don't."

"Faith," Sam grumbled. "Does it *always* have to come down to that?"

The pyramid loomed up toward them—and disappeared in a cloud of steam.

"They heard us!" Dar yelped. "They're decelerating!"

The fog cleared, and the police ship towered over them.

Sam shrank back. "I can't help it—I feel as though it's going to fall on me!"

And it did. The great pyramid sank toward them, giving them a fly's-eye view of a giant foot. Dar opened his mouth to scream just as a hatch slid open in the huge silver wall above them, swooping down to swallow them up.

"Saved?" someone croaked. Dar would've thought it was Sam, but it was coming from inside his own head.

"Just glad we were nearby." The captain poured two glasses of brandy and held them out to Sam and Dar. His insignia gleamed on the breast of his doublet—an eye-topped pyramid with "Space Police" inside it in cursive script. Arcing above it were the words, "Hal. IV," and, below it, "Falstaff." It stood out in a sea of ocher—no, maybe an ocean. The captain was obese, to say the least. So was his crew—the smallest of them was at least four feet around, and all were shorter than Dar. The captain also had the typical Haldane IV face: florid, with long curly hair and a jawline beard.

Dar accepted the brandy eagerly, but Sam held up a palm. "Thanks, but I don't believe in alcohol."

The captain blinked in surprise. "I assure you, it exists."

"We *were* lucky you were in the neighborhood," Dar said quickly.

"Well, it wasn't entirely luck," the captain admitted. "We have had reports about pirates trying to ambush merchantmen at the H-space jump points. But last week a freighter full of pickled herring that was supposed to come through this way, didn't—so we decided to guard this jump point. We only have this one patrol cruiser, so you'll understand that we couldn't guard *all* the points."

"And the load of pickled herring was *that* important?" Dar said in surprise.

"To us," said the captain, "it's vital. But what brings you to Falstaff, gentlefolk?"

" 'Falstaff'?" Dar frowned, puzzled.

"It's the local name for Haldane IV," Sam explained. "Just here to make a connection, Captain. We're inbound from Wolmar."

The captain still sat comfortably leaning back, fingers laced across his butterbelly, but suddenly he was all vigilance. "Wolmar? Really! How interesting. By the way, could I see your papers?"

"Hm? Oh, sure!" Dar slid his passport and ID out of his jacket pocket and laid them on the desk; Sam followed suit. "Sorry; we should have thought of that right off."

"Well, you were a little flustered." The captain picked up their passports and suddenly, illogically, Dar had the insane conviction that the captain had a jewler's loupe in his eye.

"Everything in order—of course." The last part lacked conviction. The captain slid their papers back to them. "We don't get many coming *from* Wolmar."

"The traffic does seem to run the other way," Dar agreed. "But our pharmaceutical materials company's getting itchy to expand, and we're heading back to the inner planets to sound out possible investors." Sam twitched; Dar reflected that he really should have told her about the cover story he was dreaming up.

"Didn't realize it was getting to be that big a business." The captain seemed genuinely interested.

Dar grinned. "It may not be—but we're sure going to find out. By the way, I was mightily relieved when you noticed our boat so quickly. Were you on the lookout for us?"

"No, not particularly." The captain frowned. "Should we have been?"

Dar sat still for a moment, letting the shock wash through him.

"Well," he said carefully, "I would've thought our courier ship would've told you we were missing."

"That *is* strange, now that you mention it." The captain

scratched his head, then looked up. "Maybe the pilot didn't notice you'd abandoned ship."

"Uh . . . could be." Dar thought of how much of a lurch the lifeboat must've given the courier ship when it blasted free. "Of course—now that I think about it, that must be it. After all, how could the pilot have noticed we were gone?"

"How *couldn't* he've noticed?" Dar raged. "When that lifeboat blasted free, it must've kicked the ship like a foundation anomaly!"

"Maybe he thought it was a blaster bolt," Sam offered. "It *was* a little hectic just then."

"And he wouldn't've checked the passengers when the action was over?" Dar shook his head. "No. It washes about as well as baked-on grease."

They were strolling through the downtown section of Haskerville, the capital of Falstaff. The street was wide, but all the buildings had a second story that projected out over the sidewalk—convenient in rainy weather, Dar was sure, but a little depressing on a sunny day. Also, it was a little strange that all the buildings were half-timbered and stuccoed.

"Well, it's a frontier planet, I guess," he said aloud.

"Not really—it's a third of the way back to Terra, and it's been colonized for four hundred years. What makes you think so?"

"The architecture." Dar pointed to the wooden beams. "Don't they know how to make steel?"

"Oh, they know how, well enough." Sam smiled. "I asked about it on my way out here. Seems there's very little free metal on Falstaff. Even the iron's all locked up in rust, in the soil."

"Oh." Dar pursed his lips. "So what do I use for money here—nails?"

Sam started, surprised. "How'd you guess?"

"You're kidding!"

"Think so, do you? Well, just try to pay for something with an I.D.E. BTU credit here."

"I'll take your word for it." Dar stopped by a storefront, looking up at the sign. "I think this is the place we're looking for. Maybe they do money-changing here."

"Makes sense," Sam agreed, "so probably they don't."

They went into the ticket office of Outworld Interstellar Starship Enterprises, Unltd.

"Help you?" the clerk grunted around his sausage, his eyes on the newsfax. He was grossly fat, and jowly, like all the Falstavians they'd seen. In fact, Dar was beginning to feel like a freak—he was slim.

"Uh, yeah. We'd like to book passage to Terra."

"Sure thing." The man pulled out two tickets without even looking. "That'll be two hundred pounds. Next ship lifts at fourteen hundred hours, May third."

Dar froze with his hand on his wallet. "May third!? But it's only April fifth!"

"Too bad, isn't it?" the clerk commiserated. "You just missed the last boat—two days ago."

"But we can't wait! We've got to get to Terra fast!"

The clerk shrugged. "I just sell the tickets, buddy—I don't schedule the ships. Y' want 'em, or not?"

"Uh, not just yet, thanks." Dar turned to Sam, looking helpless.

"Do you change money here?" she said briskly.

The clerk looked up. "Money? Yeah, sure! Whacha got?"

"I.D.E. therms—ten of them," Sam said with a meaningful stare at Dar.

"Oh." The clerk seemed disappointed. "Well, we'll take anything, I guess. Put 'em up here." He pulled out a small cloth sack and set it on the counter; it clanked.

Dar paused with his cash halfway to the counter. "What's that?"

"Money." the clerk looked up, frowning. "For ten I.D.E. therms, you get two pounds."

"*Two* pounds?" Dar bleated, aghast. "You must think your pound's worth an awful lot!"

"A pound of ten-penny nails?" The clerk eyed Dar as if doubting his sanity. "Buddy, around here, that's worth a *hell* of a lot!"

"Oh." Dar glanced at Sam out of the corner of his eye; she nodded. He sighed and laid his bills down on the counter. "Okay, here you are. Say, uh—is there *any* connection to Terra sooner than next month?"

"Well, if y' really wanna know . . ." The clerk leaned forward confidentially. "I got this buddy, see, an' he's got an inside track on this nice, used space yacht. . . ."

"Uh, thanks anyway." Dar took a step back. "I, uh, haven't done all that much piloting lately."

Sam bit the inside of her cheek.

"Oh." The clerk leaned back with a look of disgust. "No high-grade, huh? Well, suit yourself." He turned back to the newsfax.

"Uh, yeah." Dar scooped up the moneybag. "We'll, uh, get back to you."

"You an' what miner?" But the clerk lifted an affable hand anyway. "Good luck, chum."

"Well, he *tried* to sound friendly, I suppose," Dar said as they came out of the office.

"Not really. Around here, 'chum' doesn't mean 'friend'—it means 'fishbait.' The garbage kind."

"Oh." Dar frowned. "What was all that stuff about 'high-grade'? And why would we come back with a miner?"

"The kind who digs up ore," Sam explained. "High-grade ore."

Dar glanced at her, but she wasn't smiling. He shrugged. "Really serious about this iron thing, aren't they?"

A ground car went past, hissing steam from its turbine. The body was wooden; the boltheads were plastic.

"Very," Sam agreed.

Dar's head swiveled, tracking the ground car. "What do they make the engine out of?"

"A very high-temperature plastic," Sam answered. "But I understand they're short on radios."

Dar turned back to her, frowning. "That does require metal, doesn't it? But how does the newsfax work?"

"Optical-fiber cables; they've got no shortage of silicon. And it can print by heat-transfer."

Dar shook his head, flabbergasted. "Well, at least they don't have traffic jams."

"Sausage, sir?" inquired a rotund pushcart proprietor.

Dar stopped, suddenly realizing that darn near every passerby had a sausage in his mouth, chewing placidly. "Well,

I guess I shouldn't look out of place. Yeah, we'll take two."
He fished in his moneybag, and brought out . . .

. . . a large nail.

He looked up at Sam, horrified.

She frowned, and nodded toward the peddler, who was holding out two sausages on a scrap of plastic. Dar stared from her to the hotdogs and back. Then he shrugged, took the sausages, and dropped the spike in the peddler's palm. He turned away, with two three-penny nails and a brad for change. "What do they do around here when the Revenue Service comes calling?"

"They pay their tacks, like honest citizens. What's the matter? Culture shock?"

Dar shook his head. "Couldn't be; I can't find the conductor."

"Around here," Sam said slowly, "I think that's some kind of political office. You need a drink."

"Good idea." Dar nodded numbly. "I used to favor a cocktail called a 'rusty nail.'"

"On this planet, that's an obscenity." Sam steered him through a swinging door. "I think you'd better have an old-fashioned."

"I think I already have," Dar muttered.

The tavern was dim, in the best tradition of alcohol stations. They stepped up to the bar.

"Orderzh? Orderzh?" the bartender slurred, blinking.

"Uh, an old-fashioned and a martinus." Sam seemed fascinated by the blinking.

"Two bitsh." The bartender pushed buttons.

Dar laid down a ten-penny nail.

"Two from a ten-pin," the bartender muttered. Its hand sucked up the nail; a door in its chest slid open, and ejected two glasses of clear liquid and one glass of amber. It rolled away down the bar to the next customer, leaving two flat-head screws and a drill behind it.

"I'd count your change, if I were you," the patron two stools down advised. He wore a dark brown robe belted with a length of coaxial cable; the crown of his head was shaved in a neat circle. The yellow handle of a small screwdriver peeked from his breast pocket. "That bartender isn't too reliable today."

"I *thought* his lights weren't blinking in the right pattern!" Sam said triumphantly. "What's the matter with him?"

"You'd have to say he's drunk, I suppose," the shave-pate answered. "You see, the tavernkeeper couldn't afford wire for his conductors, so he had to use tubes of saline solution. Well, that means the bartender has to have a little fluid added every morning, and it seems someone spiced his morning pickup with metallic salts today. That increased conductivity, of course, and threw all his circuits off."

"Which is why I got two when I only ordered one. Oh, well." Sam shrugged and took a sip. "I should gripe?"

"Sounds like an expensive prank, for this neck of the woods," Dar commented.

"No, not really. It's *free* metal that's in short supply on Falstaff. Compounds are plentiful."

"You seem to know quite a bit about it." Dar held up his glass and peered through it warily. "From your clothing, I would've thought you were a friar—but you talk like an engineer."

"I'm both, really." The stranger grinned and held out a hand. "Father Marco Ricci, O.S.V., at your service."

"Dar Mandra." Dar shook his hand. "And this is Sam Bine. What's 'O.S.V.'?"

"The 'Order of Saint Vidicon of Cathode,'" the friar answered. "We're a society of Roman Catholic engineers and scientists."

"Oh, yeah. I should have recognized it. The chaplain on our transport was one of your boys."

"They frequently are." Father Marco nodded. "The Church tends to assign Cathodeans who specialize in astronautics to such jobs—it's one more protection in case of a malfunction."

"Yeah, makes sense." Dar nodded, and his training in Cholly's bar took over. "If you'll pardon me, though—isn't that something of a paradox?"

"What, having a priest who's a scientist? Not really. Any conflict between science and religion is simply the result of clergy who don't understand science, and scientists who don't understand religion."

"Wouldn't a scientist-religious tend to be a bit skeptical about both?"

"Indeed he would." The priest grinned. "The Vatican's habitually annoyed with us—we tend to keep asking new questions."

"Then, why do they let you keep going?"

"Because they need us." Father Marco shrugged. "Even the Vatican has plumbing."

"Well, I can see that." Dar sipped. "But why would the church ever declare a maverick like one of you a saint?"

"Oh, you're thinking of our founder." Father Marco nodded. "Well, they hadn't much choice, there. It was very clearly a case of martyrdom."

"That gives you quite a record to live up to," Sam noted.

"Oh, we don't *plan* to be martyrs," Father Marco assured them, "and I'm sure our founder would approve. After all, he was the practical sort—and a live priest can usually accomplish far more than a dead one."

Dar wondered about the "usually." "Well, we have a bit of a practical problem ourselves, at the moment, Father—and you seem to be familiar with the planet."

"But not native—as I'm sure you could tell by my size." Father Marco was only a little on the stout side.

"Yes, and that's our problem—we're not native, and we *would* like to get on with our trip."

"And the last freighter left orbit a few days ago." Father Marco nodded. "Well, I'm afraid there's not much you can do just now—especially with the I.D.E. police sealing off the planet."

"Doing *what*?"

"Sealing off the planet," Father Marco said mildly. "You hadn't heard? It was on the newsfax just a few minutes ago. The Interstels had a reliable tip that a telepath came in on the last ship, so they've forbidden anyone to leave the planet while they search for him."

"Well," Sam said slowly, "that does kind of delay us, doesn't it?"

Dar frowned. "What's this telepath done?"

Father Marco shrugged. "Nothing, so far as I know. At least, nothing was said about it."

"Then, why are they searching for him?"

"You don't know?" Father Marco asked in mild surprise. "Why, telepaths are a menace to everything any right-thinking citizen holds sacred—haven't you heard?"

"Something of the sort, yes," Sam admitted. "We didn't know it was exactly a widely held belief."

"Oh, it's been all the rage for at least a month! Telepaths invade other people's privacy, you see—you can never tell when one might be reading your mind. You could make laws against that, but there'd be no way to enforce them—unless you had telepathic police; and if you did, they'd probably side with their fellows. Those telepaths stick together, you know."

"No, I didn't," said Dar. "In fact, I didn't know there *were* any—well, almost." He remembered the Wolman shaman.

"Ah, you see?" Father Marco wagged a forefinger at him. "You've known at least one person who always seemed to know what you were thinking. So has everyone, of course."

"Of course! Who doesn't have someone who knows them really well?"

"It could be that," the priest said judiciously. "But when that person always seems to be one jump ahead of you—well, you naturally tend to wonder. Because telepaths use what you're thinking against you, you see—they have an unfair advantage in the competition of life. They always know what you're going to do, so they always know how to head you off."

"That's horrible!"

"Isn't it just? But it gets worse. The I.D.E. police are reasonably sure that telepaths all over the Terran Sphere are getting in touch with one another, forming a society of their own, conspiring to overthrow the government and take over."

"But how?" Sam frowned. "Couldn't the police intercept their messages?"

"Intercept a message from one mind reader to another? Hardly. Besides, rumor has it that these telepaths don't even need to get on a starship to get a message from one planet to another."

"What?"

"That's the word." Father Marco nodded. "Their thoughts travel from star to star almost instantaneously. You can see that would give their conspiracy a bit of an advantage over the forces of society."

"Yes, I certainly can." Dar leaned a little closer and lowered his voice. "And do I gather from your tone, Father, that you don't quite believe all this?"

Father Marco leaned over. "Frankly, I think it's the biggest pot of rotten incense I've ever smelled!"

"What I can't figure out," Sam put in, "is why people would get so worked up about something that probably doesn't even exist."

"Well, it's been known to happen before," Father Marco said judiciously. "Mass hysteria is never that far beneath the skin, I suppose. A human being is a thinking animal, but crowds don't seem to be. So I suppose it's just as well that the police are taking action, even though they're probably acting only on the strength of a rumor."

"Rumor?" Dar frowned. "How so?"

"Tips are usually hearsay, I gather. Nonetheless, better to act on a rumor than to risk a riot."

"Riot?" Sam protested. "You've got to be joking."

"Unfortunately, I'm not. If the people didn't know the authorities were on the lookout, they might try to do something on their own—then all it'd take would be one whisper that so-and-so was a telepath, and you'd have a full-scale witch-hunt to deal with. No, it's better that . . ."

"Do you mind?"

A portly gentleman had huffed up from a nearby table.

"Am I in your way?" Father Marco said politely.

"No, but you're upsetting my party quite a bit! If you must insist on discussing politics, would you please have the courtesy to do it in your own quarters? It's in frightfully poor taste, and it's ruining my digestion!"

"Oh!" Dar exchanged a look with Father Marco. "My apologies, citizen. Of course, if we're offending . . ."

"You'll keep right on!" A skinny hand clapped Dar's shoulder like a pincers. "Ay, give offense! Bother the lazy hogs out of their trough! Goad them into *doing* something—into living, for Lord's sake!" He was a short, lean, aging man, who looked to be as hard as a meteorite and as merry as a comet. And next to him . . .

Dar stiffened, eyes widening. Next to the old man stood the most beautiful woman he had ever seen, with the body of Venus outlined by a flowing, sleeveless, calf-length gown that clung to every curve. Her face was comprised of a high, smooth brow, delicate eyebrows; large, wide-set eyes heavily lidded; a small, tip-tilted nose; and a mouth with a hint of a smile that promised delights and challenged him to seek them. Tawny hair rippled down to her waist. It was the face from the dreams of his boyhood, the face that he had never thought could be, the face that could never let the grown man rest.

The unfairness of it hit him like a stiletto—that she should be with that old geezer, instead of with him!

The old geezer was turning on the portly indigestion case, who had made some outraged noises. "And *I'll* thank *you* to let *your* remarks go public! Don't you know what happens to people who won't talk politics? They stop caring about their government! And do you know what happens when they stop caring? One night, some sneaky, unprincipled scoundrel sneaks in and changes their government on them! And the next morning, they wake up and find their taxes are as high as their collarbones, and they can't go anyplace without a permit, and, taken all in all, they're not much better than slaves! And *that's* what happens when you keep your remarks to yourself!"

"Sir!" The fat one recoiled as though he'd stepped on slime. "This is obscene!"

"I'd rather be obscene, and not absurd—but since you seem to think the other way, I think my friends and I had better go look for some fresher air!" He turned to Father Marco, Dar, and Sam. "How about it, oh ones with spirit? You'll find a breeze blowing by the stage that's amazingly fresh! We're going down there, my niece and I—join us, if you're up to it!" And he turned away, limping between the tables in a rush, as though life would get away from him if he didn't hurry to catch it.

The girl turned to follow him—and did her gaze linger just a moment on Dar?

Imagination. Had to be. But . . .

She was only his niece!

"Huh? What?" His head snapped around toward Father Marco.

"I said, shall we join them?" There was a gleam in the priest's eye.

"Uh . . . yeah. Seem like nice folks."

"Why not?" Sam was a monotone in a frigid face. "It's sure to be lively."

They got up, with their glasses, and filed after the loud voice on the old legs.

"Sit down, sit down!" The geezer waved them to chairs around a large table as he slid into one himself. His niece sat demurely next to him. "So you're a Cathodean," the oldster greeted Father Marco. "What's a live order like yours doing in a dead place like this?"

"Where is a minister of Life more needed than among the moribund?" Father Marco countered.

"Wait a minute. Hold on, there." Dar held up a palm. "Back that up a few lines, will you? I think I missed something."

"What?"

"How'd you know he was a Cathodean?"

"Huh? Why, the emblem of his order, of course!" the old man exclaimed.

"This." Father Marco tapped the tiny yellow screwdriver in his breast pocket. "Used to be the sign of an electrical engineer—like a fraternity pin. We just made if official."

"Oh." Dar pulled his head down, feeling dense.

"You've got the advantage of me now," Father Marco informed the geezer.

"Yeah, I know." The old man grinned wickedly. "Ain't it great?"

"Grandfather!" the vision reproved, and the old man winced (her shoes did have very sharply pointed toes).

"Well, I can't have everything," he sighed. "I'm Whitey, Father, and this is Lona, my . . . *niece*," he added, with a glare at her.

She tried to look chastened. "Anything you say, Grandfather."

"*Must* you make me feel my age, lass?" Whitey sighed. "I know you have a fixation about absolute honesty in all the little things—but have mercy! I don't ask for much—just that you call me 'Uncle' when other people are around. Is that so much to ask?"

"Not at all, now that they know the truth." She gave the rest of the company a dazzling smile, and lied, "He's my uncle."

"Glad to meet him," Dar muttered, his eyes on Lona.

Father Marco cleared his throat and stretched out a hand. "I'm Father Marco Ricci. And this is Dar Mandra, and Sam Bine."

"Here y' are, Whitey." A waiter set a large glass of wine in front of the old man. "And you, Lona."

"Thank you." She accepted the cocktail with a smile that was polite, but warm too, then deliberately turned her eyes away. The waiter hesitated a moment hopefully, then sighed and turned away.

"Whitey the Wino?" Father Marco guessed.

Whitey held up his glass in a semi-toast and nodded approval. "You're quick."

"Not really; I've been hearing about you in every tavern and taproom for the last three parsecs. Glad I finally caught up with you."

The name fitted, Dar decided. The old man's hair was stark white, and his eyes were so light a blue that they verged on being colorless. Even his skin had a bleached look—weathered and toughened, as though it ought to have a deep space-tan; but he was almost white.

And the second name seemed to fit, too. He'd drained half the glass at a gulp.

"'Caught up with me,' is it?" Whitey grinned. "If it weren't for the cassock, I'd worry."

Father Marco grinned too. "No, I'm not the Revenue Service."

"Or an angry husband," Lona added.

"My dear!" Whitey protested, wounded. "Would I come between a man and his wife?"

"Only if you had a chance to," she murmured, and sipped at her drink.

Whitey turned to Father Marco with a sigh of despair. "Ah, the cynicism of this latter generation! Are there no ideals left, Father? No faith?"

"I believe in you implicitly, Grandfather—I'm just not saying what for."

"To move around, for one thing," Father Marco said. "You don't seem to have stayed on any one planet any longer than I have, Whitey."

The Wino nodded. "I can take any of these fat, complacent peoples, for just so long."

"Or they you," Lona murmured.

"Well, they usually do offer to pay my expenses to the next planet. I'm getting a bit restless in my old age, Father—moving outward, hoping to find a place that isn't sliding down into decadence."

"It's about time, Whitey." A tallow-ketch of a man stopped by the table.

"And I have to keep finding new audiences." Whitey slid a flat keyboard out of his tunic and stood up. "If you'll excuse me for a few minutes, folks . . ."

"You're the entertainment?" Dar said, astonished.

"Aren't I always?" he answered. Lona added, "Not much security, but it's a living."

"Better than it was in the old days, my dear," Whitey reminded her, "before I met your grandmother. I sold narcotics back then, Father—not entirely legally. Before I saw the light—when I went under the name of Tod Tambourin." He turned away toward the stage, following Lona.

Sam sat stiff and rigid, her eyes bulging. "*That's* Tod Tambourin?"

"Couldn't be." But Dar felt a sinking certainty. "Great poets don't sing in bars."

"I can think of a few exceptions." Father Marco leaned back and sipped his drink. "Let's judge the product, shall we?"

The "product" didn't bear judgment at all. Whitey settled himself on a low stool while Lona slid onto a high one, heels hooked on a rung, knees together, hands clasped in her lap. Whitey struck a rippling crescendo from his keyboard. It filled the room, leaving a moment of silence behind it. Into that silence Whitey pumped a vigorous song which had its roots in the best of the bad old days, a bit of bawdy nonsense about a lady spacer, who was scarcely a lady, and whose interest in space was confined to some interesting spaces. Lona sat through it, amused, joining in on the choruses with almost as much relish as her grandfather.

"*This* is the poet laureate of the Terran Sphere?" Sam cried, scandalized.

Dar felt a trifle disillusioned too—but not in Whitey.

The song ended with a rocketing crescendo that sounded like a spaceship taking off. The patrons roared their approval, stomping and laughing; and when the racket slackened and died, it blended into a slower, almost melancholy tune that nonetheless had a feeling of quiet certainty underlying it.

Then Lona began to sing, not looking at Whitey, gazing off into space a little above the audience's heads, in a voice as sweet as spring and as clear as a fountain. The words didn't quite register; they seemed to slide around and envelop Dar in a dazzle of consonants—but the meaning sank in: a lament for the wilderness that was, but never was, the primeval beauty that men hearkened back to when the name "Terra" was spoken.

Then Whitey joined in on the chorus, in a quiet, sad-but-satisfied judgment that the wilderness had passed, but that it had had to, as all things must. Then Lona took up the verse again, in lilting wonder that the same wilderness had greeted men anew, on distant planets, under suns unseen from Terra.

Then the chorus again, that these too had passed, as they'd had to; and another verse, another planet, a hundred more, each greeting humankind with wilderness, to tame and then destroy within the bars of hedges; then the chorus, and one final verse, in notes that soared with triumph—for bit by bit, men had learned to live within the wilderness, and preserve it—and yonder, past the marches, new planets beckoned with their forests—the ancient home of humans, which they must ever seek.

Dar sat, stunned. How could he have ever thought that poem was great when he'd read it without hearing its music?

Then the keyboard slashed out a great, jarring discord, and they were off into another bawdy song. And so it went—bits of poetry sandwiched in between carousing, continually taking the audience by surprise. When Whitey finally bade the audience give the singer time for a drink, Dar was on his feet with the rest of them, applauding wildly and shouting, "More! More!" Then Lona and Whitey came up to the table, she flushed and glowing, he smiling, grinning, and Dar felt very foolish.

"Sit, sit!" Whitey waved him into his chair. "And thousands of thanks, youngling. That's the greatest praise a singer can get—that you forget yourself in the music."

Lona didn't say anything, but she answered with a look that set Dar's blood thrilling through him and gave his teeth a tingle.

Then the waiter broke the spell by plunking glasses down in front of the singers.

"I can believe it!" Sam exploded. "I couldn't believe such a distinguished poet would be playing in taverns—but I've heard you! I believe it!"

"Well—I'm glad to know I'm still myself," Whitey said, with a twinkle in his eye. "And a poet I am—but 'distinguished' I most emphatically am not!"

"Don't let him bother you," Lona assured Sam. "You couldn't have known it was an insult."

"But what're you doing, playing in a backwater bar on a boondock planet?"

"Looking for a clean breath of air." Whitey's mouth tightened a little. "The bars on Terra, now, they're so damn polite you can't get away with anything *but* poetry, and that takes all the fun out of it. Also, they don't really listen—they just want you for background while they try to make time with each other. And say a word about politics, and wham! you're out the door! They've gone effete, they've gone gloomy, they've gone hopeless, and the finest songs in the world won't cheer 'em! Things get better as you go away from Sol—but even here, though there's some life, they've lost the sense of joy and wonder. They want to just sit back behind thick walls and taste fat meat, and they don't want to hear about hunting dragons."

"It's true enough," Lona agreed, "but you're not so young any more, Grandfather."

"That's so." Whitey nodded. "That's why I need to seek for life and freshness."

"But I *am* fresh," Lona pointed out, "and fully alive, and

no doubt of it! Just give me a try at being decadent, Grandfather—just give me a little try!"

Whitey sighed, and started to answer, but a huge slab of lard interrupted him, six feet four in height and three feet wide, four feet at the waist, with little, squinting, piggy eyes and an outhrust jaw. "Whatsa matter, singer? Don't like progress?"

Whitey's eyes kindled. "Progress? Just because you get more goods doesn't mean your soul's better!"

"So, who are you, my father confessor?" The thickened thug grabbed Whitey's shirtfront and yanked him out of his chair. "Disgusting little bastard! First talking politics, and now religion! Why, I oughta paste you up on the wall."

"Go ahead," Whitey caroled, "try!"

The thug stared at him for a moment; then his eyes narrowed, and he wound up for a pitch with a snarl.

Whitey chopped down on his elbow, hard.

The beefy one dropped him with a howl, and two more slabs of meat waded in, reaching for Whitey. Someone yanked Dar out of his chair and flipped him around with a fist to his jaw. He slammed back against the tabletop and sat up, blinking, the roar of a full-scale brawl coming faintly through the ringing in his ears. Most of the patrons were squealing and clearing back against the walls, looking for an exit. A knot of thugs kept trying to form around Whitey, but Father Marco kept roaring in, yanking them out of the way by their collars and bumping them away with his back when they tried to swing back in. The ones who did get in kept popping back as Whitey caught them with undercuts.

Sam and Lona fought back-to-back, with clips to the chin, and kicks to the shin. So far, they'd yielded a lot of hoppers.

Then Dar saw the glint of steel swinging up at Sam's belly.

He shouted and leaped forward, lurching in between Sam and her attacker. The blade slid along his side, opening the skin; he bleated in pain and anger, and pivoted to face the slice artist.

He was tall and fat, with a gloating grin. "You'll do just as well." The knife snaked out at his liver.

Dar swung to the side, grabbing the man's wrist, cradling the elbow on top of his own, and snapping down. The thug yelled, high and hoarsely; his hand opened, and the knife fell out. Then a grenade exploded on the back of Dar's neck.

He lifted his head, blinking blearily, and got a great view of feet kicking and lunging all around him. Through the singing in his ears, he heard the hoot of police horns. *About time!* Then it occurred to him that the tangling feet all around him might think he was part of the floor. He stumbled to his feet, and looked up into a breast-patch that said "Police." He looked on up to a grinning face underneath a helmet, and noticed an electroclub swinging down at him. He spun away, to find a stun-gun level with his chest, with another police-patch behind it. He yelled and leaped to the side just as the club came crashing down and the stun-gun fired. The one cop was shocked, the other was stunned, and a third caught Dar around the middle. Dar slammed a fist down—right on a helmet. The cop dropped him and leveled a stun-gun. Then the cop dropped, period, and Father Marco grabbed Dar's arm and yanked him over the scrambling uniform. "Follow me! Fast!" He turned away, and Dar stumbled after him. He bumped into Sam, coming up on his right, and caromed off Whitey on his left. Father Marco yanked open a door, and Lona darted through ahead of them. "Follow her!" the priest snapped.

Well, it went along with Dar's natural inclinations; he just wished he hadn't had so much company. He clattered down a set of narrow steps, following Lona's slim form, and came out in a cellar surrounded by shelves of kegs and racks of bottles. The door slammed behind him, and the noise of the fight diminished to a far-off rumble.

"Quick! It won't take them but a few minutes to think of the cellar!" Father Marco brushed past them, fumbled at a bolthead in the paneled wall, and swung open a hidden door. Lona darted through, and Dar followed.

Father Marco slammed the door behind Whitey, and Dar found himself suddenly in total darkness. Something soft and curved brushed against him. Lona sprang to his mind's eye, and he wished she hadn't brushed away so quickly.

"Dar?" Sam whispered, right next to him, and he fairly jumped. "Yeah, right here," he whispered back through a whirl of emotions. She'd sounded shy and unsure of herself—

feminine. It roused every protective reflex he had—and a full flood of hormones behind them. And the touch of her . . .

"Where are we?" she whispered.

"I don't know," he answered. "Why are we whispering?"

Then a spot of light glared. They turned to see Father Marco's face, illuminated from below by a tiny glow-globe in the handle of his miniature screwdriver. "The reflex is correct," he said in a very low tone. "Keep your voices down; I don't think the police know about this bolthole, but they might search the tavern basement, and we don't want them to get curious."

"Perish the thought!" Whitey agreed. "Where are we, Father? In a, you should pardon the phrase, priest-hole?"

"No, the persecutions on this planet have never been religiously oriented." Father Marco grinned. "We're in the basement of the establishment next door."

"Which one—Leong Chakov's Foot Laundry?"

"No, the other one."

"Oh, Madame Tessie's Tenderloin Chop House." Whitey raised his eyebrows, nodding. "Pretty good, Father. Even I didn't know there was any, ah, connection, between the two establishments."

The priest nodded. "Only a few select patrons know."

"*You're* one of them?"

"Well—let's just say it's surprising what you pick up in moments of confidence." Father Marco turned away, groping along the wall.

"Oh." Whitey fell in beside him. "You picked it up in the confessional."

"No, *because* of it. They had something of an emergency here last month, calling for the Last Rites and all possible discretion." There was a loud *clunk*, and the light bobbed. Father Marco hissed something under his breath. Dar wondered why "blue" should be sacred.

"I think I've found the stairs." Father Marco's voice was strained. "Slowly and quietly, now." The light began to bob upward. "The net result is, the ladies here have come to trust me. I think they'll be discreet about our passage through their quarters." His light shone on a richly-grained door. "Quietly, now," he murmured, and turned the knob.

Laughter and raucous music assaulted their ears. They stepped out into the middle of a party for the usual assortment of portly patrons and what had to be the only slender inhabitants of Falstaff. The svelte shapeliness was real, too, obviously—since they were wearing as little as possible.

"Must be later than I thought," Sam observed.

"No, it's always like this," Father Marco answered. "Come now, let's see if we can't find a quiet place to meditate."

Personally, Dar had all he wanted to meditate on right there; but Father Marco was slipping quietly along the wall toward the stairway, and Whitey was pushing from behind, so he followed suit.

"Marco!"

The priest turned just as a bosomy beldam smacked into him, lips first. She leaned back, holding him by the shoulders and laughing. "You old scoundrel, what brings you here? Interested in *our* services, for a change?"

"In a way, Tessie, in a way." Father Marco gave the madam an affectionate squeeze—on the hand. "Just looking for a place to relax and chat with a few friends, where there's a little less noise than the average tavern."

Tessie sighed and shook her head. "What a waste of a good man! And here I was getting my hopes up. I really ought to be angry with you, y'know." She gave him a coquettish flicker of eyelashes.

"Because of Rosamund, eh?" Father Marco spread his arms. "There's no help for it, Tessie. I have to do my job, even as you have to do yours."

"Yes, and usually it's all well and good—the girls get remorseful for a few days, and when they get back to work, they've got a certain freshness about them. But getting one of them to kick the trade completely? Now, don't you think that's going a bit too far?" She emphasized the point with a few strokes on his arm.

Father Marco gently disengaged her hand. "No, from my point of few, it's just enough. Where is she now, do you know?"

Tessie shrugged. "Hopped an outbound liner, that's all I can say. None of us are natives, Father."

"Father?"

"It's Father Marco!"

In a second, they were surrounded by a bevy of shapely no-longer-maidens with very long fingers. Dar thought of checking his wallet, but he was having too much fun being frisked.

The hands were all over the priest, coming on faster than he could take them off.

"Oh, Father, I'm so glad to see you!"

"Have *I* got a lot to tell you!"

"Oh, Father, it's so horrible. I tried and I tried to resist, but . . ."

"Yes, girls, I understand. Patience, patience; if I can't talk with each of you today, I'll come back another time."

"You aren't a priest's apprentice, are you?" A beautiful redhead straightened Dar's tunic with a lingering touch.

"Well, no, not really. I am interested in virtue, though."

"So am I," she cooed, "it's such a wonderful conversation topic."

Dar felt a stroke along his buttocks, and just barely managed to keep from jumping. A blond head poked over his shoulder and murmured, "Any friend of Father's is a friend of mine."

"Well, I *am* the friendly type. . . ."

There were at least five of them, all very good with innuendo, verbal and otherwise. It would've been great if they'd come one at a time; as it was, Dar was beginning to feel a little like a pound of ground sirloin at a hamburger sale.

Not that he was complaining . . .

A rippling chord filled the room. Everyone looked up, startled.

"Ladies and gentlemen!" Whitey was standing on a chair, with Lona beside him, perched on a table. "For your entertainment and delectation—the 'Ballad of Gresham's Law'!"

An incredulous mutter ran through the room—especially from the zoftig patrons, who were all in the bracket that knows some economics.

The rippling chord stilled them again, and Whitey and Lona began to sing:

"When the upright ladies come to town,
Right away they gather 'round
To form a club, and then decide
Who is out, and who's inside."

There was a tap on Dar's shoulder, and Father Marco murmured, "I hate to distract you from what looks to be a rare event, but we do have other matters to consider."

With a jolt, Dar remembered an electroclub swinging down at him. "Uh, yeah. We are in kind of a rush, aren't we?" He sidled through his circle of admirers. "Excuse me, ladies. I'm on call."

They made politely distressed noises, and turned back to Whitey and Lona eagerly. Whatever the song was, it seemed to strike a chord with them.

It seemed to be making an analogy between economics and sexual relations, but reversing what was usually understood to be a "good" woman versus a "bad."

"Look at the coin in which you pay,
The wages of a working day.
Compare it to the 'honest' bill
Of lifelong toil and thwarted will."

The patrons cheered, and the girls' faces turned very thoughtful. It occurred to Dar that Whitey might be accomplishing the same task Father Marco was trying, though by very different methods.

". . . but it is pretty urgent," Father Marco was explaining to Tessie.

She held up a palm and shook her head. "Don't explain, Father; I might be pegged for an accomplice. Besides, I've had to leave a place in something of a hurry myself, on occasion. Bring your people here." She beckoned.

They followed her around through a darkened salon. There was a squeal and a muffled curse. "As you were," Tessie ordered crisply, eyes resolutely fixed straight forward. Dar followed her example, though he was burning to look over his shoulder and make sure Sam was safely following. He felt like Orpheus on the return trip.

They turned left into what was either a small room or a very large closet—probably the latter; the walls were lined with racks of evening clothes, cut for small elephants.

"Sometimes our, ah, clients, find it advisable to leave in a different set of clothes than the one they wore on the way in," Tessie explained. "We've gathered quite a stock, over the years. Of course, you'll all need some padding, but we're not exactly short on pillows here. Let's see, now—this one ought to fit you, Father, and this one'll do for your young friend, here. . . ."

Half an hour later, swathed in evening clothes and padded out to the equator, they filed out of Madam Tessie's like a flock of pregnant penguins.

"Well, you can't deny they were hospitable," Dar said through a dazed but happy smile.

"I don't particularly care for that sort of hospitality." Sam was fuming.

Dar glanced at her, and couldn't help feeling gratified. Yesterday he would've felt downright hopeful. Today, though, he was primarily concerned with Lona, who was, unfortunately, taking it all in stride.

"They even offered me a job," she noted.

Sam hadn't been asked. "Is that what's bothering you?" Dar could at least make it sound as though she had.

"No," Sam snapped. "What bothered me was that whole scene in the tavern."

Whitey shrugged. "A brawl is a brawl—and you can't blame the cops; squelching that kind of thing is their job."

"Yeah, but they don't have to gang up three-on-one." Dar frowned, remembering. "Especially since I was losing."

"No, that *isn't* standard." Whitey frowned, too. Then he shrugged. "Anyway, *I* had a good time."

"I didn't," Sam said stiffly. "I recognized the chock who led the cops in—and he *wasn't* in uniform."

"Oh?" Dar looked up. "Anyone I know?"

"You might say that. He had a face like a rat."

"A rat! What's *he* doing here . . . ? Oh." Dar pursed his lips. "We never did see who was piloting our courier ship, did we?"

"We didn't," Sam confirmed. "I wondered why he took off and left us to the pirates, remember?"

"If you don't mind my asking," Father Marco put in, "What's this all about?"

"Our nemesis, at a guess," Sam said slowly. "We thought we'd left him back on Wolmar, with the rest of Governor Bhelabher's staff. At least, Terra sent Bhelabher out to take over the governorship; but he, ah, wound up resigning. We got the assignment of taking his resignation back to Terra."

"And we *thought* we were the only ones who left," Dar explained. "But apparently Bhelabher had a change of heart, and sent his right-hand man along to stop us."

"No, it wasn't Bhelabher." Sam shook her head. "If he'd changed his mind, all his sidekick would've had to do is order us to hand back that resignation form—or even to hand in a counter-letter from Bhelabher."

"You mean Rat-Face is doing this all on his own?"

"I wouldn't say that," Sam said slowly. "He *is* a career bureaucrat in the Bureau of Otherworldly Activities, remember. Chances are he's doing what his superiors in BOA want done."

"A man with a face like a rat, in the BOA bureaucracy?" Father Marco asked. He was frowning.

Dar nodded. "That's him. But why would he be trying to kill us?"

"*Kill* you?"

Sam shook her head. "There were two cops after me, but the worst thing they had was a hypodermic bulb."

"A hypo?" Dar looked up sharply. "They were trying to put you out and take you in?"

Sam nodded. "That's the way it looked. But it doesn't make sense. There were two of them, and they were a lot bigger than I was. Why'd they have needed a hypo?"

"And why'd their buddies be trying to put me out completely? I could swear their intentions weren't toward prolonging my life."

"Could be you're paranoid," Lona suggested.

"No doubt; but in this case, I think it doesn't matter. And I don't quite agree with *your* reading of it, Sam—one of them was trying a blade on you." He touched the bandage that Tessie had thoughtfully taped over his wound.

"No, I'm afraid you're both right." Father Marco was definitely brooding. "After all, if you think someone's a threat, and you can't capture them, what's the logical thing to do?"

"But why would they think *I'm* dangerous?" Sam wailed. "*I* don't have the papers!"

Lona was looking very interested.

"A fascinating episode," Whitey mused, "especially since I do believe I see some uniforms approaching."

All heads snapped up, and noticed the strolling pair who had just turned the corner.

"Just keep walking," Father Marco's iron tone advised, and Dar soothed his body's impulse to jump into flight.

" 'Course, it's been a while since I did this . . ." Whitey offered, and Lona coughed, ". . . but I do notice there's some sort of arcade just a few feet down, on our left. Might make a handy bolthole."

"Ideal," Father Marco breathed. "Shall we, gentlefolk?"

They nonchalantly turned into the cavelike coolness of the arcade. Its long concourse stretched away before them, lined with shops on both sides.

"Last time you did this, Grandfather, you split us up into small groups," Lona reminded.

"A good point," Father Marco agreed. "No doubt they counted noses after that tavern brawl, and came to the conclusion we'd all gone off together."

"Well . . ." Dar caught a door-handle and swung it open. ". . . see ya 'round, folks."

Sam stepped through the door before he could close it; the rest went on their way, and his team was back to its original components.

They moved down a short aisle, surrounded by skeins of yarn, squares of stiff netting, and racks of patterns. "What is all this stuff?" Dar whispered.

"Knitting, crocheting, things like that—age-old hobbies," Sam whispered back. "Ever try needlepoint?"

Dar was about to answer with a pointed remark of his own, when the proprietor popped up behind the counter at the end of the aisle, grossly fat, with the face of an aging cherub and a fringe of puffy white hair around a bald dome. "Something you'd . . . like, gentlefolk?"

"Just browsing," Dar said quickly. "Interesting collection you've got here."

"Oh yes, I try to keep it up-to-date. Had some fascinating patterns come in last week, from Samia."

"Samia?" Dar wondered, but another customer approached before the storekeeper could answer. "Ah there, Kontak! Is my order in?"

"Just an hour ago," Kontak grinned. He laid a slender parcel in plain brown wrap on the counter. "Sixty spikes, five brads, Grazh Danko."

"Samia?" Dar whispered to Sam. "Isn't that the pleasure-planet? You know, 'wrap up all your cares and clothes, and do whatever's legal'?"

Sam nodded, her eyes on the brown parcel. "And there isn't much that's illegal, except murder. I understand they don't even look too closely at that, provided the victim isn't a tourist. I think I'd like a look at the next shop."

"But this is just getting interesting," Dar protested as Sam hustled him toward the door.

"Maybe too interesting." She kept her voice low as the door closed behind them. "That was a porno shop. And did you catch the prices? For a pack of sleazy pictures? I have a sneaking suspicion we're in the middle of what they euphemistically call an 'organic market.'"

"One that charges whatever the traffic will bear?" Dar looked around him. "These innocent little shops? Illegal goods?"

"And services," Sam reminded. They went into a confectionary. The patron at the end of the counter was thumbing through a menu that seemed to be mostly bodies, while the proprietor was helping an obese, surly patron strike up an acquaintance with a slender sweet young thing. They turned around and went back out.

So it went, for the length of the arcade. Finally, in the office of the Legal Aid Society, which kept a neat list of judges, cases, and the aid the judges required to help them make up their minds about the cases, Dar exploded. "Is there *anything* that isn't for sale?"

"Haven't found anything, myself," a customer answered cheerfully, not noticing Sam's frantic shushing motions. "Of course, some commodities can't be had for cash just yet; but I understand they're working on them."

"I suppose I'm naive," Dar said slowly, "but I thought *the law* was supposed to help make people equal, not uphold the one who can pay the most."

The customer winced. "Please, young man! We must be patient with the follies of youth—but that remark was so distinctly political that I can't ignore it!"

"Don't offend the gentleman," the proprietor growled, an ugly glint in his piggy little eye.

"*That* was political?" Dar stared. While he was staring, Sam grabbed his arm and hustled him out the door. By the time he recovered enough to resist, he was in the street. Then he managed to get his mouth moving again. "*Political*? Speculating about the purpose of law is political?"

"Of course, when you say things such as 'equal,'" Sam explained. "You really must do something about that death wish of yours."

"Why?" Dar shrugged her hand off. "It puts me in phase with this whole planet!"

"Just because people don't talk politics, doesn't mean they're moribund," Sam hissed.

"No, but it means their society is! They don't even care about the law any more! Don't they realize that's what keeps a society from falling apart?"

"Oh. You're one of these people who believes that law prevents revolutions, huh?"

"Sure, by making sure no one's too badly oppressed."

"Sin?"

Dar looked up, startled; but it was just a portly passerby, chatting with a waddling clergyman. "Sin? Come now, Reverend! What a medieval idea!"

"It'll always be current, I'm afraid," the minister rejoined, "and even fashionable—though rarely as a conversational topic."

"It does lend a certain sauce to pleasure," the passerby admitted. "And, after all, the really important element in life is getting what you want—the things that make you happy."

"Of course, of course," the clergyman agreed. "Take heaven, for example. . . ."

The passerby was laughing as they passed out of hearing.

Dar shook his head. "I don't think the revolution'll wait a hundred years."

"You think this is bad?" Sam scoffed. "Just wait till you get to Terra!"

"I can wait, thank you. I'm beginning to see why you liked Wolmar so much. You know, this pretty little market couldn't be here unless the police were helping it a lot."

"Of course," Sam said brightly. "But be fair—they might not have enough officers to cover everything."

"Yeah, but which is it?" Dar muttered. He glanced up and saw a blimp of a shopkeeper leaning against his storefront. Dar stepped up to him, pointing an accusing finger and snapping, "Which is it, citizen? How can you get away with this? Don't you have any police here?"

"Sir!" The shopkeeper drew himself up, offended. "I'll thank you not to discuss such disgusting issues!" And he wheeled about majestically, slamming his door behind him.

"*I'm* not so squeamish," said an oily voice.

Dar and Sam looked up and saw a hunched old man with a lascivious grin, peering out from the shop next door. He was obscenely slender. "What's your perversion, younglings? Plato? Descartes? Machiavelli? I've got 'em all in here, all the banned books! Come in and read anything—just fifty BTUs an hour!"

"Let's go," Sam hissed. "I don't like the way your jaw is setting!"

"All right, all right," Dar growled. He turned away toward the end of the arcade, and bumped into someone. "Oh, excuse me . . ." He broke off, staring into a face like a rat's above a short, lean body.

The little man stared back at him, eyes widening in shock and horror. Then his mouth opened in a moan that turned into a scream, and he slumped to the ground, clutching his chest.

"What happened?" Dar bleated, staring at the bright redness spreading over the man's tunic from under his hands.

"Murder, I'd say."

Dar's head snapped up; he found himself staring into a very

familiar beefy face, above an even more familiar breast-patch badge.

"You're under arrest." There was another one like him on the other side of Sam. "Just hold out your wrists, now . . ." He produced a length of cable that glowed, even in daylight.

"Uh, no thanks." Dar stepped backward; he'd worn a manacle-loop before, on his way to Wolmar. Once around his wrists, the cable would virtually meld with his skin, and his wrists would stick together as though they'd grown that way. "Actually, I have an appointment at the confectionary shop, you see . . ."

"Well, I'm afraid we've got one that's a little more important. Come on now, let's not make a scene." The policeman stepped forward. Sam backed away as the shop-keeper hefted an electroclub and snapped it down against the officer's occiput. He slumped to the ground with a muted sigh as two lean and muscular types materialized out of adjacent doorways to zap the other policeman and take their places.

"Bit of a lucky thing for you we happened along," the shopkeeper observed. "From what I read on the newsfax, all the cops in Haskerville're out hunting you two. Now, if I was you, I'd be wanting a nice, safe bolthole to bolt into, and lock behind me."

"Good idea," Dar agreed. "But, personally, I go along with the idea that says the more you move around, the harder you are to find."

"I was afraid you'd make this difficult," the shopkeeper sighed. He nodded to the two gorillas. "Move 'em around, boys."

Huge arms seized Dar from behind, hoisting him off the ground and carrying him toward the open air. Beside him, Sam cursed and swore, trying to kick a shin with her heels, and missing every time.

As the toughs bundled them into a waiting car, Dar observed, "I think the cops were the better choice."

8

The sign said, "You are now leaving HASKERVILLE."

He turned to the tough who shared the back seat with them. "You must work for somebody important, to rate a car."

"Might be," the man said shortly. "Ain't so much, though."

"Well, no—it goes on wheels, not an air cushion. But it's still more than most folks have here. Must cost a fortune—all that metal in the engine."

"Metal?" The man frowned. "Where'd you grow up—on Orehouse?"

"They're doing such marvelous things with synthetics these days," Sam murmured.

"Sure, plastic," the driver confirmed. "Polythermothane. Takes all the heat we need to give it, an' more."

"Well, I suppose—for a turbine." Dar frowned. "Maybe even for a boiler. But how do you shield the fissionables?"

" 'E *is* from Orehouse," the first tough snorted. "Fissionables're metal, lunk. How'd we get 'em 'ere?"

"Yeah, I suppose it would be a little heavy on the import price." Dar scratched his head. "So what do you use for an energy source?"

"Methane."

"Methane?" Sam cried, scandalized. *"Chemicals?"*

"Uh—I hate to butt in." Dar glommed onto the tough's arm with a mastiff-grip. "But, could you say a word to your friend? We're running right into a mountainside!"

The granite outcrop towered over them, rushing down on them.

The tough nodded. "Close enough, Rog."

Rog pushed a button set into the dashboard, and the scrub at the base of the cliff swung outward and upward, revealing a huge gaping cave-mouth.

"Just a bit o' camouflage," the backseat tough explained. "Can't leave yer front door open fer just any Tom, Dick, or Paddy t' walk in, y' know."

"No, definitely not." Dar's eyes fairly bulged out of his head as the car swept into the cave, and a line of glow-plates lit up along the length of the walls, lighting their way onward. The floor sloped away in front of them, spiraling down at a thirty-degree angle. Rog held the car to a continuing hairpin turn, slowing down only as much as was absolutely necessary. Sam swung over against Dar and stayed there, which would've been very pleasant, if Dar hadn't had to keep fighting to hold himself away from the backseat tough, who might not have understood, especially since that was his gun-hand.

The ramp leveled off and the car straightened out, but Sam stayed over against Dar. He counted it a hopeful sign, but was no longer sure he cared, now that he'd seen Lona.

The tunnel flared out into a huge cavern. Brilliant glow-plates spread a cold greenish light over alleyways between towering gray plastrete slabs.

"I'd almost think those were buildings," Dar said, in hushed tones, "if they had windows."

"They *are* buildings," the tough affirmed. "What'd y' need windows for, down 'ere? Whacher gonna look at?"

Rog pulled the car into a slot between a small van and another car. They got out, and found themselves surrounded by a fleet of trucks and vans, parked in very orderly rows.

"Yes," Dar mused, "your boss isn't exactly hurting, is he?"

"Ask 'im," the tough invited. "Y've got an appointment—immediate."

* * *

The door slid aside, and they stepped into a leather-and-mahogany office with a rug as thick as graft.

"Citizens Dar Mandra and Sam Bine," said the bald man behind the acre of desktop, almost lost in the vast swivel chair. "Come in."

They came in slowly, feeling as though there were guns pointed at their backs from all angles. Ridiculous, of course; the guns were probably aimed from the front.

"Sit." It was an order, not an invitation. Under the circumstances, Dar wasn't disposed to argue. He sat at the lefthand corner of the desk; Sam sat at the right. That's where the chairs were. They didn't look as though they'd move.

"What is this—our invitation to join the Underground?" Dar joked, with a tight smile.

It died under the look the little man gave him. Did he always have to make the right guess at the wrong time?

Their host wasn't tall, but he was very broad across the shoulders and chest—and not fat. In fact, he was very hard, in the flesh—and, from the look of him, in the soul, too. He wore a quiet brown business tunic with a muted yellow ascot—conservative, punctiliously correct, with the look of a very high price. His nails were manicured, and his eyes were hidden behind brown lenses.

"You're in the House of Houses," he grated.

Dar stiffened and tried to keep his face immobile. Even buried on a prison planet, he'd heard of the I.D.E.'s biggest organized crime ring.

"The House of . . ." Sam's voice choked off. She cleared her throat. "Uh, not the head offices, of course."

The brown lenses swiveled toward her. The little man nodded slowly.

"But the head offices have to be on Terra!"

The brown lenses turned slowly from side to side. "We like it better here."

Dar clenched his fists to hide their quivering. "And, uh, whom do we have the pleasure of addressing?"

The brown lenses tracked back toward him. "I've got a lot of names."

"Any one will do." Dar tried to grin.

"Call me Sard, then—Thalvor Sard. I'm the Syndic."

"The Syndic?" Sam gasped. "The biggest boss criminal in all of Terran space?"

"A businessman," Sard said, a bit impatiently, "only a businessman. Just a little impatient with government regulation, that's all."

"Right?" His masked gaze swung to Dar.

"Right," Dar mumbled. From what he'd heard, Sard's "impatience" amounted to a running war on fifteen planets, and underground anarchy on most of the rest.

"But—*here*?" Sam spluttered. "On a frontier planet halfway to the marches?"

"Not so much of a frontier, as you've maybe noticed. The folks here like their comfort—like it enough to be glad to have us handy, and make sure their cops can't do much about us."

"And because they don't have radios," Dar guessed.

Sard's head swiveled back to him. "My, you're the quick one, though. Right, this time—radios cost so much, the cops don't have 'em. That means we can stay one jump ahead out here. Oh, they can move efficiently enough inside the town, where they can use couriers—but not out here. I'm what little law there is, outside the bounds of Haskerville."

Dar nodded slowly.

"And the law can do a lot for you." Sard nodded back at Dar. "Safety and protection, and a fat salary. What'll the town law give you, the I.D.E. law? Arrest and, probably, a quick death."

"Arrest? Whoa! What is this?" Dar protested. "We're not in trouble with the cops!"

Sard just stared at him.

"Well . . . okay. Maybe they did try to bushwhack us in that tavern," Dar amended. "And maybe they were trying to take us in when your, ah, people intervened. But we haven't done anything illegal."

"You're there," Sard said. "That's enough."

"*Why?*"

"Because you're a telepath—or your woman is. And all the government sees is that, in the wrong hands, your power could be a real threat to them." He leaned back. "They're right, too."

Dar found his voice again. "*Telepath?* Me?"

Sard shrugged. "All right, play innocent, if you want. They'll be out after you, just the same. That's why that BOA man faked being murdered right next to you—to give the cops a reason for arresting you."

"No!" Dar cried. "He's trying to stop us from taking the new governor of Wolmar's resignation back to Terra!"

"Sure," Sard said slowly. "Right."

"Uh . . . what would we have to do for this salary-plus-benefits of yours?" Sam put in.

The dark glasses swiveled toward her. "Nothing much. Just tell us what certain people are planning to do. You'd travel a lot—especially to Terra."

"Handsome offer," Sam said slowly. "Unfortunately, neither of us is a telepath."

The glasses swung toward Dar.

" 'Fraid that's true," Dar seconded. "Either I.D.E.'s got its signals crossed, or you do."

"My signals don't get crossed," Sard corrected. "I.D.E. might, but not the LORDS—and they're the ones who're out after telepaths."

"The exception proves the rule," Sam said. "This is it."

Sard shook his head slowly. "Too bad. Such nice young kids."

"*What's* too bad?" Dar felt a premonition walking up his spine.

"Your untimely deaths." Sard leaned forward. "One of you is a telepath, whether or not the other one knows it—and that telepath must've already picked up enough information to pack half of my people off to prison worlds, maybe enough to shut down the whole House of Houses. And you'd do it, too, 'cause you'd think it'd buy the LORDS off your back."

"But we're *not* telepaths."

"Sorry." Sard shook his head. "Can't take the chance. Either you join, or you leave in an urn." He pushed a button. "Don't say anything right now—think it over. This shouldn't be a snap judgment, you understand."

Two tall, muscular men, impeccably dressed, came in.

"These gentlemen will conduct you to your accommodations," Sard explained. "You'll get better ones if you join up, of course. Think it over."

* * *

The accommodations had a door made of steel bars and a very elaborate combination lock.

"Gee, I didn't know you were a telepath." Dar flopped down on a very hard bunk.

"I didn't know *you* were," Sam retorted. "Now that we've established that, shall we try to make sense out of the situation?"

"What's to make sense of?" Dar shrugged. "Somebody's spreading nasty lies about us. Probably Rat-Face. Does that make any more sense out of it?"

"Some," Sam insisted. "That gets him official help in trying to get us locked up, which keeps the resignation from getting to BOA, while he waits for Bhelabher to change his mind."

Dar snorted. "Bhelabher? He'll wait for a century. The Honorable won't change his mind as long as Shacklar's right next to him."

Sam shrugged. "So Rat-Face is doomed to failure. Unfortunately, he doesn't know that—so he still gets in our way."

"So the telepath who just landed on the planet, and for whom the police are searching, is supposed to be one of us, huh?"

Sam nodded. "Looks like it—which explains why we've seen so many of their shoestring police."

"Well, what they don't get done, the House of Houses does." Dar scratched behind his ear. "It's almost as though this planet has two governments, one inside the cities, and one out."

"Somewhat like our noble interstellar government," Sam said acidly. "There's the official government, and there's the LORDS."

"Can't stand long, can it?" Dar stretched. "Well! That leaves us two real simple problems—one, to get out of here; and two, clearing our names."

"I don't know what to do about two," Sam said, "but about one . . ." She stared off into space, eyes losing focus.

Dar frowned. What was she doing? He was just about to ask, when Sam turned and smiled brightly. "Nope, don't hear a murmur. Now, let's see . . ." She stood up, went to the door, knelt down, reached around to the front, and pressed her ear against the back of the lock. "One nice thing about a low-metal planet is the lack of modern devices."

"What're you . . . ?"

"Sh!" she hissed fiercely, and Dar shut up. She punched buttons and turned a dial for a few minutes, muttering, "No . . . no, the other way . . . there, that's right . . . there . . . there!" Triumphantly, she shoved on the door and, slowly, with a soft rumble, it slid to the side. She stepped out.

Dar stared.

Then he darted out after her. "Where did you . . . ?"

"Whisper," she hissed. "Sound carries in these tunnels!"

Dar put his lips against her ear and murmured, "Where did you learn to do *that*?"

"You pick up a lot in a government office," she whispered back, "especially if you want a look at your own personnel file. Come on, let's go!"

She led off, padding silently down the dark tunnel. Dar could remember that they had to turn left as they came out of the cell, but after that, he was as lost as Handsel and Gretel without the bread crumbs. But Sam wasn't in doubt for a moment; she paused at the corridor's end (he bumped into her. It was so dark, that was the only way he knew she'd stopped), listened a moment, then darted to her right, hauling Dar after her. They went on for what seemed a half-hour, but must've been all of five minutes; then he bumped into her again. "Sorry," he mumbled. "Sh!" she answered; then, "All clear. Come on."

Halfway down the next midnight passage, she stopped suddenly. Then she was pushing him back frantically, and shoving him into a cross-corridor. They went down it for a few steps; then she yanked on his arm, stopping him, and froze. He could tell she froze because he could see her in the first ragtag of light that hit the far wall from a handlamp. Dar froze too, plastered against the wall like a tapestry.

"Whut'ja expect?" A lean, scarred man in faded coveralls, hands handcuffed behind him, slouched forward in front of two toughs in business tunics. "A'ter all, he wint for me with a knife!"

"Y' c'n tell Sard about it in th' mornin'." One tough prodded him. "Git along, now."

The scarred one snarled, and they passed across the end of the corridor. The reflection from the handlamp wavered over the wall to Sam's right, and was gone. Dar held his breath till their footsteps had faded away, then let it out in a gusty sigh. Instantly, Sam's finger pressed over his lips, then was gone, and she was tugging on his hand again.

They turned right at the end of the corridor, and went on.

So it went, for what seemed the better part of a day. Dar was amazed at the sharpness of her hearing. Twice she pushed them into hiding in time for someone passing by to miss them, when Dar hadn't heard the faintest sound until after they were in hiding. And she never led him past an occupied cell. How could she figure out where to go?

Then, finally, she dropped down to kneel; Dar almost fell over her, but he groped back just in time. He wondered what she was doing until he heard a very faint click. Then, slowly, a slit of light appeared, and widened into a narrow rectangle that widened to a door. They stepped out into a starlit night; the door slid quietly shut behind that.

"How did you manage that?" Dar whispered. "The Labyrinth couldn't've been worse!"

"This was nothing," she snorted. "You should've seen the government building where I used to work. Come on!"

She set out at a long, catlike stride that Dar had to stretch to keep up with. They'd come out of the side of a hillock; as they rounded it, they saw nothing but a level plain, broken by the occasional outcrop, stretching away into the distance. At its limit, a feeble gleam marked Haskerville.

"Just like the early days," Dar sighed, "when the Wolmen still thought we were enemies and I had to be ready to hide, fast, whenever I went out trading!"

"Oh." Sam eyed him sideways. "You've been on the run in open country before?"

Dar nodded. "The main principle is to stay away from the roads, and stay near whatever cover there is. And, of course, if something moves, you hit the ground fast, and worry later about whether it's dangerous or good to eat. Here, I'll show you some of the fine points."

He moved off through the long grass without a breath of sound. Sam shook her head and sighed, then went after him.

As the sky lightened with false dawn, Dar started to sneak across the last yard that separated dirt track from paved Haskerville street.

Sam caught his shoulder. "Act nonchantly, gnappie. You go sneaking around like that, the first citizen who spots you'll blow the whistle."

Dar turned back. "So who's going to be awake to see me?"

"Agreed. So why sneak?"

Dar sighed and gave up.

So they strolled into town like a couple of late-night revelers returning to their hotel rooms.

"Any idea where we're going?" Dar asked. "With the authorities *and* the Underground after us, we're kinda short on hideouts."

"A point," Sam admitted. "In this town, I wouldn't even trust a cheap hotel. . . . What's that?"

Dar stopped, turning his head from side to side, and saw nothing. He strained his ears, but all he heard was a hiss of wind.

"Over there." Sam pointed towards a shopfront a block to her left. "Come on."

She set off toward the shop. After the episode in the jail-tunnels, Dar wasn't about to dispute her hearing. He followed.

They had come into a shabbier section of Haskerville. The houses were big, but they were simple frame dwellings—no half-timbering and stucco—and looked somewhat infirm. Most of them were overdue for a coat of paint—the older part of town, at a guess, built before the planet had enough surplus to worry about aesthetics in architecture.

Someone came out of the shopfront they were heading for, and turned down the street away from them. He/she was bald, and wore a gray, loose coverall.

"I think," Sam said, with a catch to her voice, "we've struck paydirt."

Dar could see her point—and now he could hear the trace she'd picked up: a low mutter of conversation, underscored by the ripple of a string instrument and a flute.

Sam swung the door open. They stepped into a room decorated in Late-Modern Junkyard. The walls were plain pastel-painted plastiboard, decorated with hangings of knotted, brightly colored twine, some of which held potted plants. The tables were plastic delivery drums, and the "chairs" were tree stumps, somewhat leveled off on the bottom. There was a counter against one wall; Dar recognized a section of it—it had "Wolmar" rolled across it. The far end was topped by an arcane plastic contraption that gave off clouds of steam and a rich, spicy aroma.

Most of the tables were filled, and all the patrons had shaved heads and loose gray coveralls. So, for that matter, did the people behind the counter. The musicians, on a small raised platform at the far end, wore the same attire.

Dar paused just inside the doorway, feeling a prickling along the back of his neck. He couldn't help it; he felt as though he'd just stepped into a village populated by a tribe he hadn't met, who might or might not be hostile.

"Don't worry," Sam murmured, "you're with me."

She sauntered over to the counter. A girl who looked enough like her to make Dar rub his eyes, came over and said, "Yeah?" in a neutral tone.

"Two cups," Sam said, and Dar felt in his purse for nails. The girl turned to the arcane contraption, picked up a cup, and pressed a valve; then she turned back to them with two steaming mugs. "New here."

"Am," Sam confirmed. "Just in from Wolmar."

Panic jammed Dar's stomach up toward his throat. Why not just send up a rocket that'd explode into the words, "Here're the suspects!"

But the girl's face came alive. "The prison planet? Where they're oppressing the natives? Hey, tell me about it!"

"Yeah, me too!" A tall, lanky man lounged up to lean on the bar beside Sam.

"Wolmar? I want to hear this!"

"Hey! The real word?"

In thirty seconds, they were surrounded by a small crowd. Dar kept trying to edge closer and closer to the counter, and to glance over both shoulders at once; but Sam launched happily into an account of her tour of Wolmar. Dar was amazed at her accuracy; under equivalent conditions, he couldn't have re-sisted the temptation to color the tale a little, probably putting in a bevy of scantily clad maidens and a hair-raising escape from a bloodthirsty tribe or two; but Sam stuck to reporting what she'd seen and heard, introducing Dar as her guide, which won him a look of respect, then glares of scorn when she mentioned his being a trader, then looks of awe when she explained his teaching function.

"You mean it's not really a prison colony?"

Sam shrugged. "Depends on how you look at it. They've all been sentenced to go there."

"They're not really oppressing the natives?" The asker sounded almost disappointed.

"No—but look what they *are* doing!" Sam fairly glowed with missionary fervor as she went into an explanation of Cholly's educational program. Dar listened, enthralled. He hadn't known he was that much of a hero.

"Hey—it sounds like heaven," said one Hume, with a shaky laugh.

"Yeah. What crime do I have to commit to get sent there?" another joked; but the laughter that followed had a rather serious echo.

"Well, don't jump too soon." Sam leaned on the counter and pushed her cup over for a refill. "The Bureau of Otherworldly Affairs sent out a new governor."

Dar was delighted at the groan.

"Bastards always gotta foul up something good when they find it," muttered one Angry Young Man.

"Establishments can't stand progress," growled another.

"Yeah, but BOA didn't figure on Shacklar." Sam sipped her refill with relish.

"Why? What could he do?" The AYM frowned.

"Well, the new governor's credentials kinda got, uh, 'lost,' before he could show them to Shacklar. And by the time Shacklar got done with him, he'd decided to resign and join the colony."

The room rocked with a hoot of laughter. The AYM smote the counter gleefully. "Go, General! The Organic Will Grow, in spite of the defoliators!"

Sam nodded. "Dar and I got the job of carrying his

resignation back to Terra. But the new ex-governor's lefthand man didn't like the whole idea, so he set out to sabotage us."

"How?" The AYM scowled. "What could he do?"

"Well, first off, he seems to have wrangled himself in as the pilot of the courier ship that brought us here—and he sicced a bunch of pirates on us as soon as we broke out of H-space."

A low mutter of anger ran around the crowd.

"Oh, it was okay—we got out of it, all right, and got picked up by a patrol cruiser. But when we got here, we found out he'd told the Haskerville government that one of us was a telepath and was a threat to social order."

"You?" a voice hooted. "*You're* the witches they're hunting?"

"What've they got against telepaths, anyway?" the AYM grumbled. "They're not hurting anybody."

"Especially when they aren't really telepaths," Sam agreed. "But the House of Houses got wind of it, too, and tried to 'script us. So we're on the run two ways, and running out of hideouts."

A chorus of protest filled the room, and a dozen Humes thrust forward with offers of sympathy.

"Sons o' sobakas," the AYM growled. "Just let one person try do do something decent, and they throw every roller they can in your way! Come on! *We'll* hide you!"

And the whole crowd swirled them out with a chorus of agreement. Dar started to dig in his heels in alarm, then noticed Sam whirling by with a delighted grin. He relaxed, and let himself be borne by the current.

It deposited them in the street outside, with only the AYM and a few other Humes.

"Come on!" the AYM declared, and he set off down the street. Dar had to hurry to catch up.

"Lucky bumping into you," Sam was saying as he came up with them.

"Not all that much luck. This's the ideal place for us—they leave us alone."

Dar could see why. The townsfolk would want to stay as far away as they could from the drab Humes and their shoestring existence. Of course, the shortage of radio communication and police might have had something to do with it, too—if the system was rigged to stay out of the way of the taxpayers' pleasures, it wouldn't be able to bother anyone else much, either.

The AYM led them into an old building that looked as though it had been an office collection in its youth, but had been converted to dwelling purposes. The liftshaft still operated, and took them up to the third level.

"Got to exploring one day." The AYM ran his fingers over the bas-reliefs that decorated the wall at the end of the corridor. "I was doing a rubbing here, and I must have pressed just hard enough on the right thing, because . . ."

Something clicked; a hum sprang up; then, slowly, a portion of the wall retracted, to leave a doorway about two meters high.

Dar stared. Then, slowly, he nodded. "A very interesting suite."

"Yeah, isn't it?" The AYM grinned. "I don't know what kind of business the office had in the old days, but they must've had some kind of a security problem. Import-export trade, at a guess."

Dar stooped through the doorway. "Don't suppose it comes equipped with little luxuries like light."

"Try the wall-plate."

It hadn't occurred to Dar that there might be one. He slid his hand over the wall until he felt the smoother rectangle. It responded to his skin temperature by glowing a small, dim plate in the ceiling into life.

Sam stepped through, too. "You knew we were coming?"

"No, but I had a notion I might need it someday." The AYM pointed to a few boxes of sealed packets and demijohns against the lefthand wall. "Made a deposit every time I could scrounge a little extra. There's a week's supply in here, at least. Pretty plain—biscuit and fruit, and some meat, and nothing to drink but water—but it'll keep you alive." He pointed to a neat stack of blankets just beyond the two straight chairs. "That's all I could scrounge for sleeping and sitting. But all I promised was a hideout."

"The way we are right now, this is a palace." Sam clasped his hand. "No way I can thank you, really, grozh."

"No need. Who knows? You may be doing the same for me someday." He squeezed her arm. "Enjoy what you can. I'll check in every now and then." He stepped back through the doorway, and the wall-segment rolled back into place.

"Of course," Dar observed, "you realize we can't get out now."

"Lesser of two evils." Sam settled herself on one of the hard chairs. "We can get him to tell us when the next ship lands, and duck out to the port."

"A *month* in this crackerbox?"

"This one, or one like it, maintained by the authorities." Sam shrugged. "Your choice. Personally, I'll take this one."

"No contest," Dar sighed, flopping down onto the other chair. "I didn't know your tribe was so widespread."

"There're a lot of us—an awful lot. Oh, there always have been some, at least as far back as the late nineteenth century—but they're always a minority, unless something's going wrong in the government. When a political system has engine trouble, alternative cultures spread."

"Until the engine starts running again?"

Sam nodded. "But the numbers have been on the increase, steadily, for more than a hundred years now."

"I always seem to come in on the end of things," Dar sighed.

"And the beginning." Sam's face lit with a rare, dazzling smile. "That's what comes after the end, you know."

The monster in his dream was knocking on his head with a very loud, hollow sound. Dar waded up out of the morass of slumber to check on the objectivity of the knocking.

Sure enough, it *was* objective—but in the drab reality of their roomlet, it sounded only as a tapping, not a booming pounding.

Dar frowned. Why would the AYM tap? He knew how to open the door!

Therefore, the tapper didn't know how.

Therefore, it wasn't the AYM.

Dar reached out and squeezed Sam's ankle. Her head came up slowly, eyes squinting painfully. "What . . . ?"

"Sh." Dar laid a finger across her lips, then pointed toward the wall/door.

She turned toward the tapping, irritated. He could virtually see her brain waking up as her eyes widened and her mind traced the same path of logic his had.

"Double-crossed?" Dar whispered.

"Can't be!" Sam scrambled to her feet. "I just won't believe it!"

The door/wall began to hum.

"Uh oh." Dar tried to get between Sam and the entryway. "He found the right leaf."

The door rolled back to show a segment of a man.

It was sort of the center stripe of a personality. Dar could see the man's face, and a little of his shoulders to either side (he had no neck), a slice of chest and belly, one knee and the other thigh, and the middle of the front of an armchair. The rest of both the man and the armchair went on to either side of the doorway and, from the look of him, went on for quite a distance. If the average Falstavian was fat, he was enormous. His face was a beachball with four chins and a blob of nose over a thin-lipped, tight mouth. But the eyes, tiny as currants in a vat of dough, were sharp and alive, quick with intelligence, chill with shrewdness. His chest and belly had been cast in one piece and, if there was a ribcage beneath, it was sunk full fathom five. His legs were sections of whale, and his foot was the whaleboat.

The chair floated a good eighteen inches off the floor—antigravity, no doubt; and the connection sparked in Dar's mind: the man couldn't get out of the chair. He couldn't move without it. *That* fat.

"Greetings," Gargantua said. "I am Myles Croft."

"Uh—a pleasure. I suppose." Dar was willing to take a chance on it; after all, the man couldn't get in. "Let me guess—you're the landlord, and it's the first of the month."

"Closer than you intended." The mouth didn't smile, but the eyes twinkled. "I have the honor to be mayor of Haskerville."

Dar levered his jaw back in place and swallowed.

"We're doing better than I thought," Sam said behind him. "The Humes're getting chummy with the mayor."

"Not particularly." The irony in Croft's voice *had* to be humor. "No one needed to tell me where you were hidden. Once I'd heard that you'd escaped from the House of Houses, it was obvious you'd be somewhere back in Haskerville—and, since I knew the lady of the party was a Hume, it was logical to conclude you'd seek refuge in this quarter."

Sam nodded. "All right, so far as it goes—but how'd you know about the two of us? . . . Hold on, cancel that! Of course. If the police knew, you'd know. But how'd you know we'd been taken to Sard, let alone that we'd escaped?"

"I have my sources."

"Interesting, interesting." Dar nodded slowly. "But how'd you know which building to look in?"

"If anyone had hidden you, it would logically be Anthony Marne, who's as much of a leader as the Humes have."

"Angry-young-man type?"

"I thought you'd met. Therefore, you'd probably be hidden in his building—so I surveyed the establishment floor by floor, until I realized one hall was noticeably shorter than the others. Beyond that, I believe you heard my search for the activating control."

Dar just stared.

Then he gave his head a quick shake. "Did you ever consider taking up detective work?"

"Frequently, young man—and I frequently do. The mayor should know *something* about the goings-on in his own city."

"But if you know all that, the House shouldn't be able to get away with anything, and ninety percent of your citizens ought to be in jail."

The huge face smiled into waves of fat. "You are observant, young man. I leave it to your imagination to determine why all are still at large. Suffice it to say that I have some rather elaborate plans, which are working rather well in practice; but they result in a delicate balance, which could very easily be upset by a new and random factor."

Dar's spine turned into an icicle. "You mean us."

Croft nodded. "It is in my interest to see that you're removed from my planet as quickly as possible."

"Shouldn't you have brought along a little protection on this jaunt?" Sam asked grimly.

"I think not. I've discussed you with a friend of mine, and he seems to have high regard for you."

"Well, it's nice to have a good reference." Dar was wary. "Who's our yea-sayer?"

"A Mr. Tambourin; he styles himself 'Whitey the Wino.' And, too, I think, all things considered, that the best way to remove you from circulation is to assist you in your progress."

"You mean you'll get us out of here?" Dar pounced on it.

"I had that in mind, yes. You've certainly done nothing meriting permanent incarceration; but the longer you're here, the more disruptive you'll be. And I don't relish having two police forces on my planet."

"Two?" Now it was Sam who pounced. "Where'd the second one come from?"

"A gentleman named Canis Destinus, I believe. He came to me yesterday morning, bearing a letter 'To Whom It May Concern,' from the Secretary for Internal Security for the I.D.E., requesting the reader to aid Mr. Destinus in any way possible. But the Secretary, as you may know, is head of the reactionary LORDS party . . ."

"I didn't," Sam said, "but I'm glad to."

"Mr. Destinus seems to be more than he appears," Dar said softly.

"Really? I thought his appearance quite indicative; looks somewhat like a rat."

"I take it you don't quite approve of the LORDS?"

"Not germane." Croft dismissed the point with a wave of his hand. "Fortunately, in such circumstances, the letter of the law requires a planetary official, such as myself, to make certain lengthy verifications of the applicant's bona fides, including the Secretary's signature; so I explained to Mr. Destinus that I would probably be able to accord him my full cooperation early next week."

"As I said." Dar grinned. "You don't approve of the LORDS."

"Be that as it may; Mr. Destinus did not seem disposed to wait. So I assumed, when I began to receive reports of pairs of police officers who were definitely not among those I had employed, that Mr. Destinus had induced my cooperation by his own initiative, possibly with Sard's assistance."

"He hired some bullyboys from the House to impersonate cops," Dar translated. "But I can see your problem; the longer we're around, the longer you've got a second, but illegal, police force."

"Of course, I have ways of making such an enterprise prohibitively expensive for Mr. Sard—but not while the LORDS' bottomless purse is open to him. However, if you depart, Mr. Destinus will leave in pursuit of you."

"Makes excellent sense," Dar agreed, "from your point of view."

"And from yours, I should think."

"As far as it goes," Sam said cautiously. "Problem is, when we *do* leave, we're a little picky about where we're going."

"Young Hume, where you go is entirely your own affair."

"Nice theory," Dar approved. "Unfortunately, once you're on a freighter, it's kind of hard to persuade it to change its destination."

"Come to that," Sam chimed in, "there aren't any ships of *any* kind scheduled to lift off for a month. How're you getting us out of here?"

Croft signed. "Haskerville is the only town of any size on the planet; we've something near ninety percent of the population here. Accordingly, I'm *de facto* planetary governor, as well as mayor. So I've authority over all I.D.E. equipment here; and part of that inventory is a small fleet of outmoded I.D.E. scout ships. I've arranged for Mr. Tambourin to buy one, as government surplus."

"To *buy* a spacer?" Dar's eyes fairly bulged. "All by himself?"

"Government surplus is ridiculously inexpensive," Croft noted.

"Even so—a *spacer*! How much money does this guy *have*?"

"Not much, after this little purchase." Sam smiled up at the mayor. "Can we hitch a ride, Mr. Croft?"

"Hey, hold on!" Dar caught her arm. "What do you mean, hitch a ride? We can't trust this man!"

Sam turned back, frowning up at him. "Why not?"

"Why *not*?" Dar spluttered. "I mean . . . look! We're on the *run*! He's the *law*!"

"That's right, he's the law. So if he says to let us go, they'll let us go."

"But . . . but . . ."

"Look," Sam said, with forced patience, "I'm a good judge of character. Have you ever known me to be wrong about who I could trust, and who I couldn't?"

Dar started to answer, then hesitated.

"Including you," Sam reminded.

Dar sighed and capitulated. "All right. You win." He looked toward Croft. "When does the next bus leave?"

With a load like Croft in it, Dar wouldn't've thought the armchair could support any more. But it had lift to spare; they glided through the deserted streets of Haskerville perched on the arms like a couple of children come to recite their Christmas lists to Santa.

After a little while, Dar said, "It occurs to me that what you've got here is a planetful of grifters and marks, about evenly divided."

Croft nodded agreeably. "An oversimplification, but accurate within its limits."

"In fact, you could almost say it's got the potential for becoming a balanced society."

"The potential, perhaps," Croft agreed.

"How do you manage to keep the House of Houses from totally destroying the citizens?"

Croft smiled, amused. "Come now, young man! You give me too much credit. Even a criminal realizes that he must take care of his geese if he wants them to grow more feathers for plucking."

"Not from what I've read," Dar said slowly. "Historically, even the organized criminals haven't cared who they hurt or killed, as long as they made a profit on it."

"Ah, but that is when they have an unlimited supply of geese!"

"Somehow, I don't think the House of Houses has quite that much foresight."

Croft nodded, amused. "I may have arranged for the odd idea to reach the House through circuitous routes. Then, too, even with a severely limited police force, there are ways of making certain activities unprofitable.''

Dar nodded, bemused. "So you've got two societies that pretty much balance each other—and it's got the potential for becoming a single, cohesive society. That would take a lot of guidance and maneuvering—but it is possible.''

Croft nodded. "Of course. *Anything* is possible—even that; with an exterior challenge and thrown back on their own resources, both halves of the population might forgo their own forms of decadence.''

"A challenge such as being cut off from the rest of the human-inhabited universe?''

Croft nodded, a slight smile on his thin lips. "You evince a definite talent, young fellow. Given time and practice, you might prove as capable of deduction as I am.''

The spaceport was guarded by a split-log fence, like an old-time Western fort. But the gate opened at Croft's approach, and they floated through, to stare at a square mile of plastrete, pock-marked with blast-pits. The two-story personnel and passenger building seemed like a miniscule bump on the fence. The only other break in the bald field was a silvery manta-ray shape tilted upward toward the stars, as though it strained to be free of the planet—an FTL scout, streamlined and planed for atmospheric capability. No ferry this time, but a ship that could go from surface to surface, though without the speed of the great liners. It was beautiful, but it seemed pathetically small and frail against the immense stretch of plastrete.

The hatch was open, and a silhouette appeared against its rectangle of yellow light as they drifted up. "As good as your word! You found 'em!" Whitey jumped down to pump Croft's arm.

"You doubted me, Whitey?''

"Not for a second! Trouble was, it was turning into hours.''

A black robe blocked the hatch, and light gleamed off a bald pate. "Welcome, wanderers!" Father Marco waved. "Come on in and tell us about your travels! We should have time; we're going seventy-five light-years!''

But Dar's eyes snapped to the figure beside the priest. Even as a silhouette, she looked wonderful.

"Good to see you again, Father." Sam hopped down off Croft's chair and strode toward the hatch. "But, why're you coming along? It's *our* misfortune, and none of your own."

"Someone has to look after your souls," the friar joked. At least, Dar hoped he was joking. "Nice of you to care, Father—but why should you?" He jumped up into the ship, carefully brushing against Lona in the process.

"Because," said the priest, "I'm a brother of the Order of St. Vidicon, and you two present a case that an engineer can't resist."

Dar didn't follow the logic, but it didn't matter; Lona was giving him the long stare. He couldn't tell whether it was admiring or accusing, but he didn't really care—so long as he had her attention.

"Well, that's it!" Whitey hopped aboard and sealed the hatch behind him. "Always helps to have friends in the right places."

"Sure does," Dar agreed, "and I'm awfully glad we've got you. But why? This isn't your quarrel, Whitey."

"It is now." Whitey flopped down into the nearest acceleration couch and stretched his webbing across. "Things were getting dull, but you two promise to make them interesting again."

"But you're heading for the frontier, and we have to get to Terra!"

"So do we—now." Whitey grinned. "As long as you promise to shake the old place up a bit. Besides, I have to see my publisher—I've suddenly run low on funds."

Dar swallowed, feeling guilty, but Whitey looked around and bawled, "Who's going to pilot this tub?"

"Who else?" Lona jumped into the pilot's couch with relish. "I'd fly a mountain to get back to some good old-fashioned decadence!" She hit a few keys, and the spacer roared to life.

"I'll take communications." Sam slipped into the couch beside Lona and keyed the talker. "What's the name of this tub?"

"I christen it *Ray of Hope*," Whitey declared.

"*Ray of Hope* to Control," Sam called, "outward-bound toward Sol."

"Uh . . . come in, *Ray of Hope*." Control was, to say the least, startled.

"Permission to lift off."

"Permission to . . . ? Uh—be right with you, *Ray of Hope*." Dar could hear a squawk in the background before Control killed its mike. "Looks like we took them by surprise," he said to Whitey.

"Not surprising enough." Whitey frowned. "Who's gotten to them?"

"Three guesses—which is two more than you need." Sam keyed her mike again. "*Ray of Hope* to Falstaff Control. What's the delay?"

"Uh . . . *Ray of Hope*," Control stammered, "it seems you forgot to file a ballistic plan."

"Ballistic plan?" Whitey bawled. "What does he think this is—a hop to the next planet?"

"*Ray of Hope* to Control," Sam said grimly. "I thought ballistic plans went out when FTL came in."

"Well—we have to make sure you don't interfere with any incoming traffic."

"Incoming traffic! *What* incoming traffic? The sky's as clear as a verdict!"

Whitey chuckled. "As owner of this ship, pilot, I order you to lift off."

"Yes, Grandpa," Lona murmured, entirely too demurely. Then there wasn't much talking, because they were plastered back in their couches for a few minutes as the *Ray* streaked up through the atmosphere.

Then the pressure eased off, and "down" gradually stopped being the back of the ship and became the deck, as ship's gravity took over from acceleration.

"Coasting at nine-tenths maximum." Lona spun her chair around and loosened her webbing. "I'd advise you stay in your couches, though; should only be about twenty minutes till we're far enough out to isomorph into H-space."

"We barely made it," Sam said with a sour smile. "Remember that squawk in the background? That was Destinus."

"Destinus?" Father Marco sat up, frowning. "*Canis* Destinus?"

"Why, yes, now that you mention it." Sam turned to Father Marco. "You know him?"

"More than that; we're related." The priest seemed suddenly saddened. "He's my father's half-brother's son."

Dar frowned. "Wait a minute—that makes him . . ."

"Half a cousin of the brother." Whitey turned to the friar. "The two of you were on the same planet, and he didn't bother to say hello?"

Father Marco nodded. "And it *would* seem that he probably knew I was here. But then, under the circumstances, I suppose he wouldn't't've wanted to be associated with me."

"Doesn't sound like the overly sentimental sort."

"To say the least," Father Marco replied grimly. "In fact, I haven't heard from him since I went into seminary; he was very upset with my choice of order. Thought I was horribly radical, that sort of thing." He turned to Sam. "He's been causing you trouble for a while?"

"Hunting us down," Sam confirmed. "He seems to be working for the LORDS."

Father Marco sighed and shook his head. "Poor Destinus! We knew he was keeping bad company, being in the government and all—but I didn't know it was *this* bad . . . well!" He slapped his knees and sat up straight. "Looks as though I made the right decision, coming along with you."

"How so?" Dar frowned. "Finding out about your half-cousin makes that much of a difference?"

Father Marco nodded. "Family obligation. It's up to me to try to counter the damage Destinus's trying to do to you."

"Well, don't be too hard on the boy." Dar frowned up at Sam. "I mean, it's not as if he were doing it on his own. He's just acting for his bosses. *They're* the ones who're going in for telepath-hunting."

"Oh, I wouldn't be too sure of that." Sam's lip curled slightly. "Do you think hardheaded politicians would really believe in telepaths? I mean, believe in 'em enough to mount a major hunt?"

"Why else would they bring in their own 'police'?"

"Because," Sam grinned, "it makes an excellent excuse to immobilize you and me, before we can get Bhelabher's resignation to BOA."

"Could a governorship of a boondocks planet be all that important?"

"To the governor's righthand man it could. Besides, even if the LORDS *are* planning to cut off all the outlying planets, that doesn't mean they like the idea of governors who're ready to get along without them very nicely, thank you."

"A point," Dar admitted. "That is a little deflating to the collective Terran ego. Which makes me think Myles Croft can't be all that popular with BOA, either."

"He always was an independent cuss, My was." Whitey grinned, leaning back with his hands locked behind his head. "Myself, I think it's just fine, seeing the outer worlds getting ready for Terra to ax 'em"

"Ready? Eager, almost." Lona was watching her data board. "About to isomorph, gentlefolk—tighten your webbing." She frowned, and peered closer at her detectors. "Strange—that blip's *gotta* be another ship lifting off from Falstaff."

"Strange indeed." Dar frowned, too. "There weren't supposed to be any arrivals or departures for a month."

"You don't think . . . ?" Sam began, but then the isomorpher kicked in, and reality turned very fuzzy for a while.

9

Out near the asteroid belt, on the Jupiter side, the solar system's tapestry of gravity begins to thin out just enough for a ship to emerge from H-space. It's not the safest thing to do, of course; there is a respectable chance of Jupiter's gravity fouling the isomorpher enough to make the ship twist into that other realm where ships that *nearly* made it back out go to. Still, probability favors success; so, if you're in a hurry, you might try it.

Dar and Sam were in a hurry, so Lona tried it.

Deceleration slammed Dar against his webbing. It was killing pressure, but it slowly eased off—very slowly; it took the ship's internal field a while to win over momentum. When he could sit back and talk again, he did. "I—I take it we made it?"

"We're in one piece." Lona sounded offended as she scanned her damage readout. "Not even a split seam."

"Didn't mean to question your ability," Dar said quickly. "It's just—well, it *was* a little risky."

Lona snorted.

"Not for my niece." Whitey leaned forward and tapped the autobar for Rhysling. "The only kind of machine Lona doesn't understand is a hammer—it doesn't have any moving parts, let alone circuits. Anyone join me?"

Red light exploded off the walls and ceiling. Lona's hands flew over her board. "That was a cannon bolt! Chug that drink and hold on!"

Something groaned, winding up to a scream as ship's gravity fought to keep up with velocity changes. But it was a losing battle; Lona was putting the little ship through so many rolls and dives, a four-dimensional computer couldn't've kept up with her.

Which, of course, was exactly the idea.

But their pursuer's battle comp was *good*; ruby flashes kept flickering off the walls, now brighter, now dimmer, now brighter again.

"How about the traditional shot across the bows?" Dar called.

"They're not big on tradition," Lona snapped, sweat beading her brow.

"I never did have much use for iconoclasts," Father Marco grumbled.

"It's a Patrol cruiser!" Sam stared at the rear viewscreen in horror. "The Solar Patrol—the ones who rescue stranded spacemen from starship wrecks!"

"And shoot down smugglers," Whitey added grimly. "But they *never* shoot without warning!"

"You've been watching too many Patrol-epic holos, Grandpa," Lona grated. "These are the *real* ones!"

"Are they?" Sam keyed the transmitter. "Let's find out! *Ray of Hope* calling Patrol cruiser! Come in, Patrol cruiser!"

An energy-bolt lanced past them as Lona rolled the ship to starboard.

"Come in, Patrol cruiser! Why're you shooting at us? We haven't broken any laws! And we're not carrying contraband!" Sam let up on the key and listened, but there wasn't even a whisper of static.

"Maybe it's broken," Dar said quickly, "not picking up their answer!"

"Dreamer," Lona growled.

"I'll try anything." Sam spun the sweep-knob, and a voice

rattled out of the tiny speaker. ". . . at the top of the roster. It's on his new holocube, 'Roll Me to Rigel!'"

"Commercial channel," Sam grated.

A new voice interrupted the announcer in mid-word. "Ganagram News Update—brought to you by Chao-Yu's Chandlers, with the latest in used burro-boat fittings!"

"Must be the Ganymede 3DT station," Whitey said, nodding. "They broadcast for the asteroid miners, mostly."

"How can you tell?"

"Who else uses burro-boats?"

"We interrupt this program to bring you a special hot flash," the radio went on. "We've just been notified that a small pirate ship with a notorious telepath aboard has just entered the Solar System. Citizens are advised not to worry, though—the mind reader's being chased by a Solar Patrol cruiser. They should be calling any minute to tell us he's been captured and locked up."

"They're talking about *us*," Dar choked.

"Correction," Lona snapped. "They're talking about *you*."

"They did say, 'he,'" Whitey admitted.

"Also, that they're going to capture us—which sounds like a fine idea, right now." Sam keyed the transmitter again. "*Ray of Hope* to Solar Patrol cruiser! We surrender! We give up! We throw down our arms!"

Red light blazed through the cabin, and the whole hull chimed like a singing bell.

"That was *really* close!" Lona rolled the ship over so fast that Dar's stomach lost track of his abdomen. "They've got a weird idea of capturing!"

"I think," Whitey mused, "that they're out to avoid the expense of a trial."

"So, what do we do?" Dar demanded. "We can't keep running forever. So far, the only reason we're still alive is their lousy marksmanship, and Lona's fantastic piloting."

"Flattery will get you an early grave," Lona snapped. "I need ideas, not compliments!"

"Well, how's this?" Dar frowned. "We came in between Jupiter and Mars, heading sunward. What's our speed?"

"We're back up to point nine seven light-speed."

Father Marco's eyes lost focus. "Let's see, that means

. . . it's been about five minutes for us, so for the people on Earth . . ."

"It's been a few weeks," Lona finished for him, "and if we don't do something soon, we're going to get punctured by a small swarm of teeny-tiny asteroids, and flattened when we run into a few big ones!"

"Asteroids!" Sam sat up straight, her eyes locking on Dar's. "We did it once . . ."

"And I'll bet the Solar Patrol aren't much smarter than pirates!" Dar turned to Lona. "Can you match velocity with an asteroid?"

"Of *course*!" Lona crowed. "Kill our power, and all we are is a new asteroid with a high albedo!"

"Not even that, if you can get a big rock between us and the sun. Can we slow down that fast?"

"Can do." Lona nodded. "It'll take most of our power, though, and it won't be very comfortable."

She had a nice knack for understatement; it was hell. Not as bad as it could've been—at least she had the courtesy to turn the ship around so she could decelerate with the main engine, and they were plastered back into their seats instead of being slammed against their webbing—but they were rammed so far into their couches that Dar could've sworn he felt the hard plastic of the frame, and held his breath, waiting for the couch to either snap or spring a leak. But it held, and he began to wonder if *he* would. His nose felt as though it were trying to flow around both sides of his face to join his ears; his eyes tried bravely to follow their optic nerves to their sources; and after a while, it occurred to him that the reason he was holding his breath was simply that he couldn't breathe. It was about three anvils, a barrel of horseshoes, two blacksmiths, and a Percheron sitting on his chest. . . .

Then the pressure eased off, and swung him against the side of the hull as Lona turned. The acceleration couch slowly regurgitated him, and he found himself staring around at a cabin that perversely persisted in looking just the way it had before they passed through the hamburger press.

Then Lona flicked a finger at her console, and the lights went out.

All he could think of was that she was over there, and he was over here, still webbed in. It was such a horrible waste of a great situation.

Into the sudden darkness her voice murmured, "I've killed all power, so they won't have any energy emissions to track us by. Don't let it worry you; you can still see out the ports. And we won't lose heat too fast; the hull's well insulated. But the air recycler's off, and this isn't all that large a cabin for five people. So do the best you can not to breathe too much. Breathe lightly—sleep if you can. And don't talk—that's a waste of air."

"If the power's off, your detectors're out," Father Marco murmured.

"Right. We won't know where they are, except by sight. Which doesn't do too much good, of course—they could be far enough away to only show as a speck of light, but they could still get here in a matter of minutes."

"So, how will we know when to turn the lights back on?" Whitey asked.

"When the air starts getting foul," Lona answered. "When you start feeling short of breath, and drowsy."

"But they might still be nearby then," Dar objected.

"Life is filled with these little chances," Lona murmured. "But let's make it as long a wait as we can. No more talking."

Sibilant silence descended on the cabin, filled with the rasp and wheeze of people in various states of health trying to control their breathing. After a few minutes, someone began to snore softly—Whitey, no doubt; Dar could only admire his composure. For himself, he was watching nervously out the nearest porthole, and, sure enough, there was the tiny dot of light, swelling rapidly, turning into a Patrol cruiser which shot by overhead so close that Dar had to fight the urge to duck.

"One pass," Lona murmured.

"Gadget-lovers," Father Marco chuckled. "They don't trust their eyes anymore; if it isn't on a sensor-screen, it doesn't exist."

"Then, pretend we don't," Sam hissed. "Shut up!"

The patrol cruiser slid out from the top of the vast asteroid that hid the *Ray of Hope*. Dar held his breath; if there were a single eye actually watching out a porthole, all he'd ever know about it would be a huge red flash that just *might* burn out his life before it melted his eyes. But, come to think of it, he didn't even *see* any portholes, and the big ship drifted on past them and disappeared into a cluster of space junk.

Sam heaved a sigh of relief, but Lona hissed, "Belay that!"

"What?" Sam protested. "Breathing?"

"You were hoping," Lona accused.

"What's wrong with that?" Sam demanded, but Father Marco assured her, "It's too soon."

And right he was, because here came the space-shark again, drifting up so closely above them that Dar halfway expected it to ask if he was interested in life insurance. But there must have been enough nickel-iron in their friendly asteroidal neighborhood to hide the *Ray of Hope*'s mettle, because the cruiser lifted its nose and rose above them, more and more quickly until it disappeared into the clutter of floating rock overhead.

A multiple sigh filled the cabin, and Whitey croaked, "Huh? Wha'sa matter? They find us? Huh? What?"

"I think they went up above the plane of the ecliptic, Grandpa," Lona assured him.

"Hoping to get a better view of the situation—looking down at us," Dar suggested.

"Can I hope now?" Sam squeaked.

A huge bass chime shook the cabin, and Lona hit the power key. "Only if we get out of here," she answered Sam. "That was our first visiting neighbor, hinting we should move out of the neighborhood."

"A little asteroid, colliding with us," Dar explained as the lights came on and gravity sucked him back down into his seat. "It's a wonder it's only the first one; they could've knocked us to bits by now."

"Not really," Lona said, punching buttons. "We came in above the plane of the ecliptic, matched velocities with this asteroid, and swooped in right next to it. Most of the local pebbles are in orbit around it. That little stone that just hit us shot in from a close bypass with another big rock. It was just a matter of time before it came calling though."

"But it won't happen again if we're going back above the plane of the ecliptic?"

"Are you kidding?" Lona snorted. "That Patrol boat's up

there! We're going *below*, sister, so we'll have the whole depth
of the asteroid belt between us and them, to foul their sensors!
Brace yourselves, everyone—this is going to be a rough ride!"

"*Nos morituri te salutamus,*" Father Marco intoned.

We who are about to die, salute thee . . . Dar shivered.
"You could've thought of a cheerier blessing, Father."

"You speak *Latin*?" Father Marco cried in surprise. "What
are you—a fossil?"

"No—I just got stoned at Cholly's a lot." Then Dar's
stomach rose as the ship sank and a huge gong reverberated
through the hull.

"Nothing to worry about." Lona's voice was tight with
strain. "It can't really hurt us unless it's as big as my head, and
I can swerve around anything that size—I think."

Then Whitey was pointing upward out the porthole and
shouting—but the gist of his comment was lost in another huge
BONG! as red lightning lit the cabin and the ship bucked like a
metal bull. Over the fading chime, Dar could hear Lona
cursing as she fought to stabilize the craft. The red glow
faded—and left them in darkness broken only by the shards of
reflected sunlight from the dancing asteroids around them. Sam
shouted in panic, and everybody started talking at once.

"BELAY IT!" Lona shouted, and a sudden, eerie silence
fell. Dar drew in a long, trembling breath. Whatever had
happened, it was really *bad*!

"They were waiting for us," Lona said into the hush. "As
soon as we fired up, their sensors locked their battle computer
on us and let loose a ball of pure energy—several, really; the
first few just vaporized the junk between us and them. The last
one knocked off our tail section. As it is, we're lucky—if I
hadn't swerved to avoid a rock, they'd have caught us right in
this cabin."

"They're rising again." Whitey had his head craned back
against the viewport, staring upward.

"Sure." Lona shrugged. "They didn't just shear away our
engines—they blew away our reactor, too. There's no power
left for them to 'sense.' Besides, why should they bother
hunting down the pieces? They know we're dead now,
anyway."

Sam strangled a sob.

"Take heart," Father Marco said sternly. "We *aren't* dead."

"We do have emergency power," Lona agreed. "It'll keep recycling air while it lasts—and the sun's radiation'll keep us warm, if we block the portholes on the far side. And we have a couple of weeks' rations."

"Will the power last that long?" Sam's voice was hollow. Lona was silent.

"It will, if we don't talk much and can do without light," Whitey answered. "Of course, we can't go anywhere."

Father Marco grunted in surprise. "I didn't know you knew any physics."

"I was an engineer before I was a bard." Dar could hear Whitey's grin. "Who else could make enough sense out of this civilization to set it to music? But I'm a gambler, too."

Dar felt the dread coalescing into terror.

"Just what kind of gamble did you have in mind?" Father Marco's voice echoed with foreboding.

"Well, we can't go *to* help," Whitey mused, "so we've got to make it come to us."

Dar cleared his throat, which pushed the fear back down. "You're talking about a distress signal."

"It'd give us a little chance, at least," Whitey answered. "Without it, we're dead—unless you can arrange a miracle, Father."

"I'm afraid my connections don't quite run that high." The priest sounded amused. "Even if St. Vidicon reaches out to us, we've got to give him a handle to grab us by—some sort of action to put us into the ring of coincidence."

"How much energy would it leave us?" Dar dreaded the answer.

"If it's going to be strong enough to do us any good, we'll have to put half our remaining power into it," Lona answered.

"A week's worth." Dar wet his lips. "That gives us a week for somebody to hear us and get here."

They were all silent.

A week! something shrieked within Dar. *Only a week to live! I've never even been in love!*

"We don't really have any choice, do we?" Sam said softly. The cabin was silent again.

Then Sam heaved herself upright and leaned forward to the communications panel. "All right. How do you want it?"

Breath hissed out in a sigh of consensus.

"Broadband." Lona slapped keys, routing the emergency power to communications. "Just the traditional Mayday, with our coordinates."

Sam leaned forward to the audio pickup and thumbed the transmit key.

"Don't give the name of the ship," Whitey said quickly.

Sam hesitated, then spoke. "Mayday, Mayday! Distressed spacer at 10:32:47 V.E., 5:22 below P.E. Mayday, Mayday! Moribund!"

Moribund. . . . "Death-bound." Dar felt the dread wrap around him, creeping up his spine.

Sam shut down her board.

"Leave trickle-power on," Lona advised. "If salvage does come, they'll need contact—a second of arc is a big distance out here."

Sam hesitated, and Dar could almost hear her thoughts—how much life-time would they lose to that trickle? But I.C. grains drew only a few milliwatts per hour, and a rescuer a mile away who couldn't spot them was no better than no rescuer at all. Sam nodded, cracked one slider, and left her main on.

The cabin was silent again; then Lona said, "Now we wait. . . ."

. . . *for death.* Dar completed the sentence in his head. "What do we do with our minds?"

The silence became acutely uncomfortable.

Then Father Marco stirred. "I do know a little about meditation. Would anyone like a mantra?"

"Burro-boat FCC 651919 to distressed spacer. Respond, please."

Dar sat bolt upright, staring at the first pair of eyes he saw—Lona's, fortunately. "So *soon*? Where was he, just around the corner?"

"It's been two hours. . . ."

"Even so. . . ."

"Burro-boat, this is distressed spacer," Sam snapped into her pickup. "Can you rescue?"

"Distressed spacer, I can rescue and am in your vicinity, but need transmission to home on. Please continue transmission of carrier wave."

"Burro-boat, will do. We await you anxiously." Sam locked down the "transmit" button, but covered the pickup with her hand and swiveled to face the others. "It doesn't *have* to be the Patrol, you know."

"If it is, we'll know in a minute." Whitey gave her a dry smile. "As soon as they get a locus on us, they'll blast us to vapor."

Sam flinched, and whirled back to her console.

"No!" Lona snapped. "It *might* be legit—and if it's not, I'd rather steam than starve, anyway!"

Sam hesitated, but she left the "transmit" button on.

"And it *could* be honest," Father Marco pointed out. "The prospectors flit all over the belt in their burro-boats. Why shouldn't there have been one two hours away?"

Lona's eyes glazed. "Well, the probabilities . . ."

"Spare us," Whitey said quickly. "Have you been praying for St. Vidicon's help, Father?"

Father Marco squirmed. "It couldn't hurt, could it?"

"Not at all. He might've stacked the deck in our favor." Whitey craned his neck, staring out the porthole. "Dar, take the starboard view. What do you see?"

"Just asteroids. . . . No, one of them's getting bigger. . . . There!"

There was a concerted rush to the starboard portholes.

"Is *that* a ship?" Dar gasped.

It was dingy gray, and it might've been a sphere once, but it was so pocked with crater dents that it looked just like any of the asteroids. Two paraboloid dishes sprouted from its top, one round for radio and microwave, the other elongated, for radar. Below them, the hull sloped down to two huge windows; the miners liked naked-eye backup for their scanners. Below *them*, the hull kept sloping until it reached the loading bay: two huge holes, housing solenoids, for small bits of ore; below it, a "mouth" for big chunks. Beneath a bulbous belly hung two pairs of pincers, one fore and one aft, for grappling onto small asteroids that were two big for loading. From the aft section sprouted a spray of antennae that set up a force-field to prevent rearend collisons by small asteroids.

"It's beautiful," Sam breathed.

The burro-boat rotated, broadside-on to the *Ray of Hope*, and a small hatch opened in its side. A magentic grapple shot out, trailing a line. It clanged onto their hull.

"Distressed spacer," said the com console, "We are prepared for boarding."

Sam dived for the console. "Acknowledge, burro-boat. We'll just slide into our pressure suits, and be right over."

Whitey swung out a section of the wall. "I hope they left the suits when they mothballed this thing. . . . There they are!"

All five crowded around, feasting their eyes on their means of escape.

"Air?" Sam said doubtfully.

Dar snorted. "So hold your breath. It's only a hundred yards!" He hauled down a suit and handed it to Sam. "Ladies first."

"Male chauvinist! *You* go first!"

"All right, all right," Dar grumbled, clambering into the stiff fabric. "Check my seals, will you? Y' know, something bothers me."

"You too, huh?" Whitey was sealing him in with a crisp, practiced touch. "You wouldn't be wondering why we haven't heard from the pilot?"

"Well, yes, now that you mention it. Or is it the custom here, to let the computers do the talking?"

"Definitely not," Lona assured him, sealing Sam into her suit. "Of course, there might not *be* a pilot."

"Could be—but not likely," Whitey grunted. "Didn't you hear the serial number? This is one of those new FCC brains— 'Faithful Cybernetic Companions,' programmed for extreme loyalty. They're not supposed to want to do *anything* without their owner's express command."

"I thought those were robot brains." Father Marco frowned. "What's it doing conning a ship?"

Whitey shrugged. "Can't say, Father. I *do* know that every scrap of junk and every used Terran part finds its way to the asteroid belt sooner or later, to get the last erg of usage out of it. . . . There!" He slapped Dar on the shoulder; it sent him spinning in the free-fall of the powerless ship. "Go out and conquer, young fella!"

"I thought I was going to be rescued," Dar grumbled. "And why do I have to go alone?"

"Because a burro-boat's lock is only big enough for one at a time." Whitey all but kicked him into the *Ray of Hope*'s airlock. "Have a good trip—and try not to breathe!"

The door slammed behind him, and the other hatch was opening; and if he didn't go out there and try to swim through vacuum to the burro-boat, he'd be killing his four friends, who couldn't go into the airlock till he'd gone. He gulped down his panic and forced himself to step through.

He held onto the line with one hand, groping frantically at his waist for the suit's anchoring cables. There! It was a snap-hook with a swivel. He pulled it out; a strong line unreeled from somewhere inside his suit. He snapped the hook onto the line. Catching the overhead line, he pulled himself back against the *Ray of Hope*'s side, bracing his feet and backing down into a crouch. Then he fixed his gaze on the burro-boat's airlock, took a deep breath, and—jumped as hard as he could.

He went shooting out along the line like a housewife's dry laundry in the first drops of rain. For a moment, he was tempted to try going faster by pulling himself hand-over-hand along the line; then he remembered that he was in vacuum, which meant no friction, but his gauntlets on the line *would* mean friction, and would probably slow him down as much as they speeded him up. So he hung on, arms outstretched in a swan dive—and began to enjoy it.

Then the burro-boat's side shot up at him, and he grabbed frantically for the line, remembering that he might have lost weight, but he hadn't lost mass—which meant inertia. If he didn't brake, fast, the next friend down the line would have to scrape a nice, thin layer of Mandra off the burro-boat before he could get into the airlock. The scream of improvised brakes squealed all through his suit, while the burro-boat's side kept rushing up at him, seeming to come faster and faster. Frantically, he doubled up, getting his feet and flexed knees between him and it. . . .

Then he hit, with a jar that he swore knocked his teeth back into the gums. But, as he slowly straightened, he realized his joints were still working, and the stars that *didn't* fade from his vision were really asteroids sweeping past. Somehow, he'd made it—and all in one piece! He breathed a brief, silent prayer of thanks and stepped gingerly through the hatch. When he was sure both of his feet were pressing down on solid metal, he let go of the line with one hand to grasp the rim of the hatchway; *then* he let go with the other, and pulled himself down into the nice, safe darkness of the interior. His elbow bumped a lever; irritated, he pushed it away—and the hatch swung shut behind him.

Darkness. Total. Complete.

That was when Dar learned what "claustrophobia" meant. He had to fight to keep himself from pounding on the nearest wall, screaming to be let out. *It's just an airlock*, he repeated to himself, over and over. *They* can't *let me out until it's filled with air. Just a few minutes. . . .*

It seemed like an hour. He found out, later, that it was really forty-two seconds.

Then a green light glowed in the darkness. He lunged toward it, felt the wheel of the door-seal, wrenched it open, and tumbled into light, warmth, and . . . AIR! He twisted his helmet off, and inhaled a reek of rancid food, unwashed body, and a sanitation recycler that wasn't quite working right. They were the sweetest scents he'd ever smelled.

A chime rang behind him. He whirled about to see an amber light blinking next to the airlock. Of course—nobody else could come in until he shut the inside hatch! He slammed and dogged it shut—and realized he'd been hearing voices as soon as he'd come in; they were just now beginning to register.

"Consarn it, 'tain't none of my affair!" a gravelly voice ranted. "Now you turn this blasted tub around and get back to my claim!"

"But under the Distressed Spacers' Law," a calm, resonant voice replied, "you are required to render assistance to the crew of any imperiled ship."

"You've said that fifteen times, hang it, and I've given you fifteen good reasons why we shouldn't!"

"Three," the calm voice reminded, "five times each, and none of them sufficient."

"*Any* of 'em's good enough! 'Tain't none of our business—that's the best one of all!"

Dar finished shucking out of his space suit and racked it, then tiptoed along the companionway toward the voices.

"Totally inadequate," the other voice answered, unruffled. "The Distressed Spacers' Law specifically mentions that a distressed spaceman is the overriding concern of any who happen to be near enough to offer assistance."

"Overriding" was the key word; it made Dar suddenly certain as to who the calm voice belonged to. He peeked around the edge of the hatchway, and saw the burro-boat's cabin, a cramped space littered with ration containers and papers, dirty laundry, and smudges of oil and grease. It held two acceleration couches, a control console with six scanner screens, and a short, stocky man in a filthy, patched coverall, with matted hair and an unkempt, bushy beard.

"Jettison the law!" he yelled. "Common sense oughta tell you that! It's the Patrol's job to take care of a shipwreck!"

"Which was your second reason." The calm voice seemed to come from the control console. "The crew of the ship in question might be those whom the Patrol was pursuing."

"If they was, bad cess to 'em! Damn telepaths, poking their noses into other people's secrets! Who do they think they are, anyway?"

"Human beings," the voice answered, "and as much entitled to life as anyone else—especially since the Patrol has apparently not accused them of any crimes."

Dar decided he liked the unseen owner of the calm voice.

"Bein' a telepath's a crime, damn it! Don't you follow the news?"

"Only insofar as it is logical—which is to say, not very far at all. I fail to comprehend how a person can commit a crime by being born with an extra ability."

Neither did Dar—and it was definitely news, at least to him. Just how powerful *were* the people involved in the plot to overthrow the I.D.E., anyway?

Apparently, powerful enough to whip up a full-scale witch-hunt, just for the purpose of catching his humble self. He realized the implications, and felt his knees dissolve.

" 'Tain't fer you or me to understand it—the goverment does, and that's enough. What—you figger you're smarter than the Executive Secretary and all them Electors put together?"

Suddenly, Dar realized why the plot had gotten as far as it had. The old man sounded more like a medieval serf than a well-informed citizen of a democracy.

A hand fell on his shoulder, and Sam snarled in his ear, "I didn't think you'd sink so low as to listen at keyholes."

Dar looked up, startled; then he smiled. "Of course I haven't. That's why I left the door open."

"That depends on your definition of intelligence," the calm voice answered.

"What difference does it make?" the old man howled. "You can't vote, anyway—you're just a damned *computer*!"

"Computers do not have souls," the voice said complacently, "and therefore cannot be damned."

"Kicked into the mass-recycler, then! Do you realize how much money you're losing me, by kiyoodling off to rescue these garbage-can castaways?"

Sam's lips drew into a thin hard line. She took a step toward the door. Dar grabbed her shoulder, hissing, "Not yet."

"Perfectly," the computer answered, "since this is the sixth time you've mentioned the fact. Considering the quality of your ore and the current price of a kilogram of nickel-iron as quoted by Ganymede half an hour ago, multiplied by my rate of excavation, this salvage mission has thus far cost you exactly 1,360 BTUs."

"There!" the old miner crowed triumphantly. "See? You know how much one thousand BTUs'll *buy*?"

"Ten cubic centimeters of hydrogen, at current prices," the computer answered, "or three ration bars."

"Damn inflation," the miner growled. "It's getting so a body can't afford a patch for the arse of his coveralls anymore."

"Be that as it may," the computer mused, "I believe a human life is worth considerably more."

"Not the life of a confounded telepath, damn it!"

Sam was trembling. She pushed Dar's hand away and took a determined step into the cabin.

"Me first," Whitey growled as he squeezed past her. "This one's more my size—or age, anyway."

He stepped into the cabin, calling out, "There aren't any telepaths on our ship, old-timer."

Looking back over his shoulder, Dar saw that Whitey was only telling the truth—Lona and Father Marco stood right behind him.

"And thanks for the rescue, by the way," Whitey finished.

The old miner spun around, staring wild-eyed. "Where in hell'd *you* come from?"

"No, we hadn't quite gotten *there* yet," Whitey said amiably. "Might have, if you hadn't picked us up, though."

The miner whirled back to his console, glaring. "Who said you could let this trash in?"

"The Distressed Spacers' Law . . ."

"Shove the law up the plasma bottle!" the old miner howled. "You're supposed to be loyal to me, not to them!"

"My initial programming included only one principle of higher priority than loyalty to my current owner," the computer admitted.

"There wasn't even supposed to be *one*!"

Whitey grinned. "Don't tell me you believed everything the used-brain salesman told you. What was the higher priority, anyway?"

"The sanctity of human life," the computer answered, "unless the human in question is attacking my current owner."

"Well, who could object to that?" Whitey fixed the miner with a glittering stare. The old man glared back at him, started to say something, stopped, and turned away, muttering under his breath.

"No, I didn't think you would." Whitey smiled, amused. "No decent person could. And we want to show you our thanks, of course."

The old miner swept a quick, appraising glance over Whitey's worn, tattered clothing. "Thanks don't mean much, unless it shows up as figgers in my credit readout."

Whitey kept the smile, but his eyes glittered again. "Well, of course. We wouldn't expect you to ship us to safety for free."

"Oh, sure! When we get to port, you'll slip your card into

my bank's terminal, and it'll read pretty—but five days later, it'll turn out that account in a Terran bank was closed out five years ago!"

Whitey didn't answer; he just slapped his jacket pocket. It clinked. The old miner's gaze fastened onto it.

"Thirty kwahers for taking each of us to Ceres City," Whitey said easily.

The old miner's eye gleamed. "Fifty!"

"Well, we don't use up *that* much air and reaction mass—and it'll have to be short rations, since you only provisioned for yourself. Call it thirty-five."

"Thirty-five kilowatt-hours apiece?" The old miner hawked and spat. "You fergit, mister—I'll have to go on short rations, too! Forty-five—and that's gifting!"

"Yes, it means I'm gifting you with an extra ten kwahers for each of us. I'll go up to forty."

"Forty kwahers apiece?" the miner bleated. "One hundred twenty all told? Mister, you know how much I'll lose from not working my claim while I haul you?"

"One hundred fifty kilowatt-hours, 3087 BTUs," the computer answered, "including reaction mass, air, and sustenance."

"There! See? I won't even break even!" The miner lifted his chin.

"But I've got five people, not three. It's two hundred kwahers total."

"Five . . . ?" The miner's gaze darted toward the companionway; Lona and Father Marco stepped into sight.

"You'll make a profit," Whitey pointed out.

"The hell I will!" The miner reddened. "That's two more for air, reaction mass, and rations!"

"Cost included," the computer informed him. "I counted the number of times the airlock door opened and closed."

The miner rounded on it, bawling, "Whose side are you on, anyway?"

"My apologies. I cannot resist accuracy in mathematics."

"Try a little," the miner growled, and turned back to Whitey. "Forty-nine kwahers ain't much of a profit, mister. Why don't you just ask me for the whole blasted boat?"

Whitey shrugged. "What do you want for it?"

The miner stared.

Then he said, flatly, "One thousand therms."

The computer said, "Current list price . . ."

"Shut up!" the miner roared. He turned back to Whitey with a truculent glare. "Well?"

"Oh, now, let me see . . ." Whitey stepped up to the console and turned the clinking pocket inside out. Coins cascaded onto the bench. He picked them up, stacking them on the console and counting slowly.

"Twenty . . . eighty . . . two hundred . . ."

The miner's eyes followed each coin, whites showing all around the irises.

"Eight hundred fifty-six . . . eight hundred fifty-seven . . . five kwahers . . . ten kwahers . . ."

The miner's mouth worked.

"Eight hundred fifty-seven therms, twenty-three kwahers, 2,392 BTUs." Whitey looked up at the miner. "Take it or leave it."

"Done!" The old man pounced on the stack, scooping them into his coverall pockets. "You bought yourself a burro-boat, mister!"

"And its computer." Whitey looked up at the grid above the console. "You work for me now."

"You were cheated," the computer informed him.

The old miner cackled.

"I know," Whitey said equably. "A beat-up old tub like this couldn't be worth more than five hundred therms."

The old miner glanced up at him keenly. "Then why'd you buy it?"

"I felt sorry for the computer." Whitey turned back to the grid. "You take orders from me, now—or from my niece, really; she's the pilot."

"Hi," she said, stepping up beside Whitey. "I'm Lona."

Dar stared, galvanized by the warmth in her voice. What a waste! All that allure cast before a machine—when it couldn've been coming at him!

Lona sat down at the console. "Let's get acquainted, FCC 651919. By the way, do you mind if I call you—uh—'Fess'?"

"Fess?" Dar frowned. "Why that?"

Lona looked back at him over her shoulder. "How would

you pronounce 'FCC'? Never mind, this's how *I'm* going to pronounce it!" She turned back to the grid. "If you don't mind, of course."

"My opinion is of no consequence," the computer answered. "My owner has delegated the necessary authority to you, so you may call me what you will."

"Not if you don't like it. A good computer tech needs a certain degree of rapport with her machine."

"Such rapport can only exist within your own consciousness," the computer replied. "I am incapable of feelings."

"All right, then, humor me; I need the illusion. Besides, since a computer's mathematical, it has to be electronically biased toward harmony and euphony. So I ask you again: does the name 'Fess' suit you?"

The computer hesitated. When it did speak, Dar could've sworn there was a note of respect in its tones. "The designation is pleasing, yes."

"Fine." Lona settled down to work, eyes glowing. "Now, Fess—how long ago were you first activated?"

"Five years, seven months, three days, six hours, twenty-one minutes, and thirty-nine seconds—Terran Standard, of course. I assume you do not require a more precise response."

"No, that'll do nicely." Lona's eyes gleamed. "And computers tend to be very durable these days; you're almost brand-new. With you in it, this burro-boat should've been worth twice what Grandpa paid for it."

The old miner cackled again.

"What's wrong with you?" Lona demanded.

The computer was silent for a minute; then it answered, "My first owner inherited vast wealth, and spent a great deal on material pleasures. . . ."

"A playboy." Dar could almost see Lona's mouth water. "I can see why he'd need a very loyal brain for his personal robot."

"Indeed. Due to his, ah, excesses, it was frequently necessary for me to assume piloting of his aeroyacht."

"Meaning he did the best he could to become a cask, and you had to fly him home when he was dead drunk."

"You choose accurate terms," the computer admitted. "On our last journey, however, he retained consciousness, though his judgment and reflexes were severely impaired. Consequently, I could not, according to my program, assume control until it became totally obvious that his life was imperiled."

"Meaning he was heading right for a collision, but you couldn't take over until it was almost too late. What happened?"

"By swerving the ship, I did manage to avoid damage to the cabin. Unfortunately, I was located in the aft bulkhead, which did suffer some impact."

Lona nodded. "What was broken inside you?"

"Nothing. But one capacitor was severely weakened. Now, in moments of stress, it discharges in one massive surge."

Lona frowned. "It could burn you out. Couldn't they fix it?"

"Not without a complete overhaul and reprogramming, which would have been more expensive than a new unit. They did, however, install a circuit breaker and a bypass, so that the capacitor now discharges in isolation. Unfortunately, I am thereby deactivated until the breaker is reset."

"If you were human, they'd call it a seizure. What'd your owner do?"

"He elected to sell me, which was economically wise."

"But lacked ethical harmony."

"Aptly put. However, there were no buyers on Terra, nor in the Martian colonies. No one wished to purchase an epileptic robot-brain."

"But in the asteroid belt," Lona murmured, "they'll buy anything."

"If the price is low enough, yes. Mine was seventeen therms."

"Of low price, but incalculable value." Lona smiled grimly. "After all, you've just saved all five of our lives."

"True, but it was a low-stress situation for me. In a moment of true crisis, I would fail, and cause your deaths."

Lona shook her head. "When things get that tense, I do my own piloting. The computer just feeds me the choices. No, I think you'll turn out to be the best thing that ever happened to me, Fess."

Which was something of a blow to Dar's ego; so maybe it was just his imagination that made the computer sound worshipful as it said, "I will do all that I can to serve you."

Lona just smiled.

"Apropos of which," the computer went on, "it might interest you to know that, while we have been talking, my former master was surreptitiously transmitting a message to Ceres City."

Every eye locked onto the old miner.

"That's garbage!" he spluttered. "You've been sitting here next to me the whole time! I didn't say a word!"

"Computers can't lie." Lona's gaze was a poniard.

"It's a breakdown! Malfunction! Programming error!"

"How'd he do it, Fess?" Lona never took her glare off the old miner.

"By pressing and releasing the transmission button," the computer answered. "That sent out carrier-wave pulses, which spelled out letters in the ancient Morse code."

"What did he say?" Whitey's voice was almost dreamy.

"'Solar Patrol, emergency!'" the computer recited, "'Burroboat FCC 651919 has just picked up five castaways. Have reason to believe they were crew and passengers of ship you were just chasing. Emergency!'"

Lona stood up with the slow, sinuous grace of a panther. Whitey stepped over beside her, his eyes chips of ice. "How do you want to be spaced—with or without your pressure suit?"

"But—but you can't do that!" The old miner cowered back against the bulkhead. "I picked you up! I saved your lives!"

"Your computer did," Lona corrected, "and it's ours now."

"The killing of humans," Fess murmured, "is the worst of crimes."

"What's your definition of 'human'?" Whitey growled, glaring at the miner.

"Treachery is right up there, too," Lona pointed out.

"True," Father Marco agreed, "but this man had no reason for loyalty to our little band—and every reason for loyalty to the government, and its Solar Patrol."

"If you can call blind faith 'reason,'" Whitey grunted. "But I guess you would, Father."

"Sir!" Father Marco stiffened. "I'll remind you that I'm an engineer as well as a priest! . . . But I am able to look at the situation from his viewpoint."

A gleam came into Whitey's eyes. "Well, then—why not let

him see things from *our* viewpoint? The one we had an hour ago."

"You wouldn't!" The miner blanched.

"Oh, don't worry." Whitey's lip curled. "They'll pick you up way before your supplies run out. What's he got on his claim, Fess?"

"A bubble-cabin ten feet down inside the asteroid," the computer replied, "with complete life-support systems and a month's rations."

"With a two-way radio?"

"No; he had mine, and didn't see the need for the expense. I do, however, have a spare emergency beacon."

"Perfect!" Whitey grinned. "He can call for help, but he can't rat on us. Oh, don't give me that terrified look, you old crawler! The patrol'll have you safe in Ceres City inside of a week!"

"Will that give us enough of a start?" Lona growled.

Whitey's lips pressed into a thin line. "It'll have to."

"Come back here, consarn you!" The voice echoed tinnily from the console's grid. "Come back here with my burro-boat, you blasted pirates! I'll have the law on you!"

"Damn!" Whitey snapped his fingers into a fist. "I should've made him sign a bill of sale! Now he'll have the Patrol hunting us down for piracy, on top of everything else."

Dar shrugged. "What does it matter? They'll chase us anyway, as soon as they pick him up and he tells them his story."

"I know, I know. But this'll give 'em a legal pretext for holding us."

"I think not," Fess demurred. "Since the transaction was a verbal contract, I recorded it as standard operating procedure."

Whitey's scowl dissolved into a grin. "Old Iron, I think you may have your uses."

"A lot of them; he wasn't really designed to pilot a boat, or even just to compute," said Lona. "He was designed as the brain of a humanoid robot."

"True, but my motor functions are adaptable to almost any sort of mechanical body," Fess explained. "I'm really quite generalized."

"And, therefore, versatile," Whitey concluded. "Well, what we need you to do most, just now, is to get us to Luna undetected."

"Why Luna?" Dar frowned. "We want to get to Terra."

"They don't allow spacers to land there," Sam explained. "Population's too dense; too much chance of a minor accident killing thousands of people. Spacers have to land on the moon, and take a shuttle down to Earth."

"Besides, we're running a little high on notoriety at the moment," Whitey added. "We need some sort of cover to let us travel—and I have a few friends on Luna."

Dar shrugged. "Why not? You have friends everywhere."

"Since you wish to avoid attention," Fess suggested, "it might be best if we wait for a large vessel to pass near, and match orbits, staying as close to it as possible, so that we're inside its sensor-range, and blend into its silhouette on any Patrol ship's screens."

Dar frowned. "Isn't that a little chancy?"

"Not for the two of us." Lona patted the console.

Dar felt a hot stab of jealousy. "What do you think that circuit-stack is—the boy next door?"

Lona gave him a look veiled by long lashes above a cat-smile. "Why not?" She turned to the console grid. "Where'd you grow up, electron-pusher?"

"I was manufactured on Maxima."

"Not exactly my home territory." Lona's eyes gleamed. "But I've heard of it. All they do there is make computers and robots, right?"

"That is their sole industry, yes. Their sole occupation of any sort, in fact."

"Sloggers," the girl translated. "A bunch of technological monks. They don't care anything about creature comforts; all they want to do is build robots."

"Not quite true," Fess corrected. "The few humans on Maxima have every conceivable luxury known—including a few unknown anywhere else, which they invented themselves. In fact, they live like kings."

"Oh, really!" Lona smiled, amused. "When're they planning to join the aristocracy?"

"Some have already begun buying patents of nobility from the Terran College of Heralds."

Lona lost her smile. "That takes *real* money! Where do they get it from?"

"From the sale of computers and robots." The computer added modestly, "Their products are already acknowledged to be the finest in any of the human-occupied worlds."

"So they sell for a small fortune each, of course. But the biggest luxury of all is servants—which they can't have, if there're only a few humans."

"True," Fess admitted, "but there are three robots to every human, on the average. They do not lack for servitors."

"Sounds like a great life," Whitey sighed, "if you don't mind settling down."

"And don't mind being stuck out in the middle of nowhere," Sam added.

"The planetoid is rather bleak," Fess admitted.

"'Planetoid'?" Lona frowned. "I thought Maxima was a world."

"It would be counted a small moon if it orbited a planet," Fess demurred. "But since it is located in Sirius's asteroid belt, it can only be counted as one of the larger of those asteroids."

Whitey frowned. "No atmosphere."

"No trees or grass," mused Sam.

"Only rocks and dust," murmured Dar.

"Only eight point seven light-years from Terra!" caroled Lona.

Dar stared. "You *like* the sound of the place?"

"It's practically heaven!" Lona squealed. "Nothing to do but design and build computers, laze around luxury, and hop around the corner to the fleshpots of Terra for the weekend! Where do I sign up?"

"Immigration is completely open," Fess said slowly, "but very few people choose to go there. It would be miserable for anyone who was poor—and only excellent cyberneticists can make money."

"I'll take it!" Lona crowed. "How do I get there?"

"That," Fess agreed, "is the rub. They will accept you—*if* you can get there."

"Grandpa!" Lona whirled around to Whitey. "Got a few royalty checks coming in?"

Whitey shrugged. "You can have the burro-boat when we're done with it, sweetheart—but first there's a little matter of saving democracy."

"Well, let's get it over with!" Lona whirled back to the console. "I want to get on with the really *important* things! Found a big liner yet, electro-eyes?"

"I have been tracking the SASE *San Martin* while we have been conversing," Fess answered. "It approaches above the plane of the ecliptic, inbound from Ganymede, and will pass us only one hundred thirty-seven kilometers away."

"Then let's *go!*" Lona grabbed her webbing and stretched it across her. "Web in, everybody!"

A chorus of clicks answered her. She grinned down at her console, then frowned at a blinking red light and looked back over her shoulder at Father Marco. "Look, Father, I know you trust in St. Christopher, and all that—but would you please buckle in?"

The monolith of a liner hurtled into eternal morning, its aft hull lost in the total black shadow of its bulging bridge. A tiny speck danced up to it from the asteroid belt, glinting in the sunlight. It swooped up to disappear in shadow under the monster's belly, where it clung like a pilot fish to a shark by the bulldog magnetic fields of the solenoids in its nose.

Inside, Dar asked, "Couldn't they spot us by the magnetic fields on their hull?"

"They *could*." Lona shrugged. "But why would they look for them?" She switched off the engines.

"It doesn't quite seem ethical," Father Marco mused, "hitching a free ride this way."

"Don't let it worry you, Father," Whitey assured him. "I own stock in this shipline."

10

The SASE *San Martin* drifted down toward its berth in the Mare Serenitatis. As it passed over Darkside, a mite dropped off its belly, falling toward the surface at no higher acceleration than lunar gravity could account for. No glint of light reflected from it to any watching eye in the shadows; and if anyone thought to glance at it on a sensor screen, they would surely think it nothing but another meteorite caught by the moon's gravity, coming to add one more crater to the ancient, pock-marked satellite.

It fell almost to the surface, so low that it was beneath the sensor-nets, and barreled over the jagged landscape.

Inside the cabin, Lona asked, "Is this what you'd call a 'stress situation'?"

"Not at all," Fess assured her. "It is simply a matter of adjusting our trajectory with the attitude jets, according to the irregularities in the landscape indicated by the sensors. At this low a speed, I always have several milliseconds to react."

"Piece of cake, huh? I think *you'd* better keep the con for this one."

"As mademoiselle wishes," Fess murmured.

He finally brought them to rest when the glittering lights of a spaceport appeared over the horizon. The burro-boat sank to the dust in the shadow of a huge crag, with the weary, thankful groan of engines idling down.

"I detected an airlock hatch in this outcrop," Fess informed them. "There is an electronics kit in the cabinet below the console; can any of you bypass the telltale on the hatchway, so that Spaceport Security will not know the lock has been opened?"

"Duck soup," Lona affirmed, "the instant kind. Where'll you be while we're gone?"

"In the shadow of a ring-wall, in a remote crater," Fess answered. "I will move as the shadows move. Next to the electronics kit, you will find a small transmitter of convenient size for a pocket. Press the button on it, and it will send a coded pulse to me. When I receive it, I will determine your location from its vector and amplitude, and bring the boat to you."

Lona opened the cabinet, pulled out the electronics kit, and flipped the recall unit to Whitey. He caught it and slipped it into a pocket inside his belt. "What's its range?"

"A thousand kilometers," Fess answered. "If you call from Serenitatis Spaceport, I will hear you."

"How about if we have to call you from Terra?"

"You will have to feed the signal through a stronger transmitter."

"We can't ask for a complete guarantee." Father Marco rose and turned toward the companionway. "I think I can remember where I left my pressure suit."

"There are ten air bottles in the locker with them," Fess noted.

"Well, thanks for all the help." Lona shooed the rest of the crew aft. "If anyone knocks while we're gone . . ."

"I will not let them in," Fess assured her.

The airlock hatch had a panel with a button inset beside it. Lona pulled out a screwdriver, tightened in the appropriate blade, and set it into the screw. It whined twice, and she lifted the panel away, handing it to Dar. Dar watched her clip a couple of leads in.

Above them, a twelve-foot parabolic dish moaned as it rotated a few degrees, and stopped.

Lona leaped back as though she'd been stabbed. Dar didn't blame her; it was all he could do to keep from dropping the plate. He wished he had; then he couldn't have heard the antenna's moan, since the sound conducted into his suit through the wires holding the plate.

Whitey leaned over, touching his helmet against Lona's. After a minute, she nodded, then stepped grimly back to the airlock. She took the plate from Dar and replaced it. Then she pressed the button, and the hatch slowly swung open. She gestured to Dar, and he stepped in. The others followed, Lona last. Whitey pressed a plate in the wall, and the hatch swung shut. Dar waited, fidgeting. Finally, the inner hatch opened. He stepped through into darkness, cracked his helmet seal, and tilted it back. He turned as a glow-light lit in Whitey's hand, saw Lona tilting her helmet back as Father Marco closed the airlock.

"What're we gonna do about the bypass?" Dar asked.

"Leave it there." Lona shrugged. "Can't be helped."

"Security patrols all the locks regularly," supplied Sam the bureaucrat. "They'll find it within a few days."

"Not exactly what I'd call a cheery thought, but it lightens the conscience. What'd you do to make that microwave dish swing around, Lona?"

"Nothing," Whitey answered. "That dish was beaming commercial 3DT programming down to the Terran satellites. When it gets done feeding its schedule to one satellite, it rotates to lock onto another one, and starts the whole feed all over again."

"3DT?" Dar frowned. "Why do they feed it from the moon?"

"Because that's where they make the programs, innocent!" Sam snorted.

Whitey nodded. "It takes a lot of room for enough 3DT sound stages to make new programming for a hundred twenty channels each, for twenty-six main cultures—and they have to make new stuff constantly. There just wasn't enough room for it in the major cities. So, bit by bit, the production companies shifted up here to Luna, where real estate was very cheap. The whole entertainment industry for the entire I.D.E. is in the moon now."

"Some say it belonged there all along, anyway," Lona muttered.

"Oh." Dar mulled it over. "So your publisher's offices are up here, too?"

"No, the print industry stayed Earthbound."

"Oh." Dar looked around at the rough-hewn tunnel walls scored with the screw-tracks of a laser-borer. "Well, not much we can do here, is there? I suppose our next step is to hop a shuttle to Terra."

"Wrong." Whitey shook his head. "That asteroid miner has probably sung the Solar Patrol a whole opera by now. Every security guard on the moon will have memorized little sketches of us. We've got to establish some kind of cover identities first, not to mention something by way of disguises."

Dar felt his stomach sink. "I should've known it couldn't be something straightforward and simple."

"Not on Terra," Sam agreed, "and the moon's just as bad." She turned to Whitey. "What kind of cover did you have in mind?"

"I didn't." Whitey started climbing out of his gear. "I recommend we rack these suits and find some place to hole up while we think about it."

Whitey had indeed emptied out his purse for the old miner— but he had another one hidden inside his belt. A brief stop at a department store turned up a coiffured wig and translucent dress for Sam, some hair dye and baggy tunic-and-trousers for Lona, some more hair dye and business outfits for the men. A somewhat longer stop at a comfort station produced remarkable changes in their appearance.

Whitey lined them up in the hallway, looked them over, and nodded. "You'll do. Just barely, maybe, but you'll do. Now, the odds are that your prints are on file somewhere—oh, you're sure of it, Dar? Well, the rest of you don't take chances, either. Don't put your thumbprint to anything. Don't look into anything that might want to scan your retinas, either—no peekholes in amusement galleries, eyepiece 3DT viewers, or lens-fitting scopes. Understand? Good. Because you're in the Big Sapphire's computer net now, folks, and every step you take is liable to monitoring by a computer tied into Terra Central.''

"Is it really that bad?" Dar asked.

"Worse," Sam confirmed.

Whitey nodded again. "Have no illusions, folks. Our chances of getting away free, back to the colony planets, are slightly worse than a dinosaur's caught in a glacier. I can only hope the gamble's worth the share-time. Okay—from now on, we're a free-lance production crew, looking for work. Anything I say about you, just confirm it, and don't look surprised. That includes your names; I'll be thinking up new ones for you as we go along. Ready? March!"

The "march" took them to a twenty-foot-high facade sheared out of the lunar rock, decorated with the modest gleam that comes of vast wealth, and the words "Occidental Productions, Inc." carved over the doorway and sheathed in platinum.

"This's just the production house," Whitey explained. "Manufactures most of the entertainment for one of the anglophone channels."

As they passed through the door, Dar found himself somehow totally certain that each person's height, weight, build, and coloring was registering in a computer somewhere deep inside the complex, which was trying to correlate it with the descriptions of all known criminals who might have a grudge against OCI. It was almost enough to make him turn right around and try to hijack the next outgoing spacer.

That didn't quite do it, but the foyer nearly did. Oh, the carpet was thick and the decoration superb; that wasn't the problem. It was the three uniformed guards, two androids, and five cameras, every one of which seemed to be looking directly at him. He stopped in his tracks, swallowing something that he hoped wasn't his heart.

But Whitey strolled ahead, confident and nonchalant, looking totally like your ordinary, everyday plutocrat.

"Service, citizen?" the lead guard asked with perfect, impersonal politeness.

"Gratitude, citizen. Mr. Tambourin, to see Mr. Stroganoff."

"Do you have an appoi . . ." the guard began, out of habit. But he closed his mouth, and gazed up at Whitey for a moment. Then he said, "Of course, Mr. Tambourin." He turned to murmur into a shielded com unit, waited, then murmured again. A delighted yelp sounded faintly from the unit. The guard listened, nodded, and turned back to Whitey. "He will be up in a few minutes, Mr. Tambourin. I regret the delay, but . . ."

"Of course." Whitey smiled indulgently. "He didn't know I was coming—but then, neither did I. Old friends, you understand."

"Perfectly." The guard was a good liar, anyway. "If you'll step into the lobby, Mr. Tambourin . . . ?"

Whitey smiled with a gracious, affable nod, and turned back to the "team." "Come along, children." He turned and ambled away toward the big interior doors.

Dar could fairly hear Sam bristling as they followed.

The androids swung the doors open, inclining in a slight bow as Whitey passed through. As Dar filed by, he definitely did not receive the expected impression of being scanned. What with one thing and another, it boosted his opinion of Whitey's status till it almost soared.

They entered a world of sybaritic luxury—parqueted walls with huge, inscrutable paintings that fairly screamed, "ART!" surrounding chairs that seemed to mold themselves around the sitter's body, a carpet so thick that it must have had a heartbeat, and a tastefully almost-dressed hostess who bent low to murmur, "Refreshment, citizen?"

A month ago, Dar would have grabbed her and enacted the wildest scene of animal lust ever recorded (which it no doubt would have been). But, with Lona in the same room, the woman just didn't seem interesting. "Yes, something to drink, thanks. Nothing too stimulating."

When she handed him the drink, he took a tiny sip—and euphoria/ecstasy/exaltation/Nirvana rose up behind his eyeballs and exploded in streamers that enveloped his brain. He sat rigid for a moment, then coughed delicately into his fist, and set the drink down. He'd had occasional experiences with the pipeweed of Wolmar, during prairie grass fires, and knew a depressant when one hit him. The lady had taken him at his word, and then some; he wondered if he'd unwittingly spoken a code phrase.

Then a medium-sized man with a giant of a personality swept into the lounge. "Tambourin! You infernal old scoundrel! Welcome back!"

Whitey stood up just in time to be almost knocked down by the dynamo's enthusiasm. All that kept him up was the bear hug as Stroganoff's rolling laughter boomed in their ears.

Then Stroganoff held Whitey back at arm's length, grinning from ear to ear. "Let me look at you, ancient my wastrel! . . . Not a day! Ten years, and he hasn't aged a wrinkle!"

"Well, I was old enough the last time I saw you." Whitey slapped Stroganoff on the shoulder. "Solid meat still, eh? You're not doing so badly yourself, David!"

"Not since they gave me that new stomach, no. But let me put on my manners a second. Glad to meet you, folks, I'm David Stroganoff. Who're your friends, Whitey?"

"Oh, this is Fulva Vulpes." Whitey stretched a hand out to Lona, whose eyes registered only the faintest of surprises. "She's my assistant director and director of editing."

Stroganoff's eyebrows went up. "Unusual combination." He pressed Lona's hand. "You must be very good with computers."

Now Lona did show surprise. She glanced at Whitey. Stroganoff chuckled. "And who's *this* enchantress?"

Sam answered the compliment with a glare, which brought even more charm feeding back from Stroganoff. "Watching to make sure the compliment's not more than its subject is worth, eh? Believe me, it's sound as an erg. What is she, Tod—your unit manager?"

"If it comes in a bureaucratic package and is wrapped with red tape, I can cut it," Sam said warily.

"Unit manager, it is! And you, citizen?"

"Coburn Helith, research and script development. Co's the one who came up with the idea for tying my verses into a story, Dave."

"Wh . . . Tod'n' I've been talking for some time now." Father Marco shook Stroganoff's hand without batting an eyelid. "I work from fundamental mythic structures—which means I have trouble thinking commercially, of course."

"Well, don't let it worry you—the myth hasn't been born

that can't be debased," Stroganoff said with a perfectly straight face. He turned to Dar. "And the young one, Tod?"

"Perry Tetic—'Pa' to us juveniles. He's the debaser you just mentioned." Whitey was obviously making it up as he went along. "The commercializer. He's very good at putting the most abstract ideas into words even the average dunce can understand."

"Oh, really." Stroganoff shook Dar's hand with guarded interest. "Let's hope we have time for a chat, Perry. I'm kind of interested in that kind of thing, myself."

"Let's *make* time." Dar was sure of being able to hold up his end of *that* conversation; anyone who'd been through Cholly's curriculum could. At least Whitey had given him a role he knew something about—and, looking back on it, he realized Whitey'd done the same for each of the others, too.

". . . a little behind the state of the art," he realized Lona was saying. "Could I have a look at your editing facilities?"

"Of course, of course! Tour of the whole place, in fact. Sound Stage Number Ten's the first stop—I just ducked out of there, and I've got to quack back to make sure everything's running smoothly. Come on, this way!"

He set off, Whitey beside him; the rest followed in their wake. They turned into a corridor that opened off the lounge, Whitey and Stroganoff talking double-speed.

"So you put together your own production unit, eh, Tod? Glad to see you were listening when I kept saying you ought to package up a tank-play—but I didn't expect you to raft your own team!"

"Only way I'll touch it, Dave." Whitey shook his head, jaw set. "With me in control over the whole thing. You may notice we're lacking a producer, though."

"Yeah, I did kind of notice that." Stroganoff grinned like a shark. "Is that an offer, Tod?"

"What do you want—thumbscrews?"

"Always the consummate diplomat. You know I can't resist a chance on something this good—but you need backing, too. You can't be crazy enough to try to finance something like this on your own."

"Well, I don't exactly have a reputation for thrift." Whitey grinned. "But I'm not *that* far gone."

"No thrift, my Aunt Asteroid," Lona muttered. "He's got enough in the Bank of Terra to buy a small planet—developed!"

It was a good chance to get close to her. Dar sidled up and whispered, "They're buddies. How come Stroganoff keeps calling him 'Tod'?"

" 'Cause he doesn't know about 'Whitey,' " Lona muttered back. "Nobody does, outside the taverns."

Well. That also explained the security problem that had been giving Dar heartburn. He'd thought Whitey was bringing sure disaster down on them by using his real name—but anyone on Falstaff who'd told Canis Destinus that Whitey the Wino was helping Dar Mandra wouldn't have known him as Tod Tambourin. So his best alias was his real name.

"Right in here." Stroganoff hauled open a door that looked like a huge airlock hatch. "Stage Ten." As Sam filed past him, he added, " 'Fraid I didn't catch your name, citizen."

"She's Ori Snipe," Whitey called back over his shoulder, and Sam forced a quick smile and handshake as she left Stroganoff in her wake.

They walked into chaos. Dar's first whirling impression was of a thousand people frantically everywhere, doing purposeless things and shouting at each other in an arcane jargon. But after a few minutes, he began to be able to make sense out of it. There weren't really a thousand people—more like three dozen. And they weren't really moving very quickly—it was just that there were so many of them moving in so many different directions that it *seemed* frantic. He locked his gaze onto one woman and watched her for a while. She was riding around on a lift, a slender telescoping column on top of a three-wheeled dolly, adjusting the lights that hung far above him. Her movements were methodical, almost plodding—nothing chaotic about them at all. He dropped his gaze to watch another person, then another.

"It may look confusing," Stroganoff said beside him, "but everyone knows what he or she has to do, and does it."

Dar glanced up at him, saw a frown. "Something wrong?"

Stroganoff shook his head. "No, it's all going smoothly. A little ahead of schedule, in fact."

"Then what's the matter?"

"Oh, nothing, really." Stroganoff forced a smile. "It's just that sometimes the phoniness of it gets to me."

Dar frowned. "But you're making stories, here—and stories have to be made-up; they *can't* be real."

"Oh yes, they can." Stroganoff pursed his lips. "There're a lot of really great stories in the history books."

The statement had a ring of familiarity to Dar; suddenly, he could almost believe he was back in Cholly's Tavern. He cleared his throat to get rid of a sudden tightness. "That almost sounds like education."

"Sh!" Stroganoff hissed, finger to his lips. He glanced around furtively, then breathed a sigh of relief. "Thank heaven! No one heard you!"

"Why?" Dar stared. "What's wrong with education?"

"Be quiet, can't you?" Stroganoff glanced around again. "Don't you dare say that word in here!"

"Why? What's the matter with ed . . . uh . . . hum . . . *you* know!"

"What's the matter with it is that it pulls low ratings," Stroganoff explained in a lowered voice. "*That* kind of program never attracts more than a handful of viewers."

"Yeah, but that's a handful of all the people in Terran space! A handful out of a trillion-and-a-half!"

"So that 'handful' is a billion or so people; yes, I know." Stroganoff nodded. "But that never sinks in, to the people who run this company. All they know is that they can get a higher price for a more popular show."

"So." Dar frowned. "You don't dare put in anything ed . . . uh . . . at all deep, or they'll cancel the script."

Stroganoff nodded. "That's the basic idea, yah."

"And you don't like it that way?"

Stroganoff hesitated; then he shook his head.

"So you don't like your job?"

"Oh, I *like* it well enough." Stroganoff looked around him. "There is still a fragrance left, out of the old glamor I thought was here when I was a kid. And it *is* exciting, putting together a story, even if it's purely trivial dross. It's just that . . . well, sometimes it gets to me."

"But *why*?"

"Because I wanted to educate." Stroganoff turned back to

Dar with a gentle, weary smile. "Not just a few interested students in a classroom—but the whole, huge mass of the audience, the billions of people who *aren't* interested, who don't *want* to learn all those 'irrelevant facts' about Socrates and Descartes, and Simon de Montfort and the Magna Carta."

"I kinda thought knowing about the Magna Carta was necessary for *all* the citizens in a democracy," Dar said uneasily. "At least, if that democracy is going to survive . . ."

"*If*," Stroganoff said, with a sour smile. "Look around you."

Dar swallowed. "I think you've got a point."

"Oh, I know I do." Stroganoff looked up at the lights on their grid of pipes, gazing at them but not seeing them. "And I knew 3DT was the perfect thing to teach with—give the people lectures, but make them so visually interesting that they'd watch it in spite of themselves. Don't just tell them about Waterloo—*show* it to them, the actual place, the way it is today, and the way it was then. Then show them the battle, reenact it, cut to an overhead shot so they can see how Wellington and Napoleon were moving their troops . . ." He trailed off, a faraway look in his eyes.

"Wait a minute!" Dar stabbed a finger at the producer. "I saw that battle! In an old 3DT program! The charge, and the horses galloping into the sunken road—then you saw from overhead, watched Napoleon's army folding in, but while you were watching it, you heard Wellington describing his strategy . . ."

"Sure you didn't read that in a book somewhere?"

"Yeah, but it didn't make any sense until after I saw the program! *Josephine's Boudoir*, that was it!"

"Yeah, it sure was." Stroganoff's mouth worked as though he'd tasted something bitter. "I'm surprised you're old enough to have seen it."

"I was way out on a, um, frontier planet. I remember it was mostly a pretty risque version of Napoleon's private life—but it did have the battle of Waterloo in it."

"Yes. It did have that." Stroganoff smiled out at the studio. "Not much education in it—but some. It'll do."

"Why didn't you go into educational programming?" Dar asked softly.

Stroganoff shrugged, irritated. "I did, fresh out of college. But they insisted that everything be dull and dry. Claimed the students wouldn't take it seriously if it was too entertaining—and they had research studies to back them up. Strange as it may seem, most people don't believe it's education if it isn't dull—and that means it reaches a very few people, indeed."

"Most of whom would learn by themselves, anyway?"

Stroganoff nodded. "The minority who read. Yes. They're wonderful people, but they're not the ones I was worried about, not the ones who endangered democracy."

Dar nodded. "It's the ones who don't want to learn that you want to reach."

"Right." Stroganoff closed his eyes, nodding. "Not that it's going to do any good, of course. Oh, if I'd started a hundred years ago, maybe . . ."

"It can't be *that* bad!" Dar frowned. "I thought a democracy had to become decadent before it collapsed."

"So?"

"But we're *not*!" Dar spread his hands, hooked into claws. "Where're the orgies? Where's the preoccupation with sex? Where're the decadent aristocrats?"

"At the I.D.E. enclave in New York." Stroganoff gave him a wry smile. "Ever seem 'em? Funny about that . . ."

"Well, okay. But the orgies . . ."

"Been looking for them pretty hard, haven't you? Well, don't worry—they don't need to be there. How many orgies do you think the average Roman shopkeeper saw? Look for the decadence in the small things—the people who don't bother to vote because the candidates're 'so much alike.' The people who think it's fine for the government to crack down, as long as it doesn't interfere with their getting their supply of their favorite euphoric. The people who think talking politics is in poor taste. *There's* the decadence that kills a democracy."

"And it traces back to lack of knowledge," Dar said softly.

"Not all of it." Stroganoff frowned; then he nodded. "But a lot of it. Yah. A lot."

"Ever hear of Charles T. Barman?" Dar said slowly.

"The rogue educator?" Stroganoff grinned. "Yeah, I've heard of him. Read his main book, even. Yes, I've followed his career with great interest. Great interest. Yes." He turned to Dar, his eye gleaming. "They never caught him, you know."

"No," Dar said judiciously, "they never did."

Dar took a sip and frowned up at Lona over the rim of his glass. "What's he doing in there?"

"Creating," Lona answered.

"For so long?"

"Long?" Lona smiled without mirth. "It's only been six hours so far."

"It takes that long to do up one of those—what'd Stroganoff call it . . . ?"

"Series format," Sam reminded him.

"Yeah, one of those."

"He finished that three hours ago." Lona took a sip. "Stroganoff needs the script for the first program, too."

"But he's just talking into a voice-writer! How can a one-hour script take more than an hour?"

"It's thinking-time, not talking-time. And don't forget, it's got to be verse. That's the only reason Stroganoff might be able to persuade OPI to do it—because it's a 3DT series of Tod Tambourin's poetry."

"And poems take a great deal of work," Father Marco said softly. "Actually, I don't see how he can possibly have a full hour's worth of verse by 10:00 hours tomorrow."

"Oh, verse he can manage." Lona glanced at the closed bedroom door that hid Whitey. "Poetry would take forever— but he isn't worrying about quality. Verse he can grind out by the yard."

"What if inspiration should strike?" Father Marco asked quietly.

"Then," Lona said grimly, "we may be in here for a week."

"Oh, well." Dar got up and went over to the bar-o-mat for a refill. "At least he gave us a nice waiting room." He looked around at the luxurious hotel-suite living room. "Come to think of it, I hope inspiration *does* strike. . . ."

* * *

Dar had a vague memory of Father Marco shepherding them all to their bedrooms, muttering something about an early day tomorrow, but it was rather fuzzy; a tide of some nefarious mist reeking of Terran brew seemed to have rolled in as the light faded. He awoke with a foul taste in his mouth, a throbbing ache in his temples, and an acute sensitivity to noises. He dropped back against the pillow, but sleep refused to return. Finally he resigned himself to having to pocket the wages of sin—though the pocket in question was feeling rather queasy at the moment—and slowly, very carefully, swung his feet over the side of the bed. He clutched his head and waited for the room to stop rolling, gulping air furiously to quiet his stomach. Eventually, it sort of worked, and he staggered to his feet. Then he had to lean against the wall, gasping like a beached fish, to wait until things stabilized again. It was a longer wait, but it worked, and finally he was able to stagger out into the sitting room.

The light had been turned down to a dim glow from the ceiling, thank heaven—but there was a babble of voices. Strangely, they didn't make his head hurt any worse—and, even more strangely, there was only one person in the room.

That person was Whitey, sprawled in a recliner with a strange glow in his eyes. He noticed Dar, cocked his head to the side, and held out a tumbler full of a thick, brownish liquid. Dar groped for it, seized it, and drank it off in one long gulp. Then his eyes bulged as his stomach gave a single, tumultuous heave. He swallowed it down and exhaled in a blast. "My lord! What *is* that stuff?"

"Uncle Whitey's Homemade Hangover Helper," Whitey answered. "Don't ask what's in it."

"I won't," Dar said fervently. He groped his way to a recliner and collapsed into it. "How'd you know I was going to need it?"

"I looked in on you halfway through the 'night.'" Whitey grinned. "You were a gas."

Dar frowned. "A gas?"

"Throughly tanked," Whitey explained.

A hazy memory of Whitney's bleached face, peering down intently, floated through Dar's mind. "Oh, yeah. I remember something about it." He frowned, then forced a feeble chuckle. "Yeah, you . . . no, it must've been a dream."

"It wasn't. Why'd you think it was?"

"Because you asked . . . and I told . . ." Dar swallowed heavily. "No. Had to be a dream."

"Asked what? Told me what?"

"Well—my mission. What I'm supposed to do on Terra."

"No dream," Whitey assured him. "And I timed it just right. *In vino veritas*."

"'In wine there is truth'?" Dar stared, aghast.

Whitey's eyelids drooped. "You *do* know a little Latin! Amazing, in this day and age. Who managed to drum it through your head?"

"My old boss, a bartender named Cholly. But . . ."

"Hm. Must be an interesting man." Whitey's eyes were glowing again. "Like to meet him sometime."

"You will, at the rate we're going. You won't have any choice in the matter." Dar swallowed. "What'd I tell you?"

"What do you remember?"

"That I had a message from General Shacklar to the I.D.E. top brass—about a plan for a coup. . . ."

Whitey nodded. "Perfect recall."

Dar groaned and crumpled, covering his eyes.

Whitey leaned forward and patted his shoulder. "Don't take it so hard, laddie—we all make mistakes the first time out. At least, if you had to spill the beans, you did it to a friend."

"'Friend'?" Dar glared up. "How can I be sure, now?"

"Because I've spent a lot of money, and put myself in quite a bit of danger, just to help you—and when I heard your story, I was glad I had. Not that I think we can succeed, mind you— but I can't let democracy go down without a fight."

Somehow, Dar believed him. He frowned up at Whitey, against his headache. "You must've had a hunch I was doing something you believed in, then—to put yourself and Lona at risk."

"Well, yes." Whitey settled back, picking up a glass. "I did have a notion the gamble was worth it. Lona's another matter, though. I didn't make her come. She could've stayed behind, with plenty of money, and she knew it."

Dar's brows pulled together. "She doesn't strike me as the self-sacrificing sort."

"She isn't. That line she feeds out, about wanting to wallow in luxury with plenty of leisure time to slaughter, is true down to the word—but she knows there are more important things. Such as having one person nearby who really cares about her— me—and freedom, without which she wouldn't have a chance at luxury."

Dar looked around. "Where is she?"

Whitey jerked his head toward the closed door. "Proofing the script."

"It's done?" Dar's gaze steadied on Whitey's face. "Any good?"

Whitey shrugged irritably. "Does it matter? It'll get you where you need to go; that's the important thing."

Suddenly, something seemed wrong. Dar lifted his head. "What happened . . . ? Oh. The voices stopped."

"Voices? The 3DT, you mean?"

"Is that where they were coming from?" Dar turned to the wall screen, and saw the word "EMERGENCY!" floating in a blue sea. A voice said, "Indulgence, citizens. We have to interrupt to bring you news of a conspiracy against the whole of the Interstellar Dominion Electorates." The word dissolved into the head and shoulders of an earnest-looking, handsome older man. "Sehn Loffer here, with news directed from I.D.E. Internal Security. We are threatened, fellow citizens— threatened by an insidious evil, creeping up on us everywhere, to choke the life out of our democracy and suck the blood of its freedom."

Whitey muttered, "Lousy prose!"

Dar stared at him, appalled. "But he's the top newsface! They're hearing him all over the Solar System—and FTL liners will take this recording-cube to all the colonies within the month!"

"Yeah. 'Nothing succeeds like excess.' "

"The villain may be your neighbor, your friend, your co-worker," Loffer went on. "No one can know where the evil ones lurk—because, citizens, they are telepaths!"

Whitey stared. Dar goggled.

"Insidious telepaths, their tendrils of thought snaking out to enfold *your* brains! All through the I.D.E. they are. How do we know? Because, for a month now, Security has been chasing a notorious telepath all the way from the marches, the outermost colonies, here to Luna itself! Time and again, they have almost caught him, only to have him whisked away into hiding, by local assistance!''

The ''local assistance'' swore under his breath.

''Who would aid a rogue telepath?'' Loffer declaimed. ''Who but *another* telepath? Wherever this monster goes, he finds help—so there must be telepaths spread throughout the I.D.E., helping him, working secretly, to undermine the foundations of our freedom and destroy our government—to take power themselves!''

''Uh—don't I detect a few flaws in his logic?'' Dar asked.

''Logic? What's that?'' Whitey snorted. ''It *feels* right, doesn't it? So it's *got* to be true—doesn't it?''

''But take heart, citizens!'' Suddenly, Loffer fairly oozed calm strength. ''Our noble Solar Patrol is pursuing this monster, and will not rest until they destroy him!''

''What does 'right to fair trial' mean?'' Whitey wondered.

Smiling confidently, Loffer dissolved into a sea of plain blue, filling the screen. A voice said, ''We now return you to 'Starship Captain's Wife.' ''

Whitey pressed the button in the arm of his recliner, and the picture faded into an assortment of fruits in a basket; the wall-screen became only a three-dimensional still picture again.

''Uh—I thought reporting was supposed to be objective, just telling you the facts they're sure of,'' Dar said tentatively.

Whitey gave him a peculiar look. ''No, you haven't been to Terra before, have you?''

''But . . . *why*?'' Dar exploded. ''Announcements like that are going to panic the public! Why get everybody into a state of terror about it?''

''I have a notion,'' Whitey muttered, ''but I hope I'm wrong.''

''It's got to be because they want to make absolutely sure they catch me. But why? Am I that much of a threat to them? And how'd they get the idea I'm a telepath?''

''Maybe they didn't. 'Telepath' is a nice scare word, conjuring up somebody poking into your most private affairs, somebody having a huge, unnatural advantage that makes everybody else feel inferior—and, therefore, all the more willing to go out and help hunt him down. Useful, if they want to make sure they catch you. And as to your being a threat, well—the answer is, you don't have to be *much* of a threat. Conspirators tend to not want to take chances, no matter how small. The LORDS party in the I.D.E. Assembly want to restrict individual rights, and they've never been so strong. Their opposition has fractured into a dozen splinter groups. If there's an opposition leader, it's Tam Urkavne, the chairman of the CPR—the Coalition for the Protection of Rights. At least he's officially the Opposition speaker. But his 'Coalition' is pretty weak—its members spend their time arguing over policy, instead of trying to *do* something."

"But the LORDS aren't trying to overthrow the whole I.D.E. government, are they?"

Whitey shrugged. "If they are, they're not saying—of course. That's high treason, boy. No, you may be sure whoever's behind the coup are keeping their lips well sealed, and want to make sure everybody else does, too."

The bedroom door opened.

"Well, enough of politics." Whitey craned around in his seat, looking back over his shoulder. "Hi, honey."

Lona swayed out into the sitting room, and the sight of her made Dar decide to stay among the living. He decided Whitey's hangover cure *was* working. But she had a kind of glassy look in her eyes, a sort of fevered brilliance. Was she ill?

"I told you, you shouldn't have stayed up waiting for me to finish," Whitey said, frowning. "You get to bed, honey; you can still catch about three hours sleep before we have to leave."

"How can I, with *this* running through my head?" Lona shoved a sheaf of papers at him.

Whitey squared the sheets on his lap, smiling up at her, almost shyly. "Liked it, huh?"

Lona nodded, with a tight smile; she looked as though she were about to explode.

Whitey grinned and turned to Dar, holding out the sheaf. "First hard copy. See what you think."

Dar took the script and began to scan it. His eyes locked in after the third line, tracking the print at speech-speed, words thundering in his head. "Whitey, this is . . ."

". . . wonderful!" Father Marco breathed, looking up from the last page. Sam looked up from her copy with a numbed gaze and an awed nod.

"Rough," Whitey grumbled, flushed with pleasure. "Needs polish. Lots of it."

"It's a masterpiece," Sam whispered.

Whitey sat still a moment, then gave a brusque nod. "Good. Yes. Rough, but—it's good. Thank you."

Lona laid a gentle hand on his shoulder. "9:30 hours, Grandpa."

"Yeah." Whitey heaved himself to his feet with a sigh. "Time to go meet Stroganoff, children—the Knight of the Shining Laser, who will do battle with the Dragon of Commerce for us. Ready?"

Dar paced the lounge furiously, hands locked behind his back. "What's he doing in there—reading them the whole script?"

"Calm down, Da . . . uh, Perry." Whitey leaned back in his chair like a cat by a fire, a tall drink in his hand. "It means it's going well. If the execs didn't like his presentation, he'd've been out half an hour ago."

The door opened, and Stroganoff shuffled in, holding the script in front of him as though it were a tray, eyes glazed.

Dar pounced on him. "Well? What's the word? They like it? They gonna buy it? What?"

Stroganoff's head swiveled toward him, but his gaze went right through Dar. Father Marco pried Dar away with a soothing murmur, and Whitey echoed him: "Calm down, Perry. They won't finish deciding for a while yet . . . How'd it go, David?"

Stroganoff's head turned toward Whitey, but his eyes still didn't quite focus. "Tod . . . why didn't you warn me?"

"Warn?" Whitey frowned. "About what?"

"About *this*!" Stroganoff held the script out reverently. "I gave 'em the overview, and the audience potential, the costminimalization, and the company-image enhancement, and they sat there looking bored, so I started reading them the first few lines, just to give 'em the idea—and I couldn't stop! I just kept going, right through the whole thing—and they didn't cut me off! Not a word! They actually *listened*!"

Whitey grinned and sat back. "Well. Nice to be appreciated."

"Appreciated! My lord, Tod, that's topping the Prize!"

Dar heaved a silent sigh. He might make it to Earth, after all.

They were laughing and chattering as they came back into their hotel, riding high on a triumph—until a grave-faced major domo stepped up to Whitey and intoned, "Mr. Tambourin, sir?"

The laughter cut off as though it had been sliced with a razor blade. Whitey turned to the man in livery, frowning. "Yes?"

"There's a call waiting, from Mr. Horatio Bocello, sir. He's been quite insistent in his demands that he speak with you."

Whitey's face cracked into a cream-whiskered grin. "Old Horatio!"

Sam was staring, shocked. Father Marco blinked. Even Lona looked impressed. Dar looked around. Then they all jumped to catch up with Whitey.

But the major domo was ahead of them. "Ah, Mr. Tambourin?"

Whitey looked back. "Yes?"

"He really has been *quite* insistent, sir. The staff would very much appreciate it if you would take the call as soon as you arrive in your suite."

"Yeah. I know what Horatio's like when he gets 'insistent.'" Whitey's grin was downright evil. "Don't worry, my good man—I'll hit the phone as soon as I'm upstairs. You can tell Terra the call's going through." His hand brushed the major domo's as he turned away; the man glanced at his palm, and his eyebrows shot up. "Thank you, sir."

"My pleasure. Come on, troops!" Whitey was striding away toward the lift tube.

His "crew" lurched into motion behind him. "Who's Horatio Bocello?" Dar hissed.

"Only the richest man on Terra, gnappie!" Sam hissed back.

"Which means, in the whole system. Devout Catholic, too. . . ." Father Marco said thoughtfully.

"Patron of the arts—especially Grandpa's," Lona added.

Dar swallowed heavily, and walked faster.

When Whitey careened through the door, the com screen was already alive with white noise, its beeper beeping. Whitey pressed the "answer" button and thumbed the toggle that uncapped his camera. The screen cleared, showing a thin, long-jawed, bony face with a receding iron-gray hairline, a blade of a nose, and burning eyes. The eyes focussed on Whitey, and the face grinned. "Tambourin, you old scalawag! Where've you been?"

"In a hundred bars on fifteen planets, Cello." Whitey grinned back at him. "You want exact figures, you'll have to tell me how long it's been."

"What—five years, this time? Why don't you write, reprobate?"

"Buy it from your book-channel, windy. How's your empire?"

Bocello shrugged, with a trace of annoyance. "You win some, you lose some, and it keeps growing, all by itself."

Whitey nodded. "No change."

"It was a lot more fun back in the Northeast Kingdom."

"I know." Whitey smiled fondly, gazing back down the years. "Running around in homemade armor, chopping at each other with rattan swords."

"And for the parties, dressing up like a fourteenth-century duke. Except you, of course. You never could decide whether you wanted to be a knight or a troubadour."

Dar nudged Lona, having a legitimate reason, and whispered, "What're they talking about?"

"A bag of mixed nuts," Lona whispered back. "Some group they both belonged to when they were young. Used to go out to a park on weekends and pretend they were still living in the middle ages."

"Well, I finally did." Whitey's smile gentled. "I swung to the troubadour—and you finally accepted your birthright obligations, and turned into a baron."

"Yes, without the title." Bocello's face clouded. "But it's not as much fun, Tod."

"You've got to lock into reality sometime, Cello. You keep tabs on the old Kingdom?"

Bocello nodded. "Still. I'm still a member. I sneak into the annual festival every now and then. You should, too."

"I do, when I run into a Kingdom. But there aren't too many of 'em on the colony planets yet, Cello. Hold onto your sword, Your Grace—you may need it."

Bocello was suddenly alert. "You see the signs, too, eh? But I don't think there'll be chaos, Tod."

"No," Whitey agreed, "just the reverse. It's a dictator that's coming, not a warlord. Can't you do anything about it, Cello? You, with all your money!"

Bocello shook his head sadly. "I always sneered at politics, Tod—and now it's too late." He frowned, suddenly intent. "*You're* not planning to try to stop it, are you? To throw yourself in the path of a runaway destrier?"

"Romanticism's for the young, Cello," Whitey said gently. "No, I just got a *modern* idea, that's all."

"Yes, I heard." Bocello's face split into a mischievous grin. "And I *love* it! *Damn* fine poem, Tod! *Damn* fine."

Whitey scowled. "Got eyes and ears everywhere, don't you?"

"Tod!" Bocello protested, wounded. "I own OPI—or fifty-one percent of it, anyway. They knew it was too hot to handle, so they bucked it on up to me fastest!"

"*You're* going to decide whether or not my epic gets made?" Dar held his breath.

Bocello shrugged impatiently. "What is there to decide? The way your last book sold, we couldn't possibly lose money on Tod Tambourin's first screenplay! All I want to know is, how quickly can you do it?"

Whitey grinned. "My crew's ready to go tomorrow, Cello."

"Wonderful. But you'll need a *little* while to cast the actors and have the sets designed and built."

"Yeah, but we can shoot the documentary sequences meanwhile. And, Cello . . ." Whitey's voice lowered. ". . . if we're going to have the I.D.E. Assembly and the

Executive Secretary in that one sequence, I think we'd better shoot them *fast*."

"Yes, I know." Bocello sobered. "The whole thing's built around the I.D.E." He leaned forward, suddenly intense, eyes burning. "*Very* fast, Tod—before the whole program's just an historical document!"

Dar fastened his webbing and looked around at the luxurious cavern of the shuttle's passenger cabin. "Little different from a burro-boat, isn't it?"

"You could put two of them inside here," Sam agreed. "Maybe three."

Dar swiveled his head to look at her, puzzled. "You've been awfully moody these past couple of hours. What's the matter?"

"Nothing." Sam shook her head with total conviction. "Absolutely nothing is wrong." But she still gazed off into space.

"It was that call from Horatio Bocello that did it, isn't it? What was so bad about it—didn't realize the I.D.E. was in *this* bad a shape?"

"*That* is saddening," Sam agreed. "But I'm not saddened."

"Then what are you?"

"Dazzled," she said frankly.

Dar stared at her for a second. Then he smiled. "Never saw anybody that rich talking just like an ordinary person, huh? Yeah, it kind of got to me, too."

"Not that," she objected. ". . . Well, maybe a little. But what got me was his *face*!"

"Face?" Dar stared again.

She nodded. "That forehead! That blade of a nose! Those cheekbones! And . . . those *eyes*!"

Dar turned his head a little to the side, watching her. "Are you trying to tell me you thought he was *handsome*?"

"'Handsome.' That's a good word for it. 'Attractive' is better. Maybe even . . . 'compelling.'"

Dar began to have serious doubts. "I thought you were supposed to be an ascetic—an anti-materialist."

She turned a gaze full of scorn on him. "You take beauty wherever you find it, gnappie, and you keep the memory of it alive in your heart. I'll probably never even talk to this man and, when this whole escapade is over, never see him again, either. But I'll never forget that I did, and the memory of it will make the rest of my life that much richer."

As they were crowding off the shuttle at Newark Interplanetary, Dar overheard some girl-talk between Sam and Lona.

"Married? Never," Lona said firmly. "Never even seen with a lady 'friend' very often. That's brought the usual run of snide comments, of course."

"About his masculinity?"

"And his sexuality, period! He reinforces that one, too—claims to be asexual. Says there's no point in sex unless you're in love."

"What a medieval romantic," Sam murmured dreamily.

Somehow, Dar didn't think they were talking about Whitey.

They strode down the concourse toward the main terminal, laughing and chattering. Dar felt heady, almost drunk. He was on Terra! The Terra of his history books, of Cicero and Caeser and the Plantagenets and Lincoln! The Terra of fable and wonder! He walked on a thick red carpet, surrounded by wall-screens flashing displays of arrival and departure times between spates of advertising—just the way he'd pictured it from his books!

Suddenly the wall-screens cleared. A giant chime sounded, reverberating throughout the entire building. All around them, conversation slackened and died; all faces turned to the wall-screens.

"Citizens," a resonant voice intoned, "the Honorable Kasi Pohyola, Chairman of the LORDS, and Majority Leader in the Assembly of Electors of the Interstellar Dominions."

A stern but gentle face appeared, surmounted by wavy, snow-white hair, gazing directly at Dar. He almost jumped out of his skin.

"Citizens," the face intoned in a deep, resonant voice, "a huge calamity has befallen us. An insidious danger stalks toward us across the stars—nay, *has* stalked us, has arrived, is even now in our midst! It may be the person beside you, or behind you—or even inside your head! For know, citizens, that there is no real guarding against this evil monstrosity, no wall that will seal it away, no shield that will stand against it—for it is a *telepath*! Even now, he may be probing your mind, wrapping his thoughts about your heart, cozening your innermost secrets!

"But worse, citizens—he is not alone! Our agents have shadowed him from the outermost colony planets, in to Terra herself—always treading upon his shadow, but never able to pounce on the creature—for always, just as they were about to close their trap, he has disappeared, spirited away by his friends and sympathizers on a thousand planets!"

"Only ninety-three," Whitey muttered, "as of last year's census report."

"Who could have assisted such a one?" Pohyola rumbled. "Who would give aid and solace to a being who could probe their innermost thoughts—save *another* telepath? That, citizens, is why we are sure there are many telepaths, spread throughout the Terran Sphere, on each and every one of its member planets—and including Terra herself!"

A horrified murmur and buzzing of oaths and curses spread through the concourse. It fairly made the hairs stand on Dar's head. He glanced at his companions—they were all watching with set, pale faces, lips drawn tight.

Except Whitey. He just looked sad.

Pohyola stared into the camera, not speaking, just holding the viewers' gazes with his own—apparently he'd been planning on the reaction. Just as it was quieting, he began to speak again. "Our vaunted I.D.E. Security Force has been impotent to stop them—these millions of highly trained warriors for whom we pay trillions of therms every year! Are they inept? No! Are they lazy or cowardly? No! They are brave, capable heroes, every one of them! Then, why have they not been able to seize this horror? Because, while he has been slipping into hiding, they have had to find a magistrate and present proof of need for a search warrant! Because they have had to waste time securing *proof* of his guilt in order to obtain that warrant—though they have *known*, all along, what he is! Because the courts will not allow these fine officers to monitor the communications between this monster and his minions!"

He glared down out of the screen in righteous wrath. "They

are impeded at every turn, they are balked at every approach! And, while the courts dither and obstruct them, the telepath moves unimpeded onto our fair mother planet!'' He shook his head slowly. "Citizens, this has gone too far! This obsession with legal pettifoggery has now imperiled your lives and mine, nay, even the fabric of our whole society! Who now can feel free to nurture secret hopes or longings, to dream of his beloved or reflect on his sins—knowing that, every moment, another's mind may have wormed its way into his, cozening up to his dearest, most cherished secrets!

"Nay! The time has come to put a *stop* to the nonsense! To purge the technicalities and loopholes that let the criminal escape while the law-abiding citizen shuffles in chains! To exorcize the demons of law! Make no mistake, citizens—a vast conspiracy of telepaths has wrapped its coils around us, and is even now beginning to squeeze the life from our democracy!

"Will they triumph? Nay!" he thundered. "We will tear their coils apart, we will rip them asunder! The law will cease obstructing the champions of justice!"

Then, suddenly, his eyes were locked onto Dar's again, burning. "But this cannot be done while Executive Secretary Louhi Kulervo dithers and vacillates! A man of decision must take the helm, a man of true strength, who does not waste expanses of time mewling about 'sacred trusts' and 'constitutionality'!"

He took a deep breath, very obviously fighting down wrath, struggling for composure, then said more calmly:

"It is for these reasons, citizens, that I will, today, demand a vote of confidence in the Assembly, and a general election. We must succeed in forcing this referendum, my fellow citizens— or we will waken one morning to find ourselves enmeshed in chains of thought! Contact your Elector, now, this minute, and tell him to demand an election. We must have it, citizens—we must have a man of decision and action to lead us—or the light of democracy will flicker out, and die!"

The image on the screen flickered out, and died.

A roar of conversation burst out all around them.

Whitey glanced back at his adrenalized crew, looking a little nervous himself. "Ah . . . I think we should just start drifting toward the main terminal . . . and try to look surprised, folks."

That wasn't hard. Dar felt as though he'd just been knocked spinning by a shockwave. It wasn't just that one fleeing little ship had been turned into a conspiracy—or that the coup was leaping out into the open. It was the idea that they might even be able to do it legally!

A very good chance, from what he was overhearing as they "drifted":

"I thought they only had a couple of telepaths in the whole sphere!" an obese commercial-type was saying.

"So did I," a slenderized companion answered, "but I guess those were just the ones they knew about—you know, *legal* ones."

"They can *really* find out your most secret memories?" This from an old harridan who obviously had one hell of a past, but didn't necessarily want it known.

"But . . . they could learn all my accounts, all the latest information I've gleaned about which stocks are due to rise!" The beefy, florid-faced individual in the conservatively expensive coverall glared in righteous indignation. "That's a completely immoral competitive advantage!"

"*Have* to be stopped," his companion agreed. . "*Have* to be."

"They could take over!" a sweet young thing shrilled, "and they might clamp down on the vice laws!"

"Telepaths certainly wouldn't want people running around with their heads full of smut." Her companion had the look of a questionable publisher. "I mean, what about civil rights?"

"But what about civil rights?" Snow-white hair, face full of authority, oozing confidence—maybe a judge?

"They'd be gone." His companion was younger, but cut from the same cloth. "Make Pohyola Exec Sec'y, give him full emergency powers—and the first thing he'll do is suspend the constitution. We'll have a full-scale dictatorship in a year."

"Are you two going to natter about technicalities at a time like *this*?" a slender, intense-type bawled, turning on them. "Do you realize what our chances of getting approval for a price-hike would be if *telepaths* were running the Department of the Economy?"

They finally broke free of the mob, into a clear space in front of a drop-tube. Whitey hit the button; time stretched out as they waited, chafing, unable to do anything. Then the doors valved open and more citizens streamed out, chattering,

". . . threat to everything we believe in . . ."

". . . probably sacrifice babies at those secret meetings they have . . ."

". . . got to vote Pohyola in!"

"Inside, folks," Whitey growled, and they sprang. The doors valved shut behind them, and Whitey hit the street-level button.

"I'm scared, Grandpa," Lona said softly.

"Comes of having brains," Whitey growled. "Me, I'm just terrified."

Sam's eyes were huge in a pale, drawn face.

Dar's voice was very low. "These people are so scared, they're actually going to be willing to give up all their rights!"

"Willing?" Whitey snorted. "They're going to rush to it!"

"Whitey . . . my mission . . ."

"Still important," Whitey snapped. "If they lose the election, they'll still try their coup. In fact, they may not wait for due process."

The doors valved open. "Walk calmly," Whitey growled. "Don't do anything out of the ordinary. Just follow Papa."

The crowd was much thinner here where people were coming into the terminal or leaving it, but there were still a lot of huddles of frantic citizens. Whitey strolled through them with his crew, retrieved his luggage, and sauntered out the ground-transport door.

A uniform stepped up to them with a man inside it. "Mr. Tambourin?"

Dar's heart jammed into his throat. Then he realized it didn't have any brass or badge; it couldn't be Security.

Whitey turned his head slowly, glowering. "Yes?"

"Mr. Bocello's compliments, sir. Would you accept his hospitality for the next few days?"

"Horatio always did have a great sense of timing," Whitey sighed, pressing back into the limousine's seat. It responded, adjusting itself to his contours.

"What's in the cupboard?" Dar nodded at a sliding panel set into the wall in front of him.

"Why not ask the driver?" Whitey nodded toward a speaker-grill. "He's just on the other side of the wall."

"Why not?" Dar pressed the panel glowing beneath the grill. "Uh, can you tell me what this little cupboard in the forward wall is?"

"A complete bar, sir," the chauffeur replied. "Please feel free to drain it. I hope we have your brands stocked."

"Oh, anything expensive is fine, thanks." Dar slid open the hatch, grinned at the gleaming panel in front of him, checked the codes listed above it, and punched up a Deneb Dimmer. "Next order?"

"Sirian Scrambler," said Lona.

"Canopus Concentrate," said Sam.

"Chateau LaMorgue '46," said Whitey.

Dar squinted at the index. "Sorry, Whitey, all they've got is a '48."

"Well, that wasn't a bad year," Whitey sighed. "It'll do."

Dar pressed in the code and glanced at Father Marco.

"Nothing, thanks." The priest raised a palm. "I only drink in the early morning."

Dar shrugged, took his tumbler out of the slot, and settled back with a contented sigh. "I'm beginning to see advantages to decadence." He beamed down on the city passing beneath them. Then he frowned. "What's that?"

Below them, a mob filled several streets, waving signs and throwing bricks.

"What?" Whitey leaned over to the window, looking down. "Hey, not bad! Let's see if we can hear them." He turned a knob and punched a button beneath the speaker grille. It filtered faint words to them:

"Espers are Ethical!"

"Don't Sell the Psis!"

"Terra for Telepaths!"

Whitey nodded with satisfaction. "A political demonstration. Nice to hear the voice of dissent."

"The bricks are bouncing back at them," Dar called. "Bouncing off of thin air, in fact. What is it, a force-field?"

"Give the man a point!" Lona said brightly. "You've got it,

sophisticate—it's a force-field. Makes sure the demonstrators don't hurt anybody."

"There're a few Security men outside the force-field . . ."

"Well, you wouldn't expect them to be inside, would you?"

"But why do they need them, with the force-field?"

"Who do you think set it up?"

"Also, they're the official sign that the government is hearing the citizens' grievances," said Sam, with full sarcasm.

"The government *approves*?"

"The government embraces it, almost to the point of lewdness. They've even written it into law—for every hundred thousand persons demonstrating for eight hours, they get one vote on the issue in the Assembly."

Dar turned to her, frowning. "Sounds a little dangerous. A fad could get voted into law that way."

"Not when you remember that the Assembly represents ninety-three human-inhabited planets with a total population of eighty billion. You have to have forty-eight votes just to get the issue onto the agenda! Not that it hasn't happened, mind you— but rarely, very rarely."

"Two of the programs based on such issues have been enacted into law," Father Marco reminded her.

"Two laws in five centuries? Not exactly a great track record, Father!"

"Well, no. It does require that the majority approve the issue."

"Yeah." Sam slid over next to Dar and stared out the window gloomily. "But some chance is better than none, I suppose. At least it gives the counterculture the illusion that they can accomplish something."

They passed over three more demonstrations on the way to Bocello's; each was huge, making the pro-telepath mob look like a handful—and all screaming for the telepaths' blood.

"What're *we* getting upset about?" Dar wondered. "*We're* not telepaths!"

"Try and prove that to Pohyola," Sam growled.

What with one thing and another, their nerves were in a fine state of disarray by the time the limo landed.

They stepped out into the midst of a tournament.

The knights had apparently unhorsed each other; the beasts

in question were standing back, watching their masters with jaundiced eyes. The knights were hewing at each other with broadswords that went CLICK! CLUNK! whenever they met. The Green Knight wore full plate armor; his opponent wore a haubergion. Behind and above them stood a scoreboard with two outline-drawings of a human form; whenever one of the knights managed to "wound" his opponent, the "wound" would show up on the scoreboard as a red light, and a chime would ring the knight's number of points.

Around them stood and sat a hundred or so people dressed in the latest fashion of the fourteenth century. Or the twelfth. Or the tenth. Or maybe the ninth. They nibbled at pasties and swigged ale, laughing and cheering, while peddlers circulated among them with food and drink, and troubadours and gleemen strolled about singing and chanting. An occasional monk stood near, inveighing against the evils of tournaments and enjoining the faithful to repent.

Lona turned to the chauffeur. "Sure you didn't take us to the wrong address? Say, maybe a mental hospital?"

"Not at all," the chauffeur assured her. "This is Mr. Bocello's house." And there it was, rising high behind the medieval crowd in full Gothic splendor, looking more like a public monument than a dwelling.

"A man's castle is his home," Dar murmured.

"Mr. Bocello is entertaining," the chauffeur explained. "Just a few friends from his club."

Dar eyed the crowd. "Not what I think of as the usual plutocrat-orgy set."

"Very few of them are wealthy, sir. But all share Mr. Bocello's fondness for the medieval. He has gathered them to celebrate the return to Terra of, ah, in his words, 'the greatest gleeman of our age.'"

A slow grin spread over Whitey's face. "Now, *that's* what I call honoring me according to my own taste and style! I *am* more of a gleeman than a poet, anyway! Come on, folks—if the man does me honor, let's honor his doing!"

A very tall, skinny man in full ducal robes shouldered his way through the crowd with a peasant lass on his arm. "Tambourin!"

"Cello, you filthy old wastrel!" Whitey reached up high to

slap the duke's shoulder. "How'd you get this crowd together on only a day's notice?"

"Oh, I had a few words with their employers, and they were more than happy to oblige. You didn't think you could set foot on old Terra again without causing a festival, did you?"

"Well, I did have some naive notion about slipping in unnoticed," Whitey admitted.

Bocello raised an eyebrow. "What is it this time—a vengeful husband, or an irate sheriff?"

"It's more like a list, really. . . ."

"Oh, is it indeed!" Horatio turned the peasant wench around and sent her off with a pat on the backside. "Off with you, child—I have a feeling we're about to be saying things that you truly want to be able to claim you didn't hear. Come now, no pouting—I saw the way you were eyeing that acrobat; deny it if you can . . ." He turned back to Whitey as the girl swept off with a blush and a giggle. "Now, then! It's been a while; perhaps you and your entourage would like a quick tour of my gardens?"

"We would indeed! Preferably out in the middle of a wide expanse of lawn, free from prying mechanical eyes and ears. . . ."

"Ah, but one can never be totally certain of that anymore." Horatio took Whitey by the arm and led him away. "They're doing such wonderful things with miniaturization these days. Still, my gardeners do, ah, 'sweep' the lawns every morning, so we've a reasonably good chance . . . By the way, what did you think of Greval's latest epic?" And they were off, happily ripping apart other artists' work in the time-honored tradition of amateur critics, as they wove and dodged their way through the crowd. The gang had to scramble to keep up with them, and by the time they came out onto the open grass, Dar was winded.

Sam was starry-eyed.

Dar glanced at her, glanced again, and scowled. What was she looking moonstruck about? He glanced around quickly, but didn't see any gorgeous hunks of manhood nearby. As a last resort, he glanced back at Sam, and followed the direction of her gaze; it arrowed straight toward Horatio. Dar felt a sudden, biting jealousy, which surprised him.

"Now, then!" Horatio stopped in the middle of a wide, open field, chewed into mud at its center. "The lists are the most private place we'll find, at least until the next joust. Let's have your list. Who's chasing you first?"

"The Solar Patrol, at the moment," Whitey answered with a grin, "cheered on by a weasel named Canis Destinus."

"Canis *what*?" Horatio frowned. "Why is *he* on your trail?"

"Because I'm helping a friend." Whitey nodded toward Dar. "And this Canis guy is chasing *him* because he's on a secret mission of some sort. It involves getting to the Executive Secretary for a few minutes."

"I think he does have an opening on his calendar, next Thursday. . . ." Horatio pursed his lips. "Still, it's a difficult appointment to make."

"Especially with Canis trying to cancel it," Whitey agreed. "We can't be sure, mind you, but we think he's the one who's been rousing the local police against us on every planet we've been to. There must be at least three warrants out for me, along my backtrail."

"Well, that's nothing new." Horatio's scowl deepened. "Still, I expect the honor's being bestowed for the wrong reasons. What charge has he drummed up?"

"Now, we're not sure, mind you," Whitey said, frowning, "but we *think* he's managed to convince the LORDS that we're a bunch of telepaths, and that we've been aided and abetted by telepaths all along our route in from the marches."

Horatio stared. "*You're* the Interstellar Telepathic Conspiracy?"

"Well, that is kinda what we think they've got in their heads, yeah," Whitey muttered.

Horatio glared down at him, his face slowly turning purple. Dar stood frozen, with his heart in his throat. If Whitey were just a little bit mistaken about his old buddy, they could all wind up in prison at the snap of a finger. He could fairly feel that restraining field pressing in on him from all sides already. . . .

Then Horatio blew. "Foul!" he bellowed, fingers clawing into fists. "How foul, how fell! That the High Gleeman of scores of worlds should be hounded and harassed like a common felon! And all for the brain-sick nightmare of a diseased and petty mind! Nay, nay! I have stood and smiled, I have gnashed my teeth whiles I watched them play their petty games of plot and counterplot; I have schooled myself to patience while the reek of their corruption stank in my nostrils—but this I cannot bear! Nay, how can there be any gram of goodness biding in a sovereignty that's so riddled with malice that it dreams up excuses to harry its bravest and best? Terra is become a stench-filled sty, a globe no longer fit for glee, a domain no longer fit for dwelling—nor can any planet be that falls within its sphere of influence!"

Whitey dug in his toes and braced himself against the gale. "Peace, now, peace, good fellow! Hope lives on yet! Even corruption has its day, and ceases, and the seeds of goodness sprout up from it, to flower again in virtue!"

"Aye, but in how many years?" Horatio glowered down at him. "Nay, centuries! I am not minded to hold my peace and bear myself in silence whiles I wait!"

Dar felt a surge of panic. Was this madman going to try a one-man rebellion, or something?

But Whitey suddenly became very casual. "Well then, if you truly feel so, flee! There be no dearth of G-type suns, nor of worlds like Terra. If you find all known worlds so swinishly unfit, go seek the unknown! Go sail into uncharted skies and find a world to make anew, after the fashion of your dreaming!"

Dar held his breath. What Whitey was saying was, in effect, put up or shut up.

But Horatio was staring at him as though he'd spoken an idea never thought of before. "Aye," he breathed. "Aye, surely!"

He whirled away toward the house, crying, "Where are these hearts? Where are my comrades?"

The whole group stared at his retreating back.

"I, ah, think we might want to go along with him," Whitey suggested. "He sometimes needs restraining when he gets into these moods." He set off after Horatio.

The troupe followed, and caught up with him.

"What's the matter with her?" Whitey muttered to Dar.

"Huh?" Dar glanced at Sam, who was moving a little more quickly than the rest of them, gaze fixed on Horatio, eyes shining. He turned back to Whitey. "Just spellbound. Money has that effect, sometimes."

But Whitey shook his head. "Not so, or she'd have gone after *me*. Would you say Sam's the impulsive sort?"

"Well . . . in a way." Dar frowned at Sam, seeing her anew. "Controls it well, though."

"And Horatio doesn't have to." Whitey nodded. "That explains a lot."

Dar was glad it did, because he didn't understand a bit of it. On the other hand, he hadn't had much exposure to women who spoke his own language.

Horatio stormed up a flight of limestone steps and wheeled through French doors into his palace. By the time the crew caught up with him, he was leaning across a Louis XIV desk, glaring into a phone screen at an image of a bulky, black-haired man with a flowing beard. "Ship?" he was saying. "Of course you can buy a ship, Horatio! The Navy has surplus dreadnoughts it would love to be rid of—but why?"

"To issue from a sty of stenches!" Horatio snapped. "What do you mean, they have ships they'd love to be rid of?"

"Always more on hand than they have buyers for. After all, who'd want a retired battleship—*without* its cannon?"

"We would! To bear a crew of colonists to a brave new world, where we may purify ourselves of this crass materialism, and rise above the suspiciousness and greed of this technological monster of a world!"

"Horatio." Blackbeard eyed him warily. "Do you speak of founding a society based on the Society?"

"Indeed I do, Markone!"

"I was afraid that this might come," Markone sighed. "You must not confuse the pleasant fantasy of our Society tournaments and moots with the reality of the real world, Horatio. That way lies madness."

"I do *not* confuse them—I wish to make the fantasy *become* real! Think of it, Markone—your barony become a reality, your vassals and serfs forever at your call!"

Markone's eyes lost focus. "A pleasant dream, Horatio—yet nothing but a dream."

"It need not be!" Horatio insisted. "Think, man! What need would we have for all our fortunes? Each could lay the half of them away for his heirs here, and take the other half to pool, to buy a ship and equip an expedition! What could it cost? Certainly no more than a hundred billion—and we must have a dozen barons in the Society who are worth more than half of that apiece!"

Markone gazed off into space. "It might be possible, at that . . . as though we were holding an extended festival abroad. . . . And 'twould be possible to return. . . ."

"Meditate upon it," Horatio urged. "Yet if 'twere done, 'twere well 'twere done quickly, Markone. You know the uncertainty of the political situation."

You could almost hear Markone's eyes click back into focus. "*Un*certainty? What's doubtful about it, Bocello? Nothing but time—and that might be as short as a few days, before these petit-bourgeois politicians in the Assembly elect the Executive Secretary to the noble post of Dictator!"

"Oh, come now," Horatio purred. "I scarcely think they'd be so blatant as to give him the title."

"No, but they'll give him the power! They're primed and ready; all they need is a trigger, some threat to all of them, and they'll cheerfully sell all their freedoms for security—and ours with theirs!"

"True, true—and we know how sensitive these lowborns are to anything that threatens their positions. When all's said and done, money is secondary to them. But give them one sign that there may be someone more powerful than they, who might usurp their powers, and they panic!"

"They do indeed—which brings to mind the latest news, Horatio." Markone glowered up at him out of the screen. "What think you of this Interstellar Telepathic Conspiracy?"

"Who could better recognize a fantasy than we? But there *is* a man of almost supernatural gifts there, as the grain of truth that rumor's wrapped around, Markone."

"Indeed?" Markone's scowl deepened. "What manner of man is that?"

"One you've met—the greatest bard of the Terran Sphere, Tod Tambourin. Government officials have been chasing him in here from the marches—secretly at first, but now openly, claiming that he and his band are telepaths."

"Chased *Tod Tambourin*?" Markone bawled. "This is too much, Bocello! They exceed excess in this!"

"They do indeed." Horatio nodded slowly, eyes gleaming. "If they will harry such a man out of pettiness and spite, what might they *not* attempt? By all the stars, Bocello—do you realize that they might come a-hunting *us*?"

"We are logical targets for envious men," Horatio purred, "the more so since we have wealth to confiscate."

"Does it begin again, then? Must we watch the bloody flag arise, and ride on tumbrels to the guillotine?"

That, Dar thought, was overdoing it a bit—though he had to agree that there did seem to be some danger in staying on Terra just now, for anyone with large amounts of money or a taste for eccentric hobbies.

"I, for one, do not intend to learn the answer," Horatio informed his phone-screen, "at least, not from personal experience. I'll buy a ship alone, if I have to, and recruit my party guests. What say you, Markone? Will you join me?"

"That I will, and see the Baronetcy of Ruddigore established in reality! Go buy your ship, Bocello—and don't lift off without me!"

The screen blanked. Horatio turned to his guests with a wolfish grin. "So it begins, and they'll fall into line quickly, I assure you; the twelve great barons of the Central Kingdom. Oh, we'll have that ship bought and outfitted within a day, and be loading passengers in two!"

Whitey spread his hands. "It was just an idea."

"You can't find enough people that fast," Dar stated flatly. "Oh, maybe you twelve rich men might be ready to jump at a moment—you know you can come back any time you choose. But it's different for the ordinary people. They'll need a long time to decide."

"They will, eh?" Horatio seized a stylus and tablet from his desk and strode to the French doors. He came out onto the terrace, hands high, bellowing, "Now I cry *HOLD*!"

The shouting chaos of laughing and singing ceased in an instant.

"They're loyal," Horatio explained over his shoulder. Then,

to the multitude: "The Baronet of Ruddigore and I have decided to take ship, and ride out to the stars, to discover a world never before seen by Terrans, there to found the Central Kingdom in reality, and live as men ought, by faith and sweat and steel. We shall need villeins and yeomen, gentlemen and knights! We shall leave in two days time; any who are not with us then, will never be! Who wishes to ride? Sign here!"

He threw the tablet down into the multitude. With a roar, they pounced on it, and the whole crowd instantly re-formed into a line, each one fairly panting in his eagerness to emigrate. Food-sellers and jugglers began to work up and down the queue.

Horatio turned back to Dar with a grin. "*That* is the mettle of my people!"

"They'll change their minds by the time they get to the front of the line," Dar predicted.

Horatio nodded. "Some of them, no doubt—but most will sign. They've wished for nothing half so much as to live in a world where folk are true, and the rulers worthy of trust. How say you, brave ones? Will you join us?"

"Instantly." Sam beamed up at him.

Horatio looked down at her, surprised. Then, slowly, he began to smile, almost shyly.

"I admit I'm tempted," Father Marco mused. "For a priest, the Middle Ages had definite advantages."

"For gleemen, too." Whitey grinned from ear to ear. "I think it's a great idea, Horatio, and I'll cheer you on every A.U. of the way—but I never was much of a joiner."

"Nor I." Lona shook her head firmly. "Stuck in a society that's never even heard of electrons? Horrible!"

Dar opened his mouth to answer, and a burring sound came out. He swallowed and blinked, then realized that the sound had come from the phone. A footman in tights and tabard stepped out to announce, "There is a Mr. Stroganoff calling, sir, for Mr. Tambourin."

Whitey looked up in surprise. "Already? There shouldn't have been any progress yet." He went back inside, with Dar trailing after.

Stroganoff was on the screen, dazed. "What's the matter, David?" Whitey asked as he came into range.

"Oh, nothing, nothing at all! Everything's just fine—in fact, *too* fine. *That's* what's the matter!"

"Glad to hear it—I hope. Want to tell me why it's gotten so hot that it's turned cold?"

"The Executive Secretary." Stroganoff swallowed. "I sent a fax to his office, right after you left. I figured the way the government bureaucracy works, I'd better start right away if we were going to have any chance of shooting him within the year."

"Wise." Whitey was poised like a hawk about to stoop. "And?"

"And his office just called. He's—he's willing to do the piece. But only if we can do it tomorrow!"

Whitey and Dar both stared.

"The primary citizen *never* says 'yes' that quickly!" Stroganoff bawled. "And even after you've talked him into it, you have to make an appointment months away!"

"And have it canceled at the last minute, at least twice." Whitey nodded, with a faraway look in his eyes. "On the other hand, I do have a certain reputation. . . ."

"Well, you're at least as famous as he is, if that's what you mean. But . . ."

"But my fame is apt to last a bit longer." Whitey mused, "and from the current political news, I'd guess the Exec isn't too sure he's going to still *be* Exec in a few months—or even *next* month, for that matter."

"Next *week*," Stroganoff growled.

Whitey nodded. "So he's making his bid for immortality. Do the piece for us, and he's guaranteed a featured place in Tod Tambourin's one and only 3DT masterpiece. Even if history forgets him, literature won't."

Stroganoff nodded slowly. "Y'know, that almost makes sense, Tod."

"Yeah, but the schedule doesn't." Whitey grimaced. "Oh, the crew can make it easily enough—all we have to do is hop into a cab, and charge it to your company."

Stroganoff shuddered. "How about first class on a public shuttle?"

Whitey shrugged. "Whatever you like. But how about equipment?"

"May have it, or may not. There's no point in dropping it down from Luna, of course; what we do is to rent it out from a dirtside company. I know a few. I'll have to make some calls, and get back to you."

Whitey grinned. "I always wanted to use a 3DT camera."

"Uh, hold on, now. Whoa!" Stroganoff held up his palm. "No can do, Tod. Cameras come with a union crew, or they don't come at all!"

"Why?" Whitey frowned. "I've got two electronics techs right here!"

"I know, but if the union finds out you've shot a sequence without them, they won't give you any tech crew for the studio segments up here. Like it or not, we've got to use them."

"Okay, I'll try to like it," Whitey sighed. "When do we meet them?"

"I'll let you know, if I manage to get them. Where'll you be?"

"Where should I be?"

Stroganoff grinned. "Thank you, Meistersinger. Be on your way to the Gamelon, will you? Call me back when you're over Lake Champlain."

11

"You're sure this's the Gamelon?" Dar muttered. "For all I can see, it could be the inside of Moby Dick."

"Moby Dick was a whale, not a snake," Whitey muttered back, "or haven't you noticed how many turns we've made?"

"Didn't look this big from outside," Dar grumped.

Father Marco had become enmeshed in a long theological discussion with two young clerks who were devout atheists masquerading as medieval monks. Lona had become enmeshed in partying, and Sam was trying to become enmeshed with Horatio. So they had come alone to the long, striplike building that had replaced New York's eastside docks, and were following a lighted bar that slid along the hallway floor in front of them, making some very unpredictable turns as it led them farther and farther into the building that housed the Central Executive Staff of the Interstellar Dominion Electorates.

Finally, it stopped next to an open doorway. Dar looked up, and met the gaze of a wide, very muscular individual dressed in a laborer's coverall. "Help you?" he rumbled.

"Somebody's got to," Dar answered. Then Whitey arrived at his elbow. "Tod Tambourin," he said, pointing to the ID tag the door-guards had hung around his neck.

"Oh yeah, the writer." The muscular one looked bored. "This your P.A.?"

"No, he's my assistant."

"Right. Well, come on in. Not much for you to do, though; we're just about ready, here."

They were, indeed. As Dar came in, he saw a huge desk sitting in front of a photomural of a starfield, with the I.D.E. spiderweb superimposed over it in lines of light. On either side of the desk, between it and the backdrop, were two slender pillars. In front were two cameras. All around were at least a dozen technicians.

Dar turned back to Muscles. "Mind if I show my ignorance?"

"That's what I'm here for," the beefy one sighed.

"What do you need so many people for?"

"Easy." Muscles pointed. "Two camera ops, one electrician, one engineer for each set of camera controls, one engineer for audio, one for the holo-mole recorder, and a staging director."

"That's only eight."

"You're good at arithmetic."

"But there're at least sixteen here!"

"Well, every position's gotta have a backup. You know, somebody might have a heart attack."

"Yeah, like the accountant who has to keep track of the budget for this show. What do you do?"

"I'm the shop steward."

"Oh . . . Uh, thanks." Dar turned away to Whitey. "You sure we didn't stumble into a mattress factory by mistake?"

Whitey frowned. "What do you mean?"

"There's so much featherbedding."

In the far corner, a small man in a business coverall came through a narrow door. "Rise, citizens, for your Executive Secretary."

Those of the crew who were sitting (twelve, at the moment) hauled themselves to their feet.

"Oh, don't be ridiculous, Hiram!" A tall man with white hair and a craggy, handsome face strode briskly in, the fabric of his modest coverall glowing with the quiet sheen of luxury.

"We don't stand on ceremony here." To prove it, he sat down at the desk.

Dar swallowed around a sudden bulge in his throat. The Executive Secretary himself! Even out on a marches planet such as Wolmar, he'd seen pictures of that face so often that virtually every wrinkle in it was embedded in his memory. To suddenly be in the same room with the man himself was unnerving; he didn't quite seem to be real.

"You've come damn near a hundred light-years to talk to this man," Whitey muttered in his ear. "Go to it!" Aloud, he said, "Go check and see if he's got any problems with his lines."

Dar swallowed thickly and stepped forward, holding the script before him like a shield. He hovered just behind the staging director, dimly aware that the lady was chatting with the Exec, but not at all sure what she was saying. Finally, the Exec nodded, and the staging director stepped back, calling to Dar, "Ready any time."

"Are there . . ." Dar's voice broke into a squeak; he swallowed and licked his lips. The Exec glanced up at him in irritation. Dar cleared his throat and tried again. "Any problems with the script, sir?" He dropped his voice down just above a whisper and poured out the rest in a sudden rush: "Boundbridge, Satrap, and Forcemain aren't going to wait for an election. They've had a coup d'etat planned for months. I have the codes that will unlock the proof of their complicity. Save democracy, sir!"

A slow grin spread over the Exec's face. "Had that memorized, did you?"

Dar swallowed, and nodded.

The Exec nodded, too, and rose, clapping Dar on the shoulder. "It's always a pleasure to meet a genuine patriot." But his hand tightened, and he called out, "Did you hook up those cameras?"

"Yes, Mr. Secretary." The staging director looked frightened. "We're patched into network. You can go live to all of Terra whenever you want."

"Good, good." The Exec let go of Dar just as harder hands laid hold of him. Looking up, he saw the shop steward and one of the assistants holding him, each one leveling a small but efficient-looking pistol at his torso. Whitey was suffering the same treatment; and the whole crew, except for the camera operators and the staging director, had pistols out.

"All right, then. Put us on," the Exec said. He smiled into the camera in front of him, seeming suddenly warm and weary, but solemn. The staging director raised a hand, palm flat and stiff, gazing off into space, listening to a voice talking into his ear-button. Suddenly his arm swung down like a sword, to point at the Exec.

"Fellow citizens," the Exec intoned, "we are happy to be able to announce that we have arrested the vile telepath who has been stalking relentlessly through the planets, to Terra. He is here."

The red light on his camera went off, and the corresponding light on the other camera glowed to life—pointing straight at Dar. With a sudden, horrible, sinking feeling, he realized everyone on Terra could see him.

"My Executive Guards caught him just in time," the Exec went on, "right here, in this studio, attempting to assassinate me."

A sudden horible chill seized Dar's intestines as he found a pistol in his hand. How . . . ?

Then, suddenly, he realized what the Exec was saying, realizing he was being identified as the horrible, vicious, telepathic assassin. He screamed, "N-o-o-o-o!" and threw his weight frantically against the hands that held him. They bit into his arms like steel clamps, and he writhed and twisted, bellowing in outrage, trying to shake them off.

"He knew what I was going to say next," the Exec said grimly, "that the danger is not over. For he has confederates, fellow citizens—traveling unseen and unknown, here on Terra itself! Where these vicious assassins will next strike, we cannot tell—nor who will be their next victim. Probably myself—but it also might be any one of you."

His voice deepened, ringing with conviction. "They must be stopped! For you, my fellow citizens, do not have a corps of guardsmen to protect you day and night. They must be stopped—but your Civil Police cannot arrest the people whom they know to be dangerous telepaths, because of the restrictions of civil rights laws! The only way to end this peril is to grant me full emergency powers, so that I can have your police clap these criminals into jails, where they belong. Today I will ask the Assembly for those powers—but I will not receive them without your support. Call your Elector now! Tell him to give me the powers I need to protect you! So that mad-dog renegades, such as this one, can be banished to the farthest reaches of Terran space!"

He stared solemnly into the camera, the perfect image of a good but troubled man, until the red light went out.

Then he thrust himself to his feet, grinning, and turned to Dar. "Thank you, young man. You timed your struggling perfectly."

"It's you!" Dar burst out. "*You're* the one who planned the coup!"

"No—but I will be the one who takes power. If there's going to be a dictator, I intend to make sure that I'm it."

"You don't even care about saving democracy!"

"Why so surprised?" The Exec's smile was gentle, sympathetic—and underscored with contempt. "You poor, naive idiot! Did you honestly think any politician really cared about anything but personal power anymore?"

Dar stared at him, horrified.

Then the frustration broke, and the rage leaped through it. He threw himself at the Exec with a howl, fingers curving into claws—but the guards' hands held him back, and a cold spray hit his face, filling his head with fumes that spread darkness through his brain.

12

"WHY DID YOU ESCAPE FROM WOLMAR?"

The voice blasted through into Dar's nice, warm nest of unconsciousness. An idiot monotone was singing in his right ear, and a cricket with absolutely no sense of rhythm was chirping into his left.

"HOW DID YOU LEAVE THE PLANET WOLMAR?"

"I hopped into a courier ship," Dar answered truthfully. He levered his eyelids open, squinting against the light.

Five of them, actually—red, blue, green, yellow, and orange—hitting him with stroboscopic flashes that didn't quite have a rhythmic pattern—but it was a different nonrhythmic pattern than the cricket's. Dar stared, dazzled.

"WHAT IS YOUR NAME?"

It was ridiculous, but he couldn't think of it. All he could think of was that he wanted someone to turn the lights off. "I don't know!"

"EXCELLENT," the unseen owner of the voice purred. "WHICH OF YOUR TRAVELING COMPANIONS WAS THE TELEPATH?"

"The *what*?"

"DO NOT SEEK TO MISLEAD US! WE KNOW THAT AT LEAST ONE MEMBER OF YOUR GROUP WAS A

TELEPATH. AND DO NOT TRY TO READ OUR MINDS;
THE SENSORY DISTRACTIONS YOU ARE EXPERIENC-
ING WILL PREVENT YOU FROM BEING ABLE TO
CONCENTRATE SUFFICIENTLY FOR TELEPATHY!"

"We hope," someone near the voice muttered.

"I can't read anybody's mind!"

"SEE?" the voice boomed to someone else. "THE LIGHTS
AND NOISES DO WORK!"

"I never *could* read anybody's mind! I'm not a telepath!"

The voice was quiet for a moment; then it boomed, "WHEN
WERE YOU LAST A TELEPATH?"

"Never! Never, so help me!"

"He could be lying," the voice muttered.

"Not with that sensory assault you've laid onto him," the
other voice answered. "Poor fellow can't even close his eyes
now. I don't think he could concentrate enough to think up a
lie."

"That was the other purpose of this system," the first voice
admitted. Then it boomed out again: "OUR AGENTS FOL-
LOWED YOU ALL THE WAY FROM WOLMAR TO
TERRA, OF COURSE. HOW DID YOU FORCE TOD
TAMBOURIN TO AID YOU?"

"I didn't! I didn't force him at all!" Then, suddenly
realizing they might accuse Whitey, Dar added, "I conned
him!"

"He *is* only a poet," the other voice murmured. "Probably
true. Besides, you'd better get back to the main question before
he goes catatonic on you."

That sent a chill trickling down Dar's spine.

"Right," the voice muttered; then, "WHO IN YOUR
GROUP *WAS* THE TELEPATH?"

"There wasn't any! There aren't any! There never have been
any!"

"WE KNOW BETTER," the voice said scornfully. "WHO
WAS IT?"

The flashing lights bit into his brain; the thousand-hertz tone
bored straight through from ear to ear, while the random clicks
tripped up every thought that tried to flow. "I can't think!" Dar
yelled. "I can't think who it could possibly be! For the life of
me!"

"IT MAY BE JUST THAT. DO YOU REALLY EXPECT US TO BELIEVE . . . ?" The voice broke off in midsentence. "WHO'S THAT? GET HIM OUT OF HERE!"

"My credentials, gentlemen." It was a fulsome voice, growing louder as it came closer. "If you doubt them, you may verify me through the computer."

"Why?" snorted the other voice. "They're computer-fed, anyway . . . *Chief Torturer*?"

"To Mr. Horatio Bocello, yes."

"He's just a billionaire, not a politician! Why would *he* need a torturer?"

"Industrial espionage, mostly."

"INDUSTRIAL NUTHOUSE," the nearer voice snorted. "HE'S ONE OF THOSE CRAZY BILLIONAIRES WHO DRESSES UP IN ARMOR AND TRIES TO PRETEND THE MIDDLE AGES'RE STILL GOING ON."

"But we can't let some civilian come in here and . . ."

"WHY NOT? MAYBE HE'S GOT JUST THE CAN OPENER WE NEED. TAKE OFF YOUR COAT AND GET TO WORK, MR. RICCI."

"Well, thank you, gentlemen. Where's the coatrack? Ah, there. Now, which way to the vict . . . ah, subject? Ah, there's the door. . . ."

Father Marco! Dar nearly yelped with joy at the thought of a familiar face. But he managed to hold it in; some wavering remnant of good sense remembered not to let the cat out of the bag.

The priest drifted into view. "Now, then, fellow! When did you stop being a telepath?"

"When did I . . . never!"

"Then you still are one!"

"No, of course not! I never . . ."

"When did you first become a telepath?"

"Never, I tell you! Never."

"When did you begin to associate with telepaths?"

"Never! Never!"

"He's being recalcitrant," Father Marco sighed, "just as I feared. Well, get rid of these lights and noises—they aren't doing any good."

"BUT . . . BUT, MR. RICCI . . ."

"Turn them off, I say! They're not getting any answers out of him—and they're driving me crazy! Turn them off!"

"WELL . . . I HOPE YOU KNOW WHAT YOU'RE DOING. . . ."

The lights and sounds died. Dar could've wept with gratitude.

"Now, then! Let's try the old-fashioned methods!" Father Marco clapped his hands, and two giants shuffled into the light. Each was a head taller than Dar, and musclebound. You could tell, because they were both stripped to the waist. On top of that, they were shaven bald. And they both wore black masks.

They unfastened the straps that held down Dar's wrists, ankles, and chest, and yanked him to his feet. "But . . . what . . . where . . ." Dar sputtered. He had his answer in a second; they hustled him through the nearest doorway while Father Marco followed, calling, "Thumbscrews! The Boot! The Iron Maiden! The Rack!"

They burst into the torture chamber, the two men rushing him so quickly that his feet scarcely had time to touch the floor. Grim, vicious-looking instruments blurred past him, covered with cobwebs and rust. In the dim light, he could see that the stone blocks oozed drops of water. Then they burst through another door and twisted down an angling corridor.

"Wh . . . didn't I miss my stop, there?"

"Nope," the black mask to his right answered. "You ain't even in your cab, yet."

And sure enough, they burst through a final door, and there stood the pregnant-teardrop shape of a cab, glistening in the muted light that filtered down to the underground cavern.

"No one'll notice y' here," the other muscleman growled. "They scarcely still know it exists." He yanked open the door, and his mate booted Dar through it. "But," the young man sputtered, "what . . . why . . . ?"

"Because Horatio Bocello promised them berths on his spaceship, of course." Father Marco slid in beside Dar. "They couldn't resist an offer like that."

"'Course not," the second man agreed, sliding into the front seat. "If anybody'd want to go back to the Middle Ages, it'd be the torturers."

"You can say that quintuply," his mate agreed, clapping a

chauffeur's cap onto his head. "These namby-pamby lights and noises and dripping water—faugh! I wanna hear those bones crunch!"

His buddy clicked the hatch closed and advised him, "You can stop acting now."

"Good." The first breathed a sigh of relief. "But I do hate this job. Me, I can't even stand to set mousetraps! Just give me a chance to escape from this sick society!"

"I did," Father Marco reminded him. "You jumped at it."

The cab swooped out of the shadows of the cavern into evening sunlight, up into clouds gilded by sunset and industrial waste.

Dar looked around him, recognizing the plush upholstery and computerized bar. "This is no cab—it's Bocello's limousine!"

"I never woulda guessed it." The righthand torturer yanked off his mask. "Pass me an akvavit, will ya?"

13

The "cab" dropped down and landed them on Bocello's back
lawn, right next to an elongated dome big enough to have been
a small spaceship. As Dar stepped out, Lona slammed into him
with a hug that would've given a grizzly lumbago. "Thank
Heaven you're safe! We were so *worried*!" Then she shoved
back, holding him off at arm's length, and he was amazed to
see tears in her eyes. "You poor, brave, dear idiot! Next time
you have to go fling yourself on a sacrificial altar, do it for
something worthwhile, okay?"

He couldn't spare the energy for an answer; he was too busy
falling into her eyes. Apparently she *had* noticed his existence. . . .

Then Whitey was slapping him on the back, and Sam was
craning up to plant a kiss on his cheek. "I should've known the
system'd swallow you up!"

He grinned back at her and squeezed her hand. "Yeah, but
you didn't let it chew me up and spit me out!"

"No." Sam caught Horatio's arm and beamed up at him.
"No, we didn't."

"Well, give some praise to the real heroes of the rescue,"
Horatio laughed, clapping Father Marco and one of the
torturers on the shoulders. "I only provided the car, and the

code for getting into the Gamelon! Hurry and change, boys—the last shuttle's lifting off in ten minutes."

The torturers grinned and trotted away.

"Nobly done, Father," Whitey agreed. "I don't know how you managed to bluff the *real* torturers."

Father Marco shrugged. "Nothing to it, when the computer said I was genuine."

"Yeah." Dar frowned. "How *did* you manage that?"

"My versatile granddaughter," Whitey sighed. "Every time I despair of her because she can't make a sonnet, she does something like this."

"Oh, it's nothing that big," Lona said, irritated. "I just made a little addition to an existing program, that's all."

"Just a 'little addition' that added Father Marco's name to a list of top security clearances," Whitey corrected.

Dar stared. "How'd she get past the security blocks?"

"Trade secret," Lona said quickly, "though I don't really see what all the fuss is about. I mean, computers may be fast, but they're really not very bright, the dear little things."

The two "torturers" came trotting back, dressed in plush overalls, and Horatio shooed them toward the dome. "Aboard the yacht, now, quickly—time's wasting! If we don't move promptly, the Executive Secretary will be the Executive Dictator, and we won't be allowed to lift off from Terra! Hurry, hurry—the *Brave New World* awaits!"

He meant it literally— the *Brave New World* was the name the dozen plutocrats had given their newly purchased government-surplus FTL spaceship. (In memory of Shakespeare, not Huxley). They saw it lying in the middle of Serenitatis Plain as they came in for a landing: a quarter of a mile long and eight hundred feet wide, glistening like a promise of the future. They landed near it and dropped down into an underground concourse with beige, textured walls and a burgundy carpet. Horatio hurried them along till the hallway widened into a circular bay with a double door in the far wall. A line of people in sturdy coveralls, with packs on their backs, was filing through it, to drift quickly upwards in a negative-gravity field.

"Up there is the ship," Horatio explained. "They should be almost done loading now. Are you sure you won't join us?"

"I'll go." Sam beamed up at him. "Anywhere you do."

He smiled down at her tenderly. "That's very touching, my dear, especially since I'm not taking my money with me. But really, I don't think you'd be very happy, stuck in a primitive society with an old goat."

"Sounds delightful," Sam pronounced. "Besides, I'll be a lord's lady."

"In a very drafty castle," he reminded her, "without central heating or air conditioning. Nor plumbing. It'll be very cold, sitting down in the garderobe on a winter's morning—and the wash basin'll be frozen."

"I'll get used to it."

"No, you won't. In effect, 'you' will cease to exist just before we make planetfall; we all will. We'll sit down under a cerebral scan and have all memories of this technological nightmare of a culture erased from our brains. Then we'll have false memories implanted; each one of us has been developing a Society persona for years. On the trip outward, each one will record the imaginary memories of his persona; and after the brain-wipe, those 'memories' will be recorded back into our brains. You won't remember Sam; you'll only remember Lady Loguire."

"Lady Loguire! Oh!" Sam breathed, nestling up against him. "It sounds wonderful. To oblivion with Sam; I never liked her much, anyway."

"*I* do," Horatio sighed, "but I trust I'll love the Lady Loguire just as dearly. Well, then, sweeting, you're one of us, now—the Romantic Emigrés; we've changed our name, effective upon our leaving the Solar system. Would anyone else like to join us?"

Lona was whispering into Father Marco's ear. He frowned, shaking his head, and whispered something back. She hissed another sentence at him, and his face broke into a wreath of smiles. He stepped forward, clasping Horatio's hand. "A delightful prospect! I'll come too, thank you!"

Horatio's face lit up, but his tone was guarded. "Are you sure, Father? I know you're a Cathodean, and that means you're either a scientist or an engineer. You'll have to have most of your memories erased too, at least the ones that have anything to do with technology. We don't want our new society to be contaminated by *any* link to this decadent, materialistic culture."

"I'm a priest before I'm an engineer," Father Marco assured him, "and the priest agrees with you: materialism is a contaminant."

"Excuse me," said Lona. "Gotta make a phone call." She swayed away to the nearest screen-booth, at her most sultry. Dar's eyes swiveled to follow her; he could almost feel them tugging at his sockets.

"Wonderful!" Horatio clasped Father Marco's hand, grinning from ear to ear. "At least our colony will have a real priest! How would you like to be an archbishop, Father?"

"That's not up to us, I'm afraid." Father Marco smiled, amused. "But I wouldn't mind being an abbot."

"As soon as we can build you a monastery," Horatio assured him. "Still, I think we might manage a bishop's miter for you; I'll beam the Pope as soon as we lift off."

Father Marco frowned. "I'm afraid it's not quite that easy to be allowed to talk with His Holiness."

"It is for me; we went to school together. Are you sure no one else would like to come?"

Dar shook his head. "Thanks anyway, Mr. Bocello."

"Me, too," Whitey agreed. "I'm having too much fun in the present. But thanks for the offer, Cello."

Lona came swaying back. "Aren't you forgetting Mr. Stroganoff?"

"My lord!" Dar cried, appalled. "He was our producer—they'll think he masterminded the whole scheme! What'll they do—torture him, or kill him?"

"Neither one," Horatio assured him, "at least, not if my chauffeur is his usual, resourceful self."

"He was."

They all swung about, to see Stroganoff puffing toward them down the concourse. "Thanks for having me kidnapped, Mr. Bocello," he panted as he came huffing up. "Probably saved my life."

"My pleasure," Horatio assured him. "I'm sorry to have been so unceremonious, but prompt action was required. Have you been briefed about our venture, Mr. Stroganoff?"

"I certainly have, and I wish you all the luck in whatever

world you find. I'd love to go along if I could bring a 3DT camera and come back—but I understand you don't want any technology developed later than 1300."

"Except for full plate armor, yes. But are you certain, Mr. Stroganoff? You don't have much of a future left, here."

"Not on Terra or Luna, no," Stroganoff agreed. "But I would like to stop by Wolmar for a few years; there's a man there I'd like to chat with."

Dar grinned.

Horatio shrugged. "Certainly. We don't much care where we exit from Terran space; one vector's as good as another."

"You're sure I won't be taking you out of your way?"

"Not at all, since we don't know where we're going. And we're doing our best to make certain nobody else does, either. We'll change directions after we pass Wolmar; but we won't decide which new heading to take until after we're out of communications range. This is going to be one 'lost colony' that will *stay* lost."

A man in uniform coveralls came running up to Horatio. "Captain's compliments, sir, and some news—right off the 3DT. The Assembly just voted the Executive Secretary full emergency powers, and the title 'Executive Director.'"

"An ominous ring to it," Horatio mused. "I think we'd better be lifting off while we still can. Farewell, good people!"

There was a quick round of hugs, handclasps, and kisses. Sam glared up at Dar with tears in her eyes. "Goodbye, gnappie, and good luck! Don't let 'em get to you!"

"I'll be kicking and screaming every centimeter of the way," Dar promised. "What *is* a 'gnappie,' anyway?"

"Someone who just sits back and lives off his GNP share, without trying to accomplish anything. You won't be that, will you?"

"Not if I can help it," Dar assured her.

Then Horatio was whirling her away, whirling all three of them away, with an arm around Sam while he burbled to Father Marco, "I'm *so* glad you decided to come, Father! After all, what would the Middle Ages be, without monks and monasteries?"

They stepped into the lift-tube, and Sam turned back to wave. Then the field bore them up, out of sight.

Whitey clasped Dar's shoulder. "Up to the observation room, quickly! This is one lift-off I want to be able to watch!"

They ran to a smaller lift-shaft back down the concourse and flew up into the observation tower. It was a wide, circular space, with a thick carpet and thicker windows. In fact, it was nothing but windows, a full circle of them, and a transparent roof above. Dar looked around at the Lunar surface outside, a crazy quilt of brightness and blackness. "Wonder why they didn't just build a clear dome?"

"The usual reason—this was cheaper." Whitey pointed at the huge sliver cigar a quarter of a mile away. "She's lifting, children."

They stared, tracking it in silence, as the *Brave New World* lifted from the Lunar surface and drifted upward, away and away, shrinking from a monster that filled half the sky, to a splendid flying hill, diminishing and diminishing, to a silver cigar indeed, then a cigarillo, then a matchstick, then only a point of brightness. Suddenly that brightness intensified; it became an actinic spark, throwing a faint shadow of the three watchers onto the floor behind them, and began to slide away across the heavens.

"Exhaust," Lona whispered. "They've ignited their interplanetary drive."

The spark moved faster and faster until it was only a streak of light, shooting off toward the unseen orbit of Pluto, a miniature sun seeking a dawn.

When it had dwindled to being only one more faint star in the millions that surrounded them, they turned away with a sigh. "I hope they make it." Dar smiled sadly. "I wonder if they'll really manage to set up their crackpot society."

"I have a notion they will," Whitey mused. "When Horatio sets his mind to something, it gets done. Just hope they'll be happy, though."

"Me, too." Dar frowned. "Especially Father Marco. How can he found a Cathodean monastery if he has his brain wiped of any engineering knowledge?"

"Oh, I wouldn't worry about that," Lona murmured, with a quiet smile.

Whitey fixed her with a jaundiced eye. "Granddaughter, lick that cream off your whiskers and tell me who you phoned!"

"Just the *Brave New World*'s computer, Grandpa—it isn't hard to get the number, if you know what to say to Central Memory."

"No, not at all—you only had to talk your way past a few dozen of the System's strongest security blocks first!"

Lona shrugged it off. "Just basic logic."

"Yes, getting baser and baser as it goes along. And just what did you and the *Brave New World* have to say to each other?"

"Oh, I just convinced it that Father Marco's the only one aboard who might stand even a remote chance of fixing it, if it ever broke down. It saw my point right away, and promised that, when it came time to wipe brains, it would skip Father Marco's."

Whitey nodded, with a wry smile. "I was wondering why he was suddenly eager to go. I could see a Cathodean being willing to leave civilization for the sake of the Church—but technology is another matter."

"I thought they ought to be able to keep *some* link to reality," Lona agreed. "And the only place they could do that, without it leaking out to the whole society, is inside the walls of a monastery."

"How pure and altruistic of you," Whitey muttered.

Lona shrugged. "I just have fun with computers, Grandpa."

"Well, enjoy it while you can," Whitey sighed. "I have a notion our new lords and masters aren't going to think too highly of fun—especially your kind."

"Yeah, I hadn't thought about the future *here*." Dar frowned. "Maybe Horatio and his buddies aren't all that much crackpots."

"Things could get rather dull here," Lona agreed. "That's why, as long as I was on the phone, I got in touch with the Bank of Terra's computer, Grandpa, and had all your funds transferred to the Bank of Maxima."

A delighted grin spread across Whitey's face. "How thoughtful of you, child!"

Dar frowned. "Maxima? The place that built Fess? He's says it's just a barren piece of rock!"

"With robot factories," Lona reminded him, "which includes computer factories. And computer technicians and cybernetics experts, of course—my kind of people."

"But I thought you wanted to participate in the life of decadence."

"I do, if I can—but if I have to choose between that and toying with circuits and programs, I know where the real fun lies. Besides, Maxima's close to Terra; I might be able to come down for a spree, now and then."

"Then why transfer the money there? *All* of it?"

"Because Maxima's the one world that might be able to keep the central government from gimmicking its computers," Lona explained. "That keeps the money intact, not to mention our privacy."

"Privacy? You think *that'll* be threatened?" Dar turned to Whitey, frowning. "You really think it's going to get *that* bad here?"

"It's called a police state," Whitey explained. "I'm sure they intend to include Maxima in it, too—in theory."

"But not in practice," Lona assured him. "At least, not if I have anything to say to the Maxima computers."

"A chip off the old bloke, if ever there was one!" Whitey grinned. "Your mama would've said just the same. Well then, if Maxima's where you're bound, we'd better get started." He pulled out the recall unit and pressed a button. "Should be here, pretty soon." He turned to Dar. "How about you? Like to lift away from here?"

"Yes, I would, thank you—very much."

"Thought so. You could go back to Wolmar, you know. The LORDS party's been saying for a long time that the frontier worlds cost too much, that we ought to just cut them off and leave 'em to their own devices. Might be some hard times coming out in the marches, but the worlds there should at least keep their freedom."

Dar nodded. "I'd thought about that. In fact, I'm pretty sure General Shacklar—our governor—has had that in mind for a while, too. Also Myles Croft, on Falstaff."

"Well, I know My's been getting strapped down and ready to go on his own, so I don't doubt your Shacklar has, too. But I take it you're not planning to go back there."

Dar frowned. "How'd you figure that out?"

" 'Cause if you were, you would've hitched a ride with Horatio and gotten dropped off with Stroganoff. What's the matter? Had a taste of the fleshpots, and decided to stay near 'em?"

"You've got me pegged," Dar admitted. "How'd you guess?"

"Believe it or not, I was young once, myself."

"The trick is, believing that he ever aged." Lona stepped a little closer to Dar, and it seemed to him that he could feel her presence as a physical pressure. And her eyes danced; she was watching him with a smile that was both secretive and amused. "Where were you planning to go?"

"Someplace," Dar pronounced, "where I'll never have to hear about that Interstellar Telepathic Conspiracy again."

"Yeah, that's a masterstroke of confusion, isn't it?" Whitey chuckled. "I never saw a Big Lie work so well—it even has some of the liars convinced! I love watching a fantasy go out of control."

"Oh, it isn't total fantasy," Dar mused. "There's a grain of substance to it."

Whitey gave him a sidelong glance. "You sure about that?"

"Well, it kinda makes sense, doesn't it?" Dar spread his hands. "With all that fuss and bother, there should've been at least one real telepath at the bottom of it all."

"Should've, maybe." Lona gave him her most skeptical look. "*Would*'ve's another matter. When it comes to telepathy, if it doesn't have integrated circuits, I won't believe in it."

"Just telepaths?" Dar gave her the skeptical look back. "I would've said that was how you looked at everything."

"There's some truth to that," Lona admitted. "I don't have too much use for dreams, unless someone's trying to make them come true. Telepathy as a dream, now, I can see that—if someone's trying to invent a way to make it happen. Or faster-than-light radio, or maybe even rearranging the bonds in a single molecule, to make it into a complete electronic circuit."

Dar's skeptical look turned into a fish-eye. "That's your idea of a dream?"

"Well, the only ones that I'd talk about in public." She had the amused, secretive look back, and her eyes transfixed him. "Don't you have any?"

Dar frowned, and his gaze drifted away, out toward the stark, cruel sharpness of the lunar plain. "No . . . I'm a little low on them, right now. I'll settle for getting away from Terra while I can."

A bulbous, pitted, teardrop fell from the starfield and drifted down, settling over the boarding-tube the *Brave New World* had used. Sensing a ship, it lifted and quested, homing automatically on the airlock, probing and touching tentatively, then locking tight.

"Fess's here," Whitey announced. "Let's go get safe, younglings."

They stepped into the drop-tube and came out into the concourse. No one talked as they walked the quarter-mile to the gate; each was wrapped in his own thoughts, realizing that he or she was leaving Terra forever. Though Lona was making plans about how to be able to come back for visits, safely; that was her only real concern with the planet. She'd been raised between the stars, after all; to her, Mother Earth had always been only an extravagant relative, to visit when you wanted a treat. Dar had never been to Terra before, and didn't particularly care to visit again; but Whitey had been born and reared on Manhome. Memories were here, many of them; but for him, now, the triune goddess had shifted; Hecate had ceased to be either mother or lover, and had become the murderess. If he came back to her arms, he would die. The children didn't know that, because they didn't know what he was planning to do; but he did.

They stepped into the gate's lift-tube, and drifted up through the airlock, into Fess's familiar frayed interior. "Ah, home," Whitey sighed, "or what passes for it these days. . . . Fess, get me a shot of real Scotch, will you? I'd like it to go with the view as we leave."

"Certainly, Mr. Tambourin. Lona? Dar?"

"Vermouth would be nice, right now," Dar mused.

"Water," Lona said firmly, "at least, until we're on our way." She dropped into her acceleration couch and webbed herself in. Dar sank down on the couch next to hers. The bar chimed softly, and he popped back up to fetch the drinks. "No, stay put, Whitey."

The bard settled back down into the couch behind Dar's with a grateful sigh. He stretched the webbing across his body and locked it in, then accepted the shot glass from Dar absentmindedly as he gazed at the viewscreen and its image of Terra, huge against the stars.

"What course shall I set?" Fess asked softly.

"Moment of decision," Lona said to Dar. "Where do you want to go?"

Dar looked deeply into her eyes. She held his gaze, hers unwavering. Her pupils seemed to grow larger, larger. . . .

"Wherever you're going," Dar said softly.

She sat still, very still.

Then she said, "Are you sure?"

"Yes," Dar said, "very."

Then they were still again, gazes locked.

Whitey cleared his throat and said, a little too loudly, "Well, you know how it is, Fess—when you're young, and all that."

"There are references to it in my data banks," the voice agreed.

"You go off to your own little dream world," Whitey explained, "even though you think you're staying in the real one. You get wrapped up in romance for a while, and you don't really relate all that well to what's going on around you."

"Similar to an artificially induced alteration in consciousness?"

"Well, that's what the drugs are trying to imitate, yeah—but you know how much an imitation's worth. Still, when they do get involved in the real thing, they're out of touch for a while, and it's up to us old folk to hold things together till they come out of their trances."

"How do you intend to hold things together, Mr. Tambourin?"

"Oh, just bumming around the Terran Sphere for a while, drifting and roaming, same as I've always done, singing innocent, apolitical songs—and gradually working my way out to Wolmar."

"Wolmar? But why?"

"Oh, to see Stroganoff again, I suppose—and this Cholly that Dar's so enthusiastic about. Seems as though they might have some good ideas. I couldn't do it the easy way, though, hitching a ride with Horatio. I mean, I've got some responsibilities. Gotta see these two young folk settled and safe before I can go kiyoodling off. And at the rate they're going now, it's going to take them a long time . . ."

"I thought you were in love with Sam," Lona finally said.

Dar shook his head. "Not a bit—at least, not after you came along. She was a good ally, when things got tense—but a lover? No. I couldn't get interested."

"Oh?" Lona said, dryly. "Why not?"

"Because," Dar said, "I just wouldn't be able to make love to someone who was reading my mind."

Lona sat very still for a few seconds. Then she said, "Sam? The real, live telepath at the bottom of the whole scare?"

"The correlations *are* rather obvious," Fess's voice murmured, "if all you've told me is accurate. Her knowing exactly where to find the credentials in the luggage of Bhelabher's staff, her ability to open a strange combination lock, to lead Dar through the dark maze of the criminals' dungeon on Falstaff, her emotional reactions to the witch-hunt. . . . What is surprising is that none of us realized it sooner."

"And that Fess knew all the facts." Lona eyed Dar suspiciously. "Didn't know you two had gotten so chummy."

"He's a very sympathetic listener," Dar said brightly.

"But nobody told him to correlate for the identity of a possible telepath." The suspicious gaze turned calculating. "When did you realize it?"

"Right after Father Marco pulled me out of that interrogation. I realized that the flashing lights and noises were an awful lot of trouble to go to if they weren't really afraid of having their minds read—so they really believed there was a telepath, and it had to have been one of our crew. Then I remembered seeing suspicious, hostile Sam falling head-over-heels in love with Horatio Bocello on a moment's notice. It just wasn't like her. She had to be seeing something in him that the rest of us didn't see—and there was only one way she could've done that."

"By peering into his mind." Lona pursed her lips, nodding. "Well, love at first second-sight, I can see."

"The Executive Director, however, does not realize that you are not the telepath," Fess pointed out. "He will no doubt be hunting you for the rest of his life—and his successor after him. A telepath would make an invaluable aide for a dictator."

"Yeah, I was thinking about that. But I think, if I find some out-of-the-way place and live quietly, I'll probably be pretty safe. Of course, I'll have to take a few standard precautions, such as changing my name . . ."

"To what would you change it?"

"Oh, nothing too elaborate; I'm kinda tired just now." Dar sighed, leaning back in his couch. "Just taking my real name and making a few changes—you know, 'd'Armand' instead of 'Dar Mandra,' that sort of thing." He turned to Lona. "You ought to think about that—you're on their list, too."

"Yes," she said, eyes glowing, "I know."

"Interested in changing your name?"

"Yes, I think I will," she said, " 'd'Armand' sounds good to me, too."